DREAMS LOVE HEALS

Kyra stiffened, and with his hand, Mac urged her to lean her head on his shoulder, then gently unknotted the fear cementing the taut cords of her neck. Regret sighed through him. Once she'd trusted him body, mind, and soul. Now she didn't even trust him with her nightmare.

"Tell me what you saw tonight, Kyra."

She shook her head against his shoulder, her hair tickling his neck. He suppressed a moan. She had no idea what she was doing to him.

"Tell me," Mac said quietly.

She turned, ready to push herself away from his arms. Mac half-dragged her into his lap and held her soothingly until her protesting grasp on his shoulders relaxed. She pressed her nose against his neck. "You smell earthy, like wild honey."

Without thinking, Mac brushed his lips lightly against hers.

"You taste so warm," Kyra whispered. Her feverish gaze blazed, sending a familiar volcanic reaction erupting deep in his core, spreading molten fire along the surface of his skin.

"Your touch makes me forget the horrible pictures in my mind." Hopelessness tinged her voice. Like a woman possessed, she clamped her fingers urgently onto the skin of his shoulders. "Help me forget, Mac."

Other *Love Spell* books by Sylvie Kurtz:
BROKEN WINGS

SYLVIE KURTZ

SILVER Shadows

LOVE SPELL ✦ NEW YORK CITY

To Chuck—because once wasn't enough.

LOVE SPELL®
May 1997
Published by

Dorchester Publishing Co., Inc.
276 Fifth Avenue
New York, NY 10001

Printed in the United States of America.

SILVER Shadows

Prologue

Park City, Utah, October 23, 1968.

Rebecca Brennan pressed the infant close to her breast and wrapped her black cape around them both. She glanced both ways before she sneaked out of her private hospital room and inched down the deserted hall. She stopped before she reached the nurses' station and waited, watching for her chance to steal by unnoticed.

When the baby fidgeted, rooting noisily for a nipple, Rebecca's heart beat a mad race. She stuck her pinkie in the infant's mouth and, even though she'd just been fed, the baby sucked greedily. When the lone nurse at the station turned to answer the phone, Rebecca slipped past the rounded desk and stole down the stairs.

The late October wind bit through her cape, but Rebecca didn't care. She was going to die anyway. The important thing was to save her baby.

Rebecca slunk from shadow to shadow, stopping every few minutes to catch her breath and to make sure she wasn't being followed. Her every footstep echoed through the rising fog, making her gasp and jump at imagined black fingers snatching at her cape. The mile and a half she traveled seemed to take an eternity to cover. When she reached her destination she slumped against the brick wall of a neighboring house to restore her drained energy.

She waited, ankle-deep in snow, in the dark between two houses, watching her goal carefully for signs of betrayal. Then she took a deep breath and braved the openness of the porch light.

She knocked and tried to melt her shape into the navy door. A minute passed before Rebecca ventured a second knock.

"Please be home," she whispered, tears choking her throat.

Soft footsteps padded to the door and stopped.

"Who is it?" a gentle voice queried from the other side.

"Miriam, it's Rebecca Brennan. Open up, please."

The door barely opened before Rebecca slipped inside, closing the door firmly behind her.

"What's wrong?" A frightened look passed over Miriam Kirtland's face.

"I need help." Rebecca sniffed, holding back the tears that threatened to fall. She couldn't give in now, not before her mission was accomplished. Not before her baby was safe.

"You're shaking. Come sit by the fire." Miriam ushered Rebecca into a living room strewn with packing cases. "Sorry for the mess, but we're moving to Florida tomorrow."

"I know. I want you to take my child with you."

"What?!"

"If you don't take her, she'll die," Rebecca pleaded.

"Rebecca?" Miriam shook her head slightly back

and forth, fright rounding her eyes.

"I don't have time to explain." Rebecca handed Miriam the sleeping child, a dry sob croaking through her parched throat.

Miriam pushed the baby back to its mother. "But we've met only once. Wouldn't a family member be better?"

"No! No one here must ever know you have my baby." With her free hand, Rebecca dug through the cape's deep pockets. "I've signed the release papers. You'll be able to adopt her legally when you get to Florida."

"But . . ."

"You must never try to contact me."

"But . . ."

Rebecca placed the child in the woman's arms, then grabbed Miriam's shoulders. "You have to take her. It's her only chance. I can't trust anyone else."

"Rebecca . . ."

"You must never tell her who her parents were. Promise." Rebecca shook Miriam's shoulders. "Promise!"

"Rebecca . . ."

Sheer panic cut through Rebecca like shards of broken glass. Her fingers turned white as they dug into Miriam's terry bathrobe, but Rebecca couldn't stop the movement borne of desperation. "Promise!"

As she saw Miriam waver, Rebecca held her breath. A million emotions passed through the woman's eyes. "Miriam, please. You're her only chance."

The moment Miriam's face showed capitulation, Rebecca relaxed her grip and allowed herself to breathe.

"Oh, Rebecca. I've wanted a child for as long as I can remember. Your daughter is a gift from God, but how will I explain her presence?"

"You're leaving tomorrow. Nobody will know she's

not yours." Rebecca dug through her cape once more. "Here; show your husband this letter. It's from my grandmother, and it'll explain everything. The threat to my baby's life isn't idle. The silver shadow's killed before. Tell no one how you got her. Tell no one who she is. You must promise."

Miriam loosened the yellow and green hospital receiving blanket that was wrapped around the infant. A smile played on her lips, and the light of desire shone in her eyes. "What will I tell her when she grows up?"

Rebecca hesitated, looking into the baby's soft green eyes. "Tell her she was loved."

Miriam shifted her hold to better support the moving infant's weight. "I can't bring danger into our home. . . ."

"We have no connection. You're moving tomorrow. The danger will follow me, and she'll be free."

Miriam searched Rebecca's face, and Rebecca could only hope Miriam saw how desperate she was. "Please, Miriam. I've no one else to turn to."

Miriam looked down at the baby in her arms. "I-I promise."

"Never tell her where she came from."

"I promise."

Relief washed through Rebecca, leaving in its wake a leaden weariness. "Thank you," she whispered.

She removed a silver chain from around her neck. From the chain dangled a moonstone trapped in the filigreed head of a key. She slipped it around the child's neck, exposing a sliver of baby shoulder with a crescent-shaped birthmark.

"She must never return to Park City. If she does, she'll die."

Miriam sucked in her breath, her pale blue eyes reflecting her fear. But Rebecca knew how important it was for Miriam to believe her warning. She kissed the baby's downy head for the last time and let her fingers linger over the soft skin of the infant's cheek.

"Good-bye, baby. I love you."

Rebecca slipped the hood of her cape back in place and left before her pain and sorrow took over. She stole one last look at her daughter before she plunged back into the cold night air. As she closed the door behind her, the infant began to wail. Rebecca's heart lurched in her chest and a small wounded cry escaped her. But she hurried on, carefully retracing her steps to the hospital. The baby's distressed cries ripped through the quiet night, tearing at her heart and reverberating through her mind, following her.

Once she was back in her bed she allowed herself to shed the waterfall of tears she'd held back.

When the tears finally ran dry, Rebecca shut down the portion of her brain holding any memory of her child. It was the only way to keep her daughter safe when the silver shadow came.

Her full breasts ached for the release of a suckling child, and Rebecca pressed a pillow into her chest to alleviate the pain. Sleep finally claimed her exhausted body.

She woke from a dreamless sleep with a cold breeze chilling her body down to her soul. She scrambled up in the bed.

"Who's there?"

When no answer came, Rebecca reached for the nurse's call button. She couldn't depress it. Then she saw the silver shadow creep across the floor.

"Where is the child?" the rough voice asked.

"She's in the nursery." Rebecca pressed her body deeper into the hard pillows.

"Where is the child?" the raspy voice insisted.

"I told you, in the nursery." She pulled the blanket up like a shield.

The shadow climbed on the bed. A cry for help

welled from deep inside but went unuttered.

"I will find her."

The cold, fetid breath tingled against Rebecca's cheek, branding her. She turned her head away and tried to scream, kicking at the blanket, seeking escape. But like a clamp, the silver shadow held her in place. Rebecca whimpered. The silver shadow crept up and settled on her throat.

"Where is the child?"

The weight on her throat increased. Rebecca knew she didn't have the energy to fight for both herself and her daughter. Her last act of courage would be to safeguard her daughter's future. As the weight squeezed at her throat, Rebecca exhaled. Unprepared for the move, the silver shadow's grip slipped, crushing her windpipe. With sheer force of will she kept her mind closed to the shadow's prying fingers.

Rebecca vaguely heard the silver shadow's angry growl resonating in her head before gray mist clouded her mind and her weariness left her.

She'd won.

She'd freed her daughter.

Chapter One

Park City, Utah, 1997

In the dreamy world created by the steam rising from the hot tub's bubbling water into the cold December air, the calming New Age music spilling over the outside speakers and the veil of falling snowflakes, Kyra Kirtland could forget.

Sighing, she leaned her head back against her small black dog, curled on the edge of the tub, using Misty as a pillow. "I'm glad we came. I feel comfortable here."

Much to her surprise, she found the statement true. She yawned, closed her eyes, and let her tense muscles relax for the first time in over a month. She was so tired, every cell of her body felt weary. Maybe here she could sleep without dreaming.

Despite the soothing warm water burbling around her, an icy shudder rippled through her. The latest installment in her series of nightmares floated up from the recesses of her mind.

Maybe she couldn't forget after all.

The too-warm air inside the trailer that housed Hadley Restoration Services' temporary headquarters had Kyra's eyelids drooping once again.

Her hand drifted from the drawing showing a wood bracket's detail. She pinched the bridge of her nose and closed her eyes, giving her fuzzy eyesight a chance to rest. If she didn't get a good night's sleep soon, she'd lose everything she'd worked toward in the past seven years. She fought the pull, but it was too strong. Resting one elbow on her drafting table, she let her head flop into her hand.

A catnap couldn't hurt. A few minutes; then she could get back to work refreshed.

She floated on cottony layers of gray. Then, like quicksand, her conscious mind was sucked into a murky past she didn't understand. She looked into her own green eyes, but her reddish curls had turned to straight brown hair twisted into a high chignon. Her cream sweater and comfortable blue pants had changed into an embroidered white shirtwaist and gored black skirt. She had no idea who the man beside her was, or why he glared at her. They exchanged heated words, but Kyra couldn't hear their voices. She could only stare aghast as the man hit her. Kyra gasped. The action jolted her head off her hand, waking her.

Keys clattered against Kyra's drafting table, slid down the incline and plopped into her lap.

"I'm working you too hard," George Hadley said. He sat in the chair next to Kyra's desk.

"I did it again, didn't I?" Kyra sighed and dropped her pencil in the holder before she rubbed her temples. With each circle of her fingers, she tried to erase the clinging dread that always accompanied the dreams that had plagued her since she'd arrived in Summit Station, Utah.

George nodded and smiled. His thin blond hair slipped into his face. He pushed it back. George was meticulously well groomed, but he'd let his hair grow long. Kyra knew it was because he'd been too busy covering for her over the past few weeks.

"I'm sorry. I won't let it happen again," she said.

"That's what you said yesterday. And the day before. And the day before that, too."

"I'm sorry." Kyra looked down at her hands in her lap and played absentmindedly with the keys that had dropped there. The small dog snoozing at her feet stirred. Misty propelled herself into Kyra's lap, faced forward, and butted Kyra's hand to be petted. Kyra obliged.

"You need a break. After we present the Summit Station project to the Utah Historical Restoration Society tomorrow, why don't you take a vacation? Our next project doesn't start until after the new year.

"My sister's got a house nearby." His chin jerked toward the keys in her hand. "Those are the keys."

"I didn't know you had a sister."

"She's ten years younger. We're not close." George shrugged and gave her a don't-ask-any-questions look. "I met her for dinner last week. I'd planned on visiting with her after this job, but she and her husband are spending the holidays in the Caribbean. I'd rather get home to the girls than spend a few days alone here. But you could go skiing, rest, and get whatever it is that's messing up your mind out of your system."

When Kyra didn't comment on his suggestion George placed his elbows on the chair's arms and tented his hands. "We're two weeks behind on this project."

"I know."

"We're known for our reliability. I can't let it get around that we can't meet our deadlines."

Kyra played with the dog's coarse black hair. George was the combination father/brother she hadn't had growing up. They'd met when she worked an internship for him while pursuing her degree in architecture at the University of Florida in Gainesville.

When she'd graduated George had attended the ceremony and presented her with a contract of employment. Liking George and the freedom he gave her with her work, she'd gladly accepted. She loved the visceral sensation bringing a neglected building back to life gave her. The way it made her feel alive and useful—needed. She wouldn't trade her job for anything in the world.

But Kyra also knew the one thing George couldn't tolerate was incompetence. And in the past month her work had fallen just short of that. It was as if her creative instinct was being sucked dry by these awful dreams.

"It's not just my reputation that's at stake. It's yours, too," George continued.

Kyra's hand stopped petting the dog, and Misty twisted around, demanding Kyra continue.

In all the years she'd known George, he'd always insisted on approving everything that went out and never letting anything go out without his name on it; his way of keeping integrity, he claimed. His obsession with a scrupulous reputation kept the personnel flowing through the door at regular intervals. Except for Betty, his secretary—the only person who dared talk back to George when he was being impossible—Kyra was the only person who'd lasted more than a year.

"What do you mean, my reputation?"

George leaned forward, his hands still tented above his lap. A mischievous grin twisted his face, taking a decade off his forty-odd years. "I was going to leave a big surprise under your Christmas tree." The smile disappeared, leaving George's this-is-serious look behind. "I think I need to let you mull over my proposition now."

"What kind of surprise?" Kyra'd never liked surprises, especially around Christmas. Those brightly wrapped packages were bound to house a few disappointments, and she'd never been good at hiding her emotions—which tended to lead to hurt feelings all around.

"A partnership." George sat back and waited for her reaction.

"A partnership?!" Kyra straightened on her stool, nearly bouncing Misty off her lap. She couldn't believe her ears. Misty nipped Kyra's hand, reminding her of her presence.

"I don't have a son to pass this business on to."

"But you're still young—"

George held up his hand to silence her. "My daughters don't seem to have an interest in what I do, so I doubt they'll care what happens to my business when I decide to retire. You love your work and you're the only person I know who understands the importance of staying true to the past when you do a restoration. It's almost as if you can see the past, see the truth, and somehow balance that with what our clients want. That's a rare gift."

"Is something wrong? You're not sick, are you?" Her mind reeled. Having recently lost her mother to cancer, the thought of losing another loved one frightened her.

"No. I'm just thinking ahead. I've got a poor track record at keeping my employees happy. You've been loyal—more like third daughter, really—and I believe in rewarding that loyalty. I'm prepared to offer you a full partnership."

Oh-oh, here comes the but.

"Kyra . . ."

That was even worse than *but*. George never used her name unless something displeased him.

"I won't give you the partnership unless you straighten out your problem. I know your mother's death's been hard on you, but to give you half my business, I've got to be able to depend on you in any situation."

Her nightmares could certainly be classified as a problem. She'd tried to cope with them, but the more she concentrated, the worse the unwanted interludes got. The more she tried to analyze them, the more confused she got. And going without sleep wasn't the answer either.

"What if I can't get rid of these nightmares?" Kyra held her breath.

George hesitated before he answered. "I'll have to let you go."

Anyone who didn't know George would be shocked by such a statement, Kyra knew, but she wasn't. She'd come to appreciate George's directness. She liked knowing where she stood, and with George she never had to wonder.

"I've got too much work lined up not to be able to depend on you," George said. "You can understand my position, can't you?"

"Yes, of course."

Kyra jingled her keys in one hand. Maybe a vacation wasn't such a bad idea. She'd hated the idea of spending Christmas at her mother's cottage in Florida, alone with her memories. Christmas spent with a throng of happy skiers might prove less depressing. Besides, with a good rest the dark clouds and mental confusion just might go away. When was the last time she'd had a real vacation?

Seven years was much too long—even if she'd had a good reason to avoid vacations.

"Are you sure your sister won't mind?"

"Lynn and Brad will be pleased."

"Why don't you draw me a map to the house, then?" Kyra reached for a piece of scratch paper on her desk and handed it to George.

George smiled. "That's a girl."

He drew a quick sketch with his bold hand. "I'd rent a four-wheel drive if I were you. I don't think your little Del Sol'll make it up the side of the mountain they live on."

"Sully can get me through anything."

"Sully isn't used to hairpin turns on a six-degree grade. I'd feel better if you rented something else. My treat."

George handed her the paper. "It's Number 196 on Timberline. It says McKane on the mailbox. Can't miss it. Is there anything else I can do for you?"

Kyra shook her head and smiled. That was something else most people didn't realize: George would give the shirt off his back for a friend. "No. I'll be just fine."

"You know where to find me if you need me." George patted her knee, then uncurled his long frame from the office chair.

"Thanks."

"You'll love Park City."

Park City! Her heart palpitated at the mention of the town. An irrational fear curled through her stomach. She'd meant to go there since she'd arrived in Utah, but they'd been too busy for her to take an afternoon off.

George was halfway out the door before he popped his head back into the trailer. "Oh, by the way . . . Brad's brother might stop by to check up on the house."

"The house or me?"

George had the decency to look embarrassed. He'd known all along she'd accept.

"I'll be fine, you know," Kyra said.

Sylvie Kurtz

"I know." George pointed a finger at her. "Don't forget to rent a sturdier car. I don't want to have to worry about you when I'm back in Florida."

"When are you leaving?" Kyra turned her attention back to her work. She whisked away the involuntary shiver by running one hand through the reassuring warmth of Misty's hair.

"As soon as we're done with our presentation tomorrow."

Kyra laughed softly, thinking how George liked to surprise his wife with his unexpected arrivals, and how much Janice hated not knowing George was on the road. "So, does Janice know this, or are you going to surprise her again?"

"Surprise her, of course. It keeps everybody on their toes."

Kyra shifted uncomfortably in the water, tamping back the memory. Misty's cold nose jabbed at her ear. "Sorry, girl."

She adjusted the hot tub's jet more to distract her thoughts than because it needed it. Misty stretched out her legs and swiveled her head to look curiously at Kyra. As Kyra lifted a hand to pet the dog, she dripped water onto Misty's coat. Her thoughts drifted once more to the dreams that were fast becoming the center of her life.

She had no idea where these dismal images of death and violence, or the feeling of terror accompanying them, had come from, or why they insisted on cluttering her mind. She only knew that because of them she had a good chance of losing the one thing she needed more than anything, especially now—her job.

But for the next few days she wouldn't think of anything except resting and relaxing. Refreshed, she could put a plan of action together and discover who she was. Maybe then she'd understand the drifting feeling that had followed her all her life.

"What do you think about skiing? I'm thinking of taking a lesson or two. Something new and different might distract me."

As Kyra sank deeper into the water, Misty's body tensed beneath her. The low rumble of a growl started deep in Misty's belly and rose to her throat in both a warning and a threat. "All right, take it easy. We'll eat in just a bit."

Misty popped to a standing position, adding menace to her growl with an occasional bark.

Kyra shifted to look at Misty. "What's wrong with you, girl?"

Then she heard the noise.

Footsteps. Stealthy, steady.

Her pulse jittered in alarm. Kyra probed the steam and snowflakes, trying to locate their direction. Her heart beat hard against her ribs, drowning the sound. A man's face swam dizzily in the mist. She shrank against the tub's side, realizing belatedly how vulnerable she'd left herself.

As he approached, the fuzzy features drifted into concrete lines—narrow chin, strong brow, clear-cut cheekbones chiseled roughly in an otherwise pleasant face, the whole softened by a full, sensuous mouth. Dark hair, smoky eyes. He moved with a primitive masculine grace she recognized only too well.

Mac Connor!

Horror washed over her. Feeling light-headed, she scrambled to get out of the tub. One foot slid from beneath her. She fell back on the seat with a splash.

Not him. Not now. Not after all this time.

Her body tensed against the avalanche of memories threatening to spill into the present. She refused to let them cascade through her brain, fought the edge of panic building in her chest. She couldn't lose control now. "What are you doing here?"

Picking up on Kyra's distress, Misty launched herself at Mac's jean-clad leg. Growling and using her thirteen-pound weight as leverage, she fought valiantly to protect her mistress.

Mac lifted his leg. Misty refused to let go and hung in midair. "You're not depending on this miniature Tasmanian Devil for protection, are you?" he asked with a deep-throated chuckle.

The sound struck Kyra with a fierce longing she thought she'd long ago set aside. Her thoughts scrabbled like mice in an attic. "Do I need protection?"

Always a man of few words, Mac didn't answer. He lowered the dog back to the deck, and Misty resumed her growling.

His silence confused her. So did his intense granite stare. She suddenly became aware of her state of undress under the frothing water. She hugged her legs against her chest, looking for the heat that had somehow vanished from the hot tub.

"Come here, Misty." The dog gave Kyra an are-you-sure look without letting go of the leg in her jaws. "It's okay. That's a good girl."

Giving a sneeze of disapproval, Misty released her prey and returned to Kyra, plunking her stout body between Kyra and Mac. She gave Mac one last teeth-baring growl. Kyra petted Misty, soothing her.

"What kind of animal is that?" he asked, watching Misty with amusement. Tall and dark, he looked like a fortress bathed in fog—solid and ephemeral at the same time.

"A Schipperke. A Belgian barge dog. You haven't answered my question." The shock of seeing him again gave way to anger. After the humiliation he'd put her through she'd hoped she'd never see him again. She resented him with the passion of a woman rejected, resented him for showing up in her life at another weak moment. "What are you doing here of all places?"

"You stole my line."

And you stole my heart, my soul. How could you leave me like that? "Don't you live in California somewhere?"

"Not anymore. I thought you lived in Florida."

"I'm here on business. Or was. I'm on vacation now. You?"

"I own a ski resort nearby."

Kyra cocked her head, scrutinizing the lines of his face, trying to imagine the intense, solitary man she'd known managing a business involving people. She couldn't get the math to add up. "You?"

"Yeah, me." He smiled, and the action transformed his face.

Kyra sucked in her breath. "What happened?" she asked without meaning to.

"It's a long story."

Kyra shrugged and glanced away. She didn't care. Really. Why should she?

Just by standing there in his black ski jacket, jeans, and boots, he overpowered the space she'd found so soothing moments ago. She wanted to escape the narrow confines of the hot tub, wanted to put layers of clothes and acres of air between them. If only there was a graceful way of doing it. But staying like this with him looking down at her with grave gray eyes made her nervous beyond reason.

Here goes nothing.

She took a deep breath, reached for the thick beach towel she'd left on the edge of the tub, and rose from the water. Fumbling for her sandals in the banked snow on the deck, she dropped one side of the towel. Mac reached over and drew the towel around her shivering body.

Their gazes met. His jaw twitched, his eyes appearing to calculate minuscule muscle contractions at high speed, like a computer sorting through data.

Kyra held herself straight, not bowing to his intense scrutiny.

"We need to talk," Mac said. His face turned to inscrutable granite once more.

"Seven years ago we needed to talk. Right now we have nothing to discuss."

"I understand you're hurt."

"Hurt! Hurt doesn't begin to describe how I felt. Do you think I've been pining away waiting for you all these years? Don't flatter yourself, Mac Connor. I got over you."

Kyra tried to move past him, but he blocked her way.

"I always expected you would, Sunshine."

Was that regret in his eyes? "Don't call me that."

Misty scrunched her way between Kyra and Mac and voiced her disapproval with a sharp yip.

Mac stepped back and raked a hand through his hair. "Listen, I know this is awkward, but we've got to deal with it. The snowstorm's made the road nearly impassable. We're stuck here together until tomorrow."

"Why are you here in the first place?"

"Part of my roof caved in, and Brad said I could use his house while he was away."

"How do you know Brad McKane?"

"Brad's my brother."

A cold chill hit her like a slap. "Your brother?"

Holding on to her towel with tight fists, Kyra backed away from Mac. "Your last name is Connor."

Brad's brother might stop by to check on the house. "You knew I'd be here." The words came out in a harsh whisper.

He reached for one of her hands. His energy rippled through the gentle caress of his fingers on her skin. Kyra found herself holding her breath once more. Desire and hatred fought a wicked battle, gushing memories of pleasure and pain, draining her of all remaining energy. Her head spun, as if some-one were twisting a kaleidoscope of her emotions, shifting them with each turn. Her overtaxed system had reached overload and threatened to crash at any moment.

"You'll catch a cold like this," Mac said gently. "Let's go inside."

"No, explain."

"My name is Owen Connor McKane."

Her body turned to ice. "And just when had you planned on telling me this? For heaven's sake, we were going to be married!"

She tried to jerk away from him. He closed the distance between them. The look in his eyes was dan-gerous, his touch possessive, his earthy scent tanta-lizing. "I couldn't tell you."

"Why? Were you some sort of spy on a secret mis-sion? What did that make me, Mac? Was I just a passing amusement?"

"No, Kyra." His voice trembled with emotion. His hands skimmed up her toweled arms, to her neck, and stopped. He cradled her face with his thumbs. His fingers on her nape played havoc with her senses.

"Don't, Mac. Don't touch me." Panic slithered through her like a striking snake. She didn't want to fall so easily a second time. Not with this man.

"I had no choice, Kyra. I had to leave."

She shook her head, fighting the pain, the humil-iation, the tearing loss battering the barely healed wound on her heart. "But not at the altar, not with no explanation. What you did was unspeakably cruel."

"I had no choice."

She looked deep into the melting glaciers of his eyes, looking for the potent stability that had grounded her so powerfully seven years ago, know-ing it had proved an illusion as formless as the steam surrounding them. "There's always a choice."

"And I made the wrong one."

"Why come back now?"

"Kyra . . ."

His lips covered hers gently. She realized with horror that she didn't feel disgust but pleasure. He'd betrayed her. She needed to hate him. Yet her body remembered his heat, his strength, and responded to him the way it always had. It melted against him, seeking his warmth, his energy, his bold passion. She wanted to cry with joy, with pain. Could he still care?

His mouth on hers shut down the reasoning part of her brain. As if a few days had gone by instead of seven years, her hands, of their own volition, splayed over his jacketed chest and drank in the warmth of him. The exploration of his hand on the small of her back, his fingers tangled in her hair, eclipsed the years with a river of memories. An impossible yearning seared her soul.

No! She was furious at her loss of control. She wouldn't put herself through the heartache again. Mac Connor didn't honor commitment. Mac Connor didn't honor love. After a month of hard work, no sleep, and terrifying nightmares she was in no shape to handle him.

She snapped their invisible connection. Every nerve in her body tingled, leaving her feeling adrift. The misty world she'd found so safe started to spin like a planet gone out of control.

"Kyra? Are you all right?"

His words sounded far away, yet they pounded like a jackhammer on her eardrums, pulsating between the *whoosh whoosh* of her blood. Suddenly, the whole situation was more than she could bear. As she turned away from him, the world dipped crazily to the left. She bumped her leg against the edge of a deck chair and stumbled to the door like a drunk.

"Kyra?"

She lunged for the door and hurried to her room.

With a swipe of her arm she sent her unpacked suitcase flying to the floor and fell into bed. She rolled the blue-and-white monkey wrench quilt around her. She needed warmth. She needed comfort. She needed safety. And she would find none of those in Mac Connor's arms.

Silent tears flowed down her cheeks. Why had he come back? Why now?

They'd betrayed her. They'd lied to her. Her mother. Mac. And unless she could find herself again the nightmares would cost her what little she had left. She wouldn't let Mac, or Owen, or whatever his real name was, cheat her out of her future.

"Are you all right?" Mac asked, concern in his voice.

Kyra hadn't heard his footsteps and started. "I'm fine. I just need to rest. I haven't had much sleep lately." A long rest with no dreams.

"We need to talk."

"I don't think so. I think you should leave. And now sounds like a real good time."

"It's not that simple."

"It never was with you." She was amazed at the cool control of her voice.

"There was a lot at stake."

Kyra shot him a glance over her shoulder. "For me too, Mac."

He nodded, backing off for now. "We'll talk after you sleep."

If she ignored him, would he go away? Ignoring hadn't worked for her mother's betrayal. It hadn't worked for the nightmares. It probably wouldn't work for a man with Mac Connor's assurance either. He'd be there when she went back into the other room, waiting.

Misty jumped onto the bed. After licking the salty tears from Kyra's face she snuggled at the crook of

Sylvie Kurtz

Kyra's legs. Kyra heard the gentle click of her bedroom door closing.

She thought of their whirlwind romance, their explosive passion. He'd wanted her, pursued her, and won her. She'd had no defenses against his relentless energy then. Now, her defenses were shaky at best. He could still get to her, hurt her. And where would that leave her?

Dark clouds drifted over the gray sky, blanketing out the afternoon light. She'd thought she'd be safe here. The house had seemed to welcome her. From the rough-hewn cedar planks on the chalet-style house, to the snowdrifts banked cozily around the house, to the interior's inviting balance of colors and textures, she'd sensed this house was just what she needed to whisk away the darkness that had plagued her since she'd arrived in Utah last month.

But the McKanes' home wouldn't be the perfect place to rest. Not with Mac here.

A vicious chill wrapped itself around Kyra's shoulders. She shrugged it away and reached for the flannel nightgown inside her suitcase. Curling up in the quilt once more, she sighed. She wouldn't think of Mac. She wouldn't think of her mother. She wouldn't think of betrayal at the hands of the people who'd said they loved her.

As she concentrated on blanking her mind, she stared at the lulling display of snowflakes drifting by her window. After what seemed an eternity Kyra's heavy eyelids closed. *Please God, don't let me dream.*

As if in answer, the whole mountain on which the McKane home stood shook in a low, resonating rumble.

Lost in the swirling mist of impending sleep, Kyra's last conscious thought was the deep-seated, absurd feeling that the mountain on which this house stood was hollow and hungry and that it wanted her—and that Mac would lead her there.

Chapter Two

Mac stood by the floor-to-ceiling windows in the living room, resting his forehead against the cool glass pane, watching the wet snowflakes slap and slide against the window.

The plan had seemed so simple when he'd hatched it over dinner last week. George hadn't known Mac and Kyra knew each other. Of course Mac hadn't filled him in on all the little details. He'd told him only that he'd met Kyra years ago and would like to have the chance to see her again. George had agreed a distraction of the heart might be exactly what Kyra needed right now, and together they'd set her up.

But a lot had happened since then. A week ago it had seemed as if his life were being handed back to him—a second chance on a golden platter. Then yesterday everything had fallen apart.

As a reminder, the mountain rumbled below his feet. He felt its shaky movement through the glass and cursed. The destruction was starting already.

How long would be it be before the whole thing crumbled, taking with it innocent lives?

He should have known better. He should have stayed away. But he couldn't help himself. The thought of holding Kyra once again had blurred his judgment.

He raked a hand through his hair and massaged the knot at the base of his neck. It had been a long day. Hell, it had been a long week. He still couldn't believe he'd agreed to let the Institute reinstate him. They'd known exactly which string to pull, hadn't they? Now the machinelike ability to search and destroy the Institute had trained into him was the only thing that stood between the life or death of people he cared for.

To top things off, the roof heating system on his house had failed and the past few days' heavy snowfall had caved in part of the ceiling. According to the contractor, the roof and the mess in his living room were going to take a week to clean up and repair.

And now Kyra had arrived.

The right wish fulfilled at the wrong time and the wrong place. But then, life had chosen to teach him that particular lesson exceedingly well, hadn't it? There never was a right time for anything. Too bad he hadn't realized that seven years ago.

As if the whole messy situation wasn't enough, he had a pounding headache and wanted nothing more than to relax in the hot tub with the beer he'd picked up on his way here.

Instead, he found himself ambling to Kyra's bedroom and opening the door. He advanced with no trace of noise, careful not to disturb the sleeping woman or the snoring dog.

Mac's gaze strayed to her lips. Like ripe fruit, her slightly parted mouth begged to be tasted. Deep inside, a familiar stirring shifted, then grew, twisting his gut with the deepest hunger he'd ever felt. Kissing her earlier, he'd felt her unguarded reaction, seen the fire ignite in her eyes. And he'd also seen the pain, raw and open.

Her wild strawberry-blond hair reminded him of autumn leaves tousled by the wind. Alive with color and possibilities, fascinating, disorienting. Desire fierce and strong pierced through his savage hunger.

Her skin seemed too pale to be healthy. He remembered her golden tan and how it had made her glow with an airiness that lifted the heavy weight of his conscience. The dark circles beneath her eyes looked like bruises. He wanted to smudge the marks away, to see the spring green of her eyes vibrant again with the promise of life. As it had seven years ago, anguish rippled down to his stomach. He'd had no choice. Standing by her that day would have signed her death warrant.

Regret sang through him.

A woman like Kyra wasn't meant for a man like him.

He'd known that even as he'd pursued her. He'd known that even as he loved her. He'd known that even as he allowed himself to believe in a future with her. But after what had happened to Alek, he'd known he could never jeopardize her life just because she added so much to his miserable one.

And as wrong as he was for her, he still wanted her, needed her. She held the key to the peace he'd yearned for so long.

He rubbed his throbbing temple with the fingers of one hand. He'd managed to find her, to start hoping and dreaming again, only to be put in the same position he had been in seven years ago. The knowledge weighed on him like a ton of avalanched snow.

But this was the last time, wasn't it? After this mission he could put his Institute days behind him forever. And this time it was him against the mountain—nothing and no one else.

She'd be safe. He'd make sure.

He snaked a finger around a strand of reddish gold hair and reveled in its softness. He'd lost as much as she had. Maybe more. She'd had her mother to support her. He'd had only his broken illusions. Over the years he'd grown weary of battles that could never be won, battles where innocents were used as pawns. Wasn't that why he'd quit and bought the broken down ski resort he'd christened Mountain Swift?

After screwing up his life royally he was given a second chance all around. He had to take it. He simply couldn't let her go again.

Misty cocked an eye open and gave a guttural growl. Mac splayed his hands up in a sign of surrender and backed away. "I'm leaving," he whispered and backed out of the room.

He headed for the fridge. One more mission and he'd be free. His concern had to be for the present.

He took out a bottle of beer, ripped off the cap, swallowed a swig, then set it on the counter.

She didn't need to know. He could do what he needed to without her being the wiser. He could find the entrance, retrieve the data box, and seal the mine. Then, when it was over, he'd have a chance to win her again.

Having heard the fridge open, Misty popped up on a stool and looked at him expectantly. When he didn't move she licked her chops to make her meaning clear. Absently, Mac reached for a cookie jar and offered her a whole-wheat cracker. She sneezed.

"You're right. It needs cheese," Mac said, realizing he was hungry.

He pulled a lump of cheddar from the fridge and cut some slices for himself and the dog. As she waited for her share, Misty drooled.

"I have a feeling I'm going to have to work very hard to win Kyra back."

Misty ignored him and wolfed down her cheese and crackers.

Be patient, he advised himself. *Take it slow.*

The problem was, he'd been patient for seven long years. He was tired of being alone. And he didn't want to fail again. Not when the price was so damn high.

I've got her where I want her, the silver shadow thought. The last of the line and my revenge will be complete.

He slunk closer to the window and melted through the glass. His dark finger skimmed the snow white skin. With his breath, he ruffled the long hair from Kyra's neck. He smiled. The crescent-shaped birthmark designated her as one of Hallie's descendants. The last one. And his task would be complete.

Liebliche Kyra, I've waited for you for such a long time.

She stirred in her sleep, and the silver shadow crept back. It was too early. She had to come to him willingly—as they all had. He'd make sure she understood the whole story. But not right now. First he would take everything from her. Her love, her happiness, her life. Just as Hallie had done to him all those years ago.

Ich werde meine Rache haben, Liebchen. Yes, revenge was the panacea for all that ailed him, and Kyra was his last link to eternal peace. Her life force would rescind his dark exile, repair his deep loneliness, resurrect his life.

His finely tuned senses picked up an unexpected presence down the hall.

Time to go.

For now.

Welcome to Park City, Liebchen. *I will make sure you never leave.* His cold kiss branded her cheek. He wanted her to know he'd been here, and his mark should stir fear into her soul. *Dream, liebliche Kyra. Dream of me. I'll be back.*

He drifted across the floor and through the closed window. His fluid form left no trace on the virgin snow.

Blood. Everywhere. It dripped from her hands, stained her shirt and pooled at her boots. "Go away!" she yelled as the rivulets of red streamed through her fingers. She wiped the offending sticky mess back and forth across the front of her skirt. "Leave me alone!"

Strong hands reached for her and pulled her up from darkness back into reality. The boots shimmered away, the skirt turned back into her soft flannel nightgown, and the sea of red wavered, then became black. "I never asked for you to come."

"I know, but I'm here, so let's just make the best of it." A man's voice echoed eerily in her confused mind. Familiar, that voice, but wrong, terribly wrong. Kyra pushed away from the sturdy wall of chest, but insistent fingers still bit into the tender flesh of her arms. Something clawed at her legs and yipped.

Kyra blinked and tried to force her mind to focus. The nightmare still resonated through her body. Usually the colors were muted, but this time the red had been bright and very real. When she closed her eyes she could still see it on her hands, feel its sticky mess between her fingers, hear it fall in drips at her feet, and smell the stench of it as it coagulated on the cavern floor. The dream had felt so real, Kyra wondered who she'd murdered and why. She shuddered.

She hadn't meant to fall asleep. She'd only meant to rest her eyes for a minute or two. But the bed had been so comfortable and the quilt so warm. With Misty's rhythmic snores and the hypnotic dance of falling snowflakes outside her window, sleep had snuck up on her and claimed her.

And the nightmare had come again.

Now Misty barked threateningly at the window, the room felt evil, and the quilt did nothing to rid her of the chill that froze her to the marrow of her bones.

She shivered, suddenly aware of her head resting against a warm shoulder, of the solid flesh beneath her palms, of gentle hands holding her. Mac. She didn't want to cry, but she couldn't stop the tears.

"Aw, Kyra, don't cry." Mac held her tightly, trying to stop the convulsive shudders that racked Kyra's body. He'd never been good at lending a shoulder to cry on. He was used to being in total control, and the feeling of helplessness coursing through him was highly uncomfortable. "Tell me what happened."

Kyra shook her head and her heart pounded erratically against his chest. As he felt a fresh wave of panic claw through her, she wound her arms around his neck, her fear of the nightmare outweighing her hatred of him.

"Just hold me." She hiccuped.

No, this wouldn't do. He couldn't hold her. He'd promised himself he'd go slow, earn back her trust. He couldn't let her melt his resolve with her soft body and passion-flower scent. He had to get it right this time. What he needed to do was distract her, distract them both.

"Hey, do vegetarians drink hot chocolate?" he asked in a teasing voice, remembering her dislike of his carnivorous tastes. He pulled her away from his shoulder and looked into the watery green of her eyes. He was rewarded with a teary half smile.

"This one does." Kyra wiped her wet cheeks with the back of her hand. "I have an incurable sweet tooth."

"I remember. I've never seen anybody consume as many of those sickly sweet shaved ices as you did."

35

Misty jumped on the bed and poked her nose at her mistress's arm, demanding attention. Kyra obliged by petting Misty's head.

"Come on." Mac wrapped the quilt tightly around Kyra and guided her to the kitchen. The *click click* of Misty's paws followed them. He flipped on lights as he went, sensing the brightness would offer her some reassurance. He settled her on a stool, then headed to the fridge for milk. Misty hopped on the stool next to Kyra's and waited expectantly for a handout.

The night's cool air chilled the damp tracks of Kyra's tears on his skin and made him wish for a sweatshirt, but he didn't dare leave her alone. Not when fear still rippled so visibly through her. He wanted answers about the nightmare; he couldn't give her the chance to retreat.

"Do you like marshmallows?" Mac asked as he rummaged through the pantry.

"What's hot chocolate without marshmallows?" she answered. Her attempt at a laugh drifted away uneasily.

"My mother used to make the best hot chocolate. This is her personal recipe." Mac grabbed a can of cocoa and the bag of miniature marshmallows. "We lived in the northeast when I was a kid. Brad and I would go sledding or skating in the winter, and when we came back in Mom always had steaming mugs waiting for us. I can't decide if it was the warmth of the mug that was so good, the taste of the chocolate, or the fact that Mom always remembered I liked marshmallows and Brad didn't."

Of course, that was in the good old days before his rebellious teenage years. It wasn't that he'd been bad, but he'd made life difficult for the whole family. Mac firmly pushed the thoughts away. He had to concentrate on Kyra.

As he talked and prepared the drink, Mac watched

her out of the corner of his eye. Her eyebrows knit together even as she tried to lighten her features. She was trying for the sunshine even with the gray clouds around her. He needed to divert her thoughts away from her nightmare and give the natural cheer he remembered a chance to heal her. "Tell me about your memories of hot chocolate."

She wrapped her hands around the mug he offered, then sipped the hot liquid. "In Florida we didn't have the snow to use as an excuse to indulge, but after Dad died when I was thirteen I had trouble sleeping, and Mom started our tradition of late-night hot chocolates. She'd use her best cups and float the marshmallows on top. We'd sit for hours and talk. About everything. I know most teenage girls hate their mothers, and God knows we didn't agree on everything, but I loved our evenings together. She was a good friend."

As she spoke, Mac realized how little he knew about the woman he'd loved too much; about her childhood, her friends, her life. "Sounds like you have a special mother."

The creases in her forehead deepened. "I did. She died two months ago."

"I'm sorry." George had mentioned how hard her mother's death had been on her. "Tell me more about her."

Kyra looked deep into her cup and gave a sharp, short laugh. "In the end she betrayed me, the way you did." She didn't give him a chance to respond, but barreled on. "So what am I supposed to call you? Owen?"

Ignoring the pointed barb, Mac made a face at the mention of his given name. "My mother's the only person alive who can get away with calling me Owen. Most people call me Mac. How did your mother betray you?"

Kyra shrugged. "She wasn't my mother and never

bothered to tell me. At least the humiliation wasn't public. It came in the privacy of a lawyer's office. Why the name change, anyway?"

He felt the pain she tried to hide and kept his voice soft. "It was part of the job."

Her chin came up stiffly. "Was *I* part of the job?"

"No. You're the reason I quit."

She fell silent. Her gaze dropped to her cup, looking, it seemed, for answers in the chocolate sludge at the bottom.

Mac reached across the counter and rubbed circles on the creases of her forehead with an index finger. It was then he noticed the mark on her cheek. "Where did you get the freeze burn on your face?"

"What freeze burn?"

Mac traced the wavy double line on her skin. "Here."

Her fingers rose to touch the mark and brushed his, causing an instantaneous internal contraction. "I-I don't know."

She sounded thunder-struck. He dropped the subject. "Tell me about your dream, Kyra."

She broke the contact and shook her head. "I can't."

"It might help. Like those nights with your mother. I'm a good listener." They hadn't done much talking in their two weeks together, but the memory of those heated nights had sustained him for years.

"You're not a friend." Kyra took another sip of her drink. A single tear slid down her cheek. The stubborn tilt of her chin dared him to argue her claim.

"I'm not the enemy."

Kyra turned her haunted green gaze at him, and a weight settled at the pit of his stomach.

"Come on. Try me," Mac urged. He smiled teasingly. "I can be a gentleman."

Kyra huffed her disagreement. "You were never a

gentleman. As I recall, your first words to me were, 'I want you.' "

"To which you promptly reacted by putting on a T-shirt over your tank top and a long-sleeved cotton shirt over *that*."

She unconsciously pulled the quilt tighter around her until not a millimeter of skin below the neck showed. "Then you said, 'I'm going to have you.' "

"And you would have added several layers of clothes if you'd had any left. But you had to settle for sunglasses."

"Then you told me your first lie. You said you'd be patient."

"I usually am." He chuckled. "I've a reputation for it."

"You weren't patient that time."

"No," he conceded. "I guess I wasn't. But I don't recall you minding too much."

She blushed and turned away from him. "Well, that's another story altogether."

Mac rounded the counter and helped her off the stool. He walked her to the sofa, dogged by Misty's feet clicking on the hardwood floor.

"Sit next to me." He patted the green leather cushion beside him, deliberately keeping her hand in his.

She tried to pull away, but he tugged on her arm and she flopped down beside him. Misty jumped up to join them, but Mac shooed her away. With a snort of disgust, the dog settled on the recliner, turning her back to them. He gently pulled Kyra against him and massaged the tension from her shoulders. He enjoyed the feel of her body against his after all the years of waiting, making him wish the circumstances were different.

"How come you're not going home for Christmas?" Mac eased into the conversation.

"George offered me the use of this place and I

jumped at the chance for a white Christmas. I've never had one before."

"What were you doing in Park City?" Mac's hand slid up and tangled into her cloudlike red-gold curls. He swallowed his sigh of pleasure.

"We were doing a restoration project in Summit Station." She laughed mirthlessly. "George was going to offer me a partnership, you know."

Knowing of George's obsession with his job, the offer of a partnership surprised him. Kyra must be good at her job to have earned such a prize. "What made him change his mind?"

"The nightmares."

"This isn't the first?"

She shook her head, rippling her soft hair against his chest. His breath caught in his throat for a heartbeat. "They started not long after we set up our temporary office in Summit Station." A dejected look crossed Kyra's face and she fell silent. Mac felt her muscles tighten beneath his fingers. He gently kneaded at the tension.

"Tell me about your nightmares."

Her whole body stiffened. She sat up and turned to face him. She probed deep into his eyes, as if to see whether his interest was genuine. Then, as if coming to a decision, she sighed and relaxed against him. Slowly, methodically, he massaged away her defenses.

"The worst part is that they don't make sense. It's like I'm sucked into the past. Memories that aren't mine. Can't be mine. I see myself, but it's not really me." Her hand moved in a helpless gesture.

"My clothes are from a different era," she continued. "There's this man. Dark hair and beard streaked with gray. He's got a sharp, pointed nose and ears like Spock on 'Star Trek.' And his eyes; they're so hard and cruel." A fearful shudder echoed through his body.

40

"I have no idea who he is, but he's mad at me. He rants and he raves, but I can't hear what he's saying."

Kyra's fingers unconsciously grasped the material of Mac's sweat pants, bringing an instant reaction she didn't notice. Mac pushed away the erotic images his mind conjured up.

"I've seen him hit me," Kyra said.

"And tonight?" He stroked her arm.

She stiffened again, and with his hand, Mac urged her to lean her head on his shoulder, then gently unknotted the fear cementing the taut chords of her neck. Regret sighed through him. Once she'd trusted him body, mind, and soul. Now she didn't even trust him with her nightmare.

"Tell me what you saw tonight, Kyra."

She shook her head against his shoulder, her hair tickling his neck. He suppressed a moan. She had no idea what she was doing to him.

"Tell me," Mac said gently.

She turned, ready to push herself away from his arms. Mac half-dragged her into his lap and held her soothingly until her protesting grasp on his shoulders relaxed. She pressed her nose against his neck. "You smell earthy, like wild honey."

Without thinking, Mac brushed his lips lightly against hers.

"You taste so warm," Kyra whispered. Her feverish gaze blazed, sending a familiar volcanic reaction erupting deep in his core, spreading molten fire along the surface of his skin.

"Your touch makes me forget the horrible pictures in my mind." Hopelessness tinged her voice. Like a woman possessed, she clamped her fingers urgently into the skin of his shoulders. "Help me forget, Mac."

This was crazy. She wanted a distraction, and he wanted her to see him clearly, not through the misty veil of desperation. "Are you offering me your body?"

She blinked in confusion. "No. No, I . . . you . . .

I'm scared, Mac. I'm scared the nightmare won't go away. I'm scared of what I'll see. I'm scared to go to sleep."

She clutched him like a lifeline, desperation, fear, and pain twisting her face into a mask of terror.

"Tell me what you saw."

"Tonight . . ." She gulped a mouthful of air. "Tonight there was blood everywhere. He wanted to kill me. I saw it in his eyes." She shook her head. "We were in a cave somewhere. But what kind of cave has an elevator?"

The old Easton mine, his mission's goal, had an elevator. Mac didn't like the chill of premonition making the hair on the back of his neck stand up.

"I-I think I killed him instead," Kyra whispered harshly.

"Nightmares don't always make sense."

She buried her face into the angle of his neck. "Hold me."

"As long as you want." Mac resumed his calming caress, his thoughts roiling.

Ten minutes later Mac shifted Kyra's weight and noticed that her breathing had grown shallow and even. She'd fallen asleep. Her body warm and soft against his had him believing in the future again.

Suddenly her dark lashes fluttered against her pale skin and her forehead crinkled in anxiety. The fingers of one hand dug painfully into his biceps.

"Mac?" she asked in a sleep-laden voice.

"Umm. I'm right here."

"Don't let him kill me. Don't let me die."

Chapter Three

Kyra woke to Misty's cold nose jabbing her hand and Mac's warm body spooned against hers on the sofa; his arm wrapped protectively around her waist and his breath soft against her hair. An almost imperceptible tensing of muscle and intake of breath signaled the instant Mac awoke, but he didn't move.

As she realized she'd spent the night cuddled with a man she'd vowed to shun, a burning flush swamped Kyra's face. This wasn't like her at all. She eased from beneath the quilt, letting Mac's arm fall gently as she moved. What had she done?

She tried to escape to her room, but Misty sank her teeth into the hem of her flannel nightgown and with a low growl told Kyra that she was ready for her breakfast. Mac stirred on the sofa, increasing her need to flee.

"Not now," Kyra whispered irritably.

Misty insisted.

After scooping a cup of dog food into Misty's bowl

and freshening her water, Kyra almost ran to her room. She wasn't ready to meet Mac's keen gaze. As she closed her own door, she heard him pad to his room across the hall.

"Phew! Too close."

She erased the last bitter traces of her nightmare with an invigorating cold shower, then dressed in her softest, most comfortable clothes. She built the layers like a mason bricking a wall—silk long underwear top, a cream turtleneck, a heavy fuchsia sweater, silk long underwear bottoms, forest green Lycra ski pants, and thick, cream-colored slouch socks. How could she ever face Mac again after what she'd done last night? She'd found something about the masculine strength of him, the earthy scent of him very reassuring—as she had all those years ago. But turning to him had been a mistake.

Kyra, you've really lost it. You've got to get a grip. You can't fall for him again.

She tried to tame her unruly curls into some semblance of order, gave up, and bound them into a French braid.

The best thing to do would be to leave Utah and never come back. But as much as she feared the nightmares, she had to find out why she'd been given away as a baby, and why the shadow of death skirted her life in this corner of the world. She'd never find her mental balance unless she faced the monster of her nightmare and the hole that had been left in the fabric of her past. Every instinct told her this was the right decision, but fear made her want to shut the door to her dreams and run away as fast as she could.

Every time she thought about the nightmares a shudder of dread shook her body. Every time she thought of Mac's arms holding her, a fiery blush heated her cheeks. How could she have let Mac comfort her like that? She sighed. And how long would it last? She'd have to watch out for those instinctive responses of hers or they'd get her in trouble all over again.

Then it hit her that in Mac's arms she'd had her first good night's sleep in nearly a month. The edge of continual weariness was gone, and she had more energy this morning than she'd had for a long while.

The braid was crooked. Kyra unwound it and started over.

Her work was important and satisfying and she had friends to keep her from getting lonely. She didn't need a man to make her happy. Or marriage and children to satisfy her. She was, after all, a modern woman.

Her reflection in the mirror called her a liar.

"What do you know?"

Apparently a lot.

Mac's hands massaging away her fears, Mac's lips kissing away the horrid images reminded her that something was missing from her life—the physical connection with another human being that her nature craved.

But not with Mac.

Kyra wound a pink rubber band around the end of her braid. On the other hand, dealing with him for a few days could bring the closure she needed to heal once and for all the wound he'd left behind.

She sighed, feeling as if she sat on both ends of a seesaw. She was damned if she did, damned if she didn't. The painful fact was that she couldn't ignore either the nightmares or Mac. Both would haunt her unless she dealt with them. But how? And where to start?

When she dared to return to the living room and face Mac, she found Misty perched on one of the stools at the counter and Mac lecturing the dog on the art of flipping pancakes.

"I didn't know pancake flipping was an art," Kyra

45

said, flashing Mac a reluctant smile. She went to the fridge in search of orange juice, poured herself a glass, and sat on the stool next to Misty's. Mac had changed into black Dockers, a white turtleneck, and a red sweater. The ends of his still damp hair curled at the base of his neck.

"Oh, it is," Mac said. He proceeded to pick up the pan, flip the pancake it contained, and catch it expertly. Misty, thinking a breakfast bonanza would soon befall her, hopped off the stool and raced to Mac's feet.

"I told you I was good," he said to the dog. Disappointed, Misty returned to her position on top of the stool.

He gave Kyra a quick once-over. "So how many layers do you have on this morning?"

"I don't know what you mean." The wings of her shoulders rounded protectively forward in response.

One of Mac's eyebrows lifted with incredulity. "I'd say six or seven. What are you afraid of?"

"Nothing." She shrugged and gulped her orange juice.

"Me?"

Who else? You already have me feeling as if I'm about to shake hands with a high-tension wire. "Of course not."

"You're afraid I'll hurt you again."

He'd always been sharp. That keen vision of his had latched onto her as easy prey, and he was doing it again. She scowled at him. "I won't let you."

"I think you're still attracted to me—"

"Your ego amazes me—"

"Why else would you be wearing so many layers?"

"Maybe I'm cold."

"Uh-huh." He walked to the fridge. "Do vegetarians like blueberry pancakes?" Mac placed a bottle of maple syrup in front of her.

"You're going to rub that in, aren't you, Mr. Carnivore? I suppose you'll be frying some bacon to go along with those pancakes?" Kyra teased back, glad to take the conversation into a light direction. She could handle pointless banter much better than inquiries into her psyche. Much better than her undisciplined thoughts of Mac and his hands and where she'd like to feel them.

"Nope. Sausages. Found them orphaned in the back of the freezer." Mac dropped half a dozen links on the sizzling grill. "I just had to rescue them."

The smell of the hot grease and singed meat made Kyra's empty stomach lurch. "Don't you know those things are lethal?"

"Yeah, but I love to live dangerously. How about you?" Mac leaned across the counter and ran a finger softly along her jaw.

Kyra forced herself not to lean into his touch. "It depends on how you define danger."

Mac went to the freezer and got out a bag of coffee beans. "Excitement. Thrill. A rush of adrenaline. The breaking of rules. Testing your limits and knowing that brain and brawn got you out safely." He measured a scoop of beans into the coffee grinder, the whirring noise temporarily drowning out any comment.

Kyra thought about her job. Except for the brawn, her work encompassed all of the above. "I live that way every day."

He dumped the grinds into the filter, poured water into the coffee maker, and turned it on. "As an architect? Or do you live a double life?"

She couldn't help laughing. "What's that supposed to mean?"

The coffee gurgled into the glass pot and the enticing aroma excited the last of her sleepy brain cells into awareness.

He poured a cup of coffee and lifted it in her direction. "Coffee?"

"I'd love a cup." She smiled coyly. Even though she preferred tea in the morning, she played along. "With cream. I like to live dangerously, too."

As he poked his head in the fridge for some cream, Mac laughed with deep-hearted abandon. Kyra found herself wanting his laughter to go on forever. She loved the way the rippling sounds floated inside her like a caress. She loved the way the freeness of it drove the nightmares into the deep, dark corners of her mind.

"You're a strange bird, Kyra Kirtland."

So are you. How could she possibly be attracted and repelled by the a person at the same time? It didn't make any sense.

Mac placed the cup of coffee before her and followed it soon after with a plate of pancakes.

"Sausage?" He dangled a sausage on a fork in front of her nose, his wide grin teasing.

Kyra glared at him and pushed the fork away, wrinkling her nose in disgust. She had a hard time suppressing the laugh bubbling in her chest and stuffed a forkful of pancake in her mouth to stop her amusement from spilling out and negating her stern intent.

"You don't have to cook for me," she said. Misty leaped into Kyra's lap and watched each forkful with hopeful anticipation.

"I like to. I'd like to do a lot of things for you, Kyra."

His voice was husky. His eyes gleamed with sexuality. Desire shivered through her. Kyra chose to ignore him, ignore her own feelings. "Where'd you learn to cook, anyway?"

"I taught myself." Mac sat down with his own plate. "I love to eat and going out every night got boring after a while."

"These are really good." The heavy coat of hair on

top of all her layers of clothing suddenly became uncomfortably hot. Kyra returned Misty to her stool and firmly insisted she stay there.

In the silence, the feel of her blood bumping against her pulse points had her shifting uncomfortably in her seat. She wished for his earlier silliness so she wouldn't have to deal with her growing awareness of him, of the sensual memories he stirred.

"So, how come some lucky girl hasn't snatched you up and put you to work in her kitchen?" Kyra moved her food around the plate.

When he looked at her over the rim of his cup his eyes shone like polished silver. "I'm still single, if that's what you're getting at."

"Of course not." She felt her cheeks burn. "Our relationship is dead. Over. Done with."

"I want another chance."

Not in this lifetime. "Another chance at what? Breaking my heart?"

"At loving you. The right way."

She didn't say anything—couldn't say anything for the lump in her throat.

"So, what are you going to do?" he asked.

"Ignore you, and hope you go away." She stabbed a stack of pancake bits to hide her uneasiness.

"About your nightmares."

Her fork hung in midair. Dread leadened the pancakes in her stomach. She shrugged and dropped her fork to her plate.

"Have you seen a doctor about them?"

"No, and I'm not going to either." She'd dealt with enough doctors in the past year, during her mother's illness, to know how little they could truly do. And she couldn't stand the thought of a stranger calmly telling her she was going crazy. "It's something I have to work out on my own."

Mac's gaze returned to her face. "So, you've got a plan."

49

"I'm working on one."

She felt his suppressed sigh and melted back to her childhood and her father's frequent disappointment at her inability to come to an instant decision. She couldn't bear to look in Mac's deep gray eyes and see disappointment, so she stared at the muddy contents of her coffee cup.

"You can't just do nothing," Mac said.

"I can't rush into anything either. I have to think."

Mac pushed his plate away from him. "Thinking won't get anything done. By the time you decide which car to take, the train'll have left without you."

Anger tensed every one of her muscles into knots. "Well, it's better than jumping blindly at the train and hoping I hit an open door."

Mac refilled his coffee cup and sat back down. "So, what are you going to do?"

"Mac!"

"Why don't you talk your thoughts out? Maybe I can help you."

"I don't want your help." Kyra pushed a piece of pancake around in a lake of maple syrup. "And I don't like to be pushed."

"I'm not going to push you into anything you don't want."

His gaze was intent. Her insides fluttered. "Are we still talking about my nightmares?" She had the distinct impression they weren't.

"Listen, Kyra, this problem of yours is obviously causing you a great deal of emotional pain. I don't believe in destiny or fate or anything like that, but last night when you had your nightmare you trusted me. Trust me now."

Kyra looked deep into his silver eyes and found honesty. Maybe it would be different this time. Maybe he would stay longer than a honeymoon. More than anything she wanted to believe him. She had known then she would never love anyone as viscerally, as completely as she'd loved Mac. But experience had taught her a painful lesson. She was in no hurry to repeat it.

Mac took her delving stare like the solid walls of the mountains outside the window. How could she ever have fallen in love with someone like him? He never seemed unsure, making her wish he had some sort of endearing little quirk, a weakness of some sort to make him more human. The old hurt and rage welled up again.

She wouldn't fall for him again. History didn't have to repeat itself. She could use him, use his grounding strength and prove to herself the stitches on her heart were strong enough to withstand him. Then she could leave, without looking back, just as he had done.

"Why should I trust you again?" she asked.

"Who else have you got?"

Who, indeed? She didn't have anyone left in the whole world. Her father was dead. Her mother was dead. George was her friend and mentor, but he wouldn't suffer weakness of any kind. Wasn't that why he'd sent her away? To get strong again. Her hollow sigh echoed the emptiness of her heart. Alone. Unless she placed her trust in the one man she couldn't afford to trust. Did that make him a skewed balance or a counterweight? She couldn't decide.

"I have a feeling I'll regret this," Kyra said finally.

She slid off her stool, taking her coffee cup with her, and headed for the window. The snow had stopped falling and the sun shone, sparkling the white crystals like fool's gold, melting the snow-laden boughs into long, treacherous icicles whose stark shadows blotted at the snow like black daggers.

A movement among the pines caught Kyra's attention. From behind a tree trunk a silver shadow in the shape of a wolf shimmered. It moved into the open until it stood by itself, with no apparent reason for its presence. If a shadow could stare, this one stared straight at her.

A face flashed in her mind: the man in her dreams. She dropped the cup. It shattered against the floor. One hand flew to her mouth to stifle a gasp.

"What's wrong, Kyra?"

"That wolf shadow." She pointed out the window. "He's part of the nightmare. He's the one."

"The one what?"

"The one I killed."

"Kyra, there are no wolves in Utah." Rag in hand, Mac joined Kyra at the window. He peered out into the sun-sparkled snow and saw nothing. "See, there's nothing out there. It was probably just the neighbor's German Shepherd."

Mac kneeled to pick up the pieces of broken ceramic.

"It wasn't a dog. And I didn't say I saw a wolf. I said I saw a shadow shaped like a wolf." Kyra crouched down to take the rag from him. "Here, let me do that."

"I've got it." Mac plucked the last piece from the floor and wrapped it in the rag. "Don't you see that your nightmares have you jumping at every shadow? You've got to do something about them before they control your life."

"He was there." Kyra straightened up to stand, crossing her arms under her chest and turning her watery gaze out the window.

Damn, she was shutting him out. Mac dumped the broken cup into the garbage, then gathered the plates Misty was busily licking clean. Misty glanced up at him, a sticky doggy grin plastered on her face. He shooed her off the counter and let her out the back door before he turned his attention back to Kyra. She still stared at the pristine snow. Had her fatigue caused her to hallucinate?

"He's still there," Kyra said. "Behind that tree. Can you see him? He's staring at me." Her voice was sure and challenging.

Mac came up behind her, gathering her in his arms as he looked over her shoulder at the spot she pointed out. His skin tingled everywhere they touched. He reveled in the feminine softness of her body, remembering the unbridled passion he'd savored from it so long ago. Too long.

He'd dreamed so often of finding her again. None of the reunions he'd imagined had played out this way. He'd expected her to be wary. He'd expected to have to earn her trust and her love all over again. He'd never expected to find her so troubled. His arms tightened around her protectively. He wanted to see her smile again—that dazzling smile of hers, as brilliant as midday sunshine, the one that made him feel so potently male, the center of her world.

The reflection of her face in the window looked so fragile, on the brink of shattering from the force of her tension, but Mac sensed in her an inner strength. Somehow he had to draw on that power and make her confront her nightmares. This haunting sadness didn't belong in someone of such brimming life.

"There's nothing there, Kyra," Mac said with a gentleness that disguised his taut nerves.

"Even Misty sees him. Look how puffed up her coat is. She's growling."

"There's a squirrel in the tree." Mac turned her around in his arms. "Ah, Kyra, don't cry. I hate tears." He hated *her* tears and the way they reminded him of how he'd failed her.

"What if it's more than a nightmare? What if what I'm seeing is real?" Kyra dropped her head against his shoulder, a small, trusting gesture he cherished like a gift. "Am I going crazy?"

"No, you're not. Not yet. But you will drive yourself

over the edge if you just wait for things to happen to you." His hand slid down the bumpy track of her golden-red braid. The strands shone like liquid gold in the morning sun streaming through the window. A waft of passion flowers reached his nostrils, transporting him to paradise and the tangle of their warm bodies on a cool moonlit beach.

He wanted her. Badly. He wanted her in a way that had a lot to do with sex and everything to do with the complete and utter paradox of inner peace and fiery sunshine he'd found in her arms. Why did so much have to stand between them?

"Talk to me, Kyra. Tell me what's going on?" *Distract me from your magic and keep me from rushing you like a fool.*

Her fingers dug into his arms, mirroring her frustration. "I don't know. If I knew what was happening, then I could do something concrete about it, but nothing makes sense."

"Are you willing to try?" Mac asked.

He pushed her slightly away from him so he could read her green eyes. He felt torn between his two duties. Seven years ago he'd chosen his duty to the Institute over his duty to her and broken her heart. Now neither she nor the mountain could wait. Somehow he'd have to help both of them at once.

"How about it, Kyra?"

"I don't have much of a choice."

Mac let out the breath he hadn't been aware he'd held. "Good." He understood action. "Let me get you a fresh cup of coffee and we can sort this out."

While Kyra went back to the kitchen, Mac answered Misty's scratch at the back door. Misty sniffed around the kitchen. When she found no interesting scraps on the floor, she headed for the living room and settled on the recliner.

Mac placed a steaming mug of coffee in front of Kyra and added a generous dollop of cream. Where had the woman he'd loved disappeared to? He found he was annoyed with her, and it took some effort to keep his voice calm and even. "How long ago did these nightmares start?"

Dealing with facts allowed him to concentrate and temporarily forget his perilous flights of fancy. Patience, he reminded himself, patience.

"A month." Kyra wrapped her hands around the proffered mug.

Mac emptied his cup into the sink and refilled it with hot coffee. "Have they changed?"

Pain flashed in Kyra's eyes and a worried crease wrinkled her forehead. He resisted the urge to kiss it smooth. "Yes. They've gotten stronger and more frequent over time."

Mac sat in the stool facing Kyra's and carefully watched her body language as he trained his ears to filter her words. "What about the nightmare last night? Was there anything new?"

"Last night's was the worst. It was so real." A shudder racked her body and Kyra sipped from her cup, as if to quell the cold shivers.

"Do you suppose your mother's recent death has anything to do with what you're dreaming?"

Kyra's indignant glare spiked his face. A spark. It was a start. "I'm not that impressionable."

"I'm not passing judgment. I'm just exploring all angles. The way you like to operate."

"You're right. I'm sorry." She sipped her coffee pensively, shifting her eyes down and to the left. "No, I don't think my mother's death is what triggered these dreams. They have nothing to do with her. It's like I'm caught in a story that took place a long time ago."

"Do you know these people?"

"No. Although . . ." Kyra shook her head.

Why was she mistrusting her instincts?

"Although, what?" " Mac pressed.

"The woman. I feel connected to her. She sort of looks like me."

Her cheeks flushed a delightful pink, and Mac couldn't help thinking that they should always glow that healthily. A thought zipped through her mind, and Mac could see it wasn't a pleasant one by the way her face turned deathly pale.

"What is it, Kyra?"

She shook her head again and turned her gaze to her cup.

"Come on. We're getting somewhere."

Kyra hesitated and pushed her hands, still holding her coffee mug, so that the backs of her fingers touched his. Electricity still existed between them, and the faint pulse vibrating along his skin held a world of promise.

"Right after my mother died . . . I found out I was adopted."

The last part spilled out from her like a cascade, and Mac experienced the betrayal she'd endured at the revelation. Now he understood her doubts about her instincts. She thought they had failed her at important times. Intuitively, he knew her instincts weren't to blame, but the good intentions of people who loved her and had tried to shelter her were. What reason had her mother had to keep such a secret?

"Do you think that maybe this woman in my mind is related to me somehow, and that's why I'm picking up her image?" Kyra's worried gaze rose to meet his. "Last night I saw someone new. For some reason I was sure she was my natural mother."

A thrill of excitement rang through Mac's body and he recognized it as the feeling he always got when he was on the right track.

"Did she say anything?" he asked.

Kyra tried to disconnect their touch, but Mac trapped her hands in his, offering his silent support.

"She said, 'Go in for the kill.' Right after that my adoptive mother told me to get out of Park City or I would die."

This new twist to her dreams worried him. The dreams had seemed out of character to start with for someone as practical as Kyra, but now the sense of wrongness about them increased. "What else?"

"Nothing. Except the adoption papers said I was born in Park City."

"That's it, then."

"What?" Kyra looked at him with frightened eyes. Not the innocent fear of a woman on the brink of tasting passion for the first time, but a primal fear that had banked that passion to cold embers.

She needed a push in the right direction. He had enough sense to know that he couldn't get all of Kyra's attention until she'd solved the mystery of her dreams, and to stir her generous passion to life he would need her full attention. Sitting here talking wasn't going to get them very far, but finding the source of her nightmares and confronting it would dissipate it. Mac had seen it happen often enough in his long career to know that it was the truth. He'd give her a day before he tackled the mountain.

"We're going to Park City."

Chapter Four

Park City! Familiar dread swamped through Kyra. No, she couldn't go there. She wasn't ready yet.

The sunshine seemed to fade from the kitchen, leaving her chilled to the bone. Even the warm coffee in her cup offered no solace from the ice of primal fear.

Park City. The town named on the adoption papers she'd seen in the lawyer's office after her mother's funeral. How could her mother have kept something like that from her? Kyra tightened her hold on her cup. Her throat constricted and her heart felt as if it were bleeding. She loved her mother, but she couldn't help the betrayal she felt every time she thought about the fact that her adoption had been hidden from her all of her life.

Get over it, Kyra! You're all grown up now, what difference can it make?

"When?" she asked.

"No time like the present." Mac's voice was too

bright, his smile too cheerful. He took her cup from her and set it in the sink.

Losing the anchor of the cup, Kyra knotted her fingers in her lap. "What's the plan?"

"We'll wing it."

Every step of her job required careful thought—from the first germ of an idea down to the meticulous specifications needed to transform her drawings into concrete objects. The process of thinking and planning gave her comfort and confidence. Going off to Park City without a series of steps and alternatives inspired nothing but apprehension.

Then a tremor of anger rumbled through her. At herself or Mac? It didn't matter. She lashed out at him. "Just who do you think you are, making decisions for me?"

Mac leaned across the counter separating them and stared straight at her, his gaze sharp, intent, and more than a little annoyed. "Someone who remembers the spunk below all those layers of protective clothing. What I see now is a pale ghost of the woman I remember—"

"That's really none of your—"

"—Don't interrupt me while I'm on a roll. I've waited for you too long to watch you fade away. If you won't go see a doctor, then I'm going to drag you kicking and screaming if I have to, but you are going to look for that monster hiding in your mind. Do you understand?"

She swallowed hard. The determination of his gaze competed for intensity with the mass of dread gurgling through her stomach, making her want to throw up. Impulsive actions always got her in trouble. But in this case she knew she had no choice. Mac was right. Faced with her fears, she had to look at them. She could find betrayal, sorrow, and misery, but she could also find hope. Mac was offering her that hope.

"Okay," Kyra said. "Let's go."

He nodded stiffly, then got ready to leave.

As they wound their way down the mountain, Kyra decided Mac's truck matched his personality perfectly. Red, his favorite color, shone from a highly polished exterior. The deceptively comfortable interior of muted tan sported an instrument panel rivaling that of any personal jet. He seemed to drive for the sheer pleasure of it, rather than seeing it as a way to get somewhere, the way she did. A complicated man with many surprising facets—rugged, comfortable, exciting—like his mode of transportation.

Classic rock boomed from a series of speakers that surrounded them with sound, and warm air blew from carefully monitored vents. But the warmth didn't reach Kyra's cold body. And the bright sunshine outside couldn't hide the dark cloud that seemed to have settled over Eaton Peak since she'd spotted the wolf shadow this morning.

Kyra couldn't wash away the sticky apprehension that had attached itself to her the minute Mac had started the truck. Not all of it because of the wolf shadow, she realized. Danger as well as raw sensuality had practically pulsated from Mac the first time they'd met. Both had thrilled and frightened her, but in the end her curiosity about such magnetic energy had won over her fear. Just as her need for an anchor seemed to override her better judgment today. How big a price would she pay for momentary comfort this time around?

She missed Misty's rough hair and the relaxing effect petting her four-legged friend gave her. They'd left the dog in the laundry room, comfortably surrounded by her toys, to keep her nosy snout out of trouble. Now Kyra wished she'd insisted on taking her along.

A mile past the base of Eaton Peak, Mac slowed his mad pace on the service road long enough to point out a chalet surrounded with glass sides. Kyra could see a massive fireplace in the middle of the room. The place buzzed with cross-country skiers getting ready for an outing.

"Debbie must've booked a tour for this morning," Mac said. "The Christmas holidays are usually our busiest time. That's also the reason I'm banned from there."

Kyra was momentarily shaken out of her unease, so surprised was she by his comment. "Banned? Don't you own the place?"

"Yeah, but I'm not too patient with those sissy city folk who think they know it all. Debbie banishes me to my office whenever a tour comes in. She actually got down on her knees and thanked God when my roof caved in and I told her I was taking time off. She's lucky she's a great manager or she'd have found herself without a job."

Kyra laughed softly at the idea of anyone telling Mac what to do and decided that this Debbie must be someone special. When her thoughts strayed to wondering how special her cheeks flamed. It's none of your business, she reminded herself.

Mac pointed to a string of condos at the edge of a tract of wood. "My condo is the one farthest from Mountain Swift."

"Mountain Swift?"

"My ski resort."

"I would've thought you'd have picked a more down-to-earth name like . . . Blue Spruce Ski Center or something just as plain, not a bird."

"Sometimes I can be downright poetic." Mac grinned widely. "Does that surprise you?"

"Frankly, yes."

He chuckled.

Perhaps there were facets of Mac she hadn't yet discovered, she thought, but solving two mysteries in one day was asking too much of her. The lid would remain tightly shut on the one labeled *Mac*.

She tried to keep her concentration on the passing scenery but couldn't. Her rising blood pressure made her face flush hot and her pulse thump painfully around her skull. Unconsciously, her hands gripped the sides of the leather-upholstered bucket seat of Mac's Range Rover.

Mac looked at her quizzically. "Are you all right?"

Kyra forced a smile. "Perfect."

Perfectly horrible. She was sure she'd be sick any minute. She squeezed her eyes shut tight. Maybe if she filled her mind with pretty pictures she could calm her jangled nerves. But even images of her mother's cottage along Cocoa Beach, with its calming sounds of surging sea, couldn't alleviate the deep-set anxiety.

Kyra opened her eyes just as Mac sped onto the highway, barely missing an oncoming car. Her patience with his mad-hatter driving snapped. "Where on earth did you learn to drive? That guy had the right of way."

"I had plenty of room."

"You could've gotten us killed."

"No chance of that, Kyra. Not a chance." His low rumbling chuckle, instead of pleasing her as it had earlier that morning, grated on her already raw nerves. "I'm in complete control."

And he was. He had both his hands on the wheel and steered with an ease that reflected skill. An air of casual power surrounded him, making her feel as if this man could handle absolutely anything that came his way. The realization took the wind out of the sails of her anger, but stubbornness made her push on.

"Then why do I feel as if we're an accident waiting to happen on the last lap of the Indy 500?" she asked.

He grinned at her, and she saw the speedometer's needle creep down slightly. "Because you've been living in that safe little world of yours for too long."

"Don't feel like you have to inject any excitement into my life. I've got quite enough, thank you."

His grin turned wicked. "But not the right kind."

"And I suppose you think you know exactly what I need."

"You need me. I'm just the man for you, Kyra." He cast her a sidelong glance. "You might as well get used to the fact that I won't leave this time."

She didn't want to analyze the rush of heat flowing through her or the highly charged undercurrents of their conversation. It was safer to change the subject. "So, how's the ski business this year?"

Mac gave her an odd look. "Nervous?" He glanced pointedly at a tight twist that had only minutes ago been a pair of gloves.

"A little," Kyra admitted after a moment. She sighed heavily. She didn't like the whirlwind of emotions blowing through her this morning, but she hadn't yet found the key to abating its destructive force. The snow-covered countryside blurred past her window.

"Cheer up, Sunshine. Things aren't as gloomy as you make them out to be. We'll get this whole mess straightened out in no time."

Mac's bright smile did nothing to calm her mounting apprehension. Nor did it appease the growing feeling that Mac was turning her into some sort of project. Was he trying to redeem himself by playing knight in shining armor? Did he think it would make her forget the pain he'd caused her?

"Is that a guarantee?" Kyra probed Mac's unreadable profile, looking for she wasn't sure what. Maybe she did want reassurance that everything would finish with a happy ending.

"Word of honor."

The way he looked at her caused memories of Hawaii to float up from her subconscious. Mac could be loving and caring. He could make her feel alive in a way no one else had. Trust, a small voice told her. Then she saw herself full of joy, waiting for him at the back of the small white church. And waiting. He could also hurt her like no one else could.

Mac kept up a stream of chatter about the area they were driving through. He was trying to distract her, Kyra realized, but even Mac's cheery demeanor couldn't keep naked fear from coiling like a snake at the pit of her stomach. With each click of the odometer the snake squeezed her intestines tighter, while the rattler's tongue flicked painfully against the sensitive tissues and its noisy rattle resonated through her gut. How could Mac possibly believe that dragging her through Park City would do any good? Relaxing in the McKanes' comfy home would certainly have been easier than this gut-wrenching ordeal.

But she wanted her life back. The easy way out wasn't an option.

Mac's hand, loose on her leg, was too intimate a gesture for the strangers they'd become, yet Kyra drew a measure of comfort from this connection. It was real when nothing else seemed to be right now. Part of her wanted more of this reality, more than the fringe of warmth he offered. Part of her wanted to relive the passionate recklessness that had brought her completely to life all those years ago. She fought the memories, but when she failed to suppress them, she luxuriated in them.

Between the droning sounds of the engine, her warm memories, and the compelling, calming effect of Mac's voice, the snake in her guts slowly uncoiled and she relaxed. Her head rested against the window and her eyelids grew heavy.

Could fire be solid? she wondered in a dozing haze. Mac's fire had branded her soul, and his solid strength was helping her keep her feet firmly on the ground. She smiled at the image of Mac's silver eyes ablaze with desire. The full power of the remembered gaze still held a dizzying kind of attraction. Yes, fire could be solid. She sighed.

The right feeling. The wrong man.

Slowly, the picture shifted. Amazing, she thought, even with my eyes closed I can see the scenery outside. Fields of snow. Houses with smoke coming out of their chimneys. Old-fashioned trucks. Horses drawing buggies.

Mac turned off the highway at the Park City exit, still only marginally following the speed limit, from the way the landscape sped past. Something wasn't right. Wasn't there a shopping center here? Why were the streets so muddy?

She could hear her heart beat hard against her ribs. She tried to pry her heavy lids open but couldn't. Mac rounded a corner. She twisted her head to look at him, but couldn't see him. Panic zigzagged through her like an out-of-control skier on a steep slope. Her tongue felt thick in her mouth. "Mac?"

"We're almost there."

She turned toward the voice coming to her in a fog. She desperately tried to lift her heavy lids. She could hear him, but couldn't see him. Instead she took in the sight of an old livery stable. *This is not real. This is not happening. This does not make sense. Concentrate on Mac's voice. That's real.* "I didn't know Park City still had a livery stable."

"They don't, as far as I know." Mac braked to slow his speed.

"We just passed one."

"The Kimball Art Center?"

Why did he sound so far away? "No. There." How could he miss the big brown building with the white lettering?

"Watch out!" Kyra yelled. She launched herself in the direction of the steering wheel, gripped it and twisted it in time to avoid a quaintly dressed man on a ragged chestnut horse. "You almost hit that guy on the horse!"

As they came to a jarring halt, Mac forcefully grasped the wheel away from her. "What horse?"

"Over . . . there . . ." Her voice trailed off. The muddy street had turned into asphalt covered with slushy snow, and Kyra realized her eyes were wide open.

An angry Mac glared at her.

She blinked and looked back at the livery stable. The brown planks were lighter and the white sign announcing the livery had changed to black letters that clearly read KIMBALL ART CENTER. Bewildered, Kyra slumped against the back of her seat.

What had just happened?

Mac deftly maneuvered the truck out of the snow-bank she'd steered them into and drove into a nearby parking lot.

"Don't ever do that again!" Mac jumped out to check the damage to his front fender.

He seemed more annoyed with a possible dent on his precious truck than in her trespass on the wrong side of sanity. It was ridiculous to feel that way, of course, but at least her side trip into self-pity was taking the edge off the impossibility she'd just lived through.

"You're lucky there's no dent." Mac slammed the truck's door shut. The roll of the idling engine filled the heavy silence between them. "What on earth were you thinking of?"

She'd been thinking she'd avoid sending a horse to the glue factory. Only the horse wasn't real, and she could have gotten Mac and herself hurt. What she was thinking now was that it wouldn't be very long before men dressed in white offered her a nice strait-jacket and a ride in a padded truck. It didn't make sense. Why were these images invading her mind when she hadn't even been sleeping?

"What happened, Kyra?"

She tried to find the words to explain what had happened to her, but only nonsensical pictures came to mind. With a frustrated groan she gave up and tried a different tack.

"Was there ever a livery stable where the Kimball Art Center is?" Kyra asked.

"I don't know." With a finger, Mac pushed back a stray curl from her cheek. Kyra stiffened, and his finger fell away. She didn't need the extra jumble of Mac's touch added to her already scrambled mind.

"There's a visitors' center and museum up the street," Mac said. "We'll ask there." He paused. "Tell me what happened, Kyra. Trust me."

What else could she do? If she didn't try to explain to him what had happened, he'd wonder why she'd acted like a perfect idiot. "I . . . saw a muddy street, a man on a horse crossing the street toward the train depot, and a livery stable where the art center is."

Mac's arched eyebrow and the slight movement of his shoulders away from her said it all. He didn't believe her. And why should he? She could hardly believe it herself.

"That doesn't make any sense," Mac said. Kyra had to give him credit for keeping his voice even and devoid of sarcasm.

"I know that! But I know what I saw. Maybe I'm going insane. I don't know. I only know that when you rounded that corner I couldn't open my eyes, but I saw something that had to be some sort of time warp. And that's scary as hell, because I wasn't sleeping this time."

"I don't like this."

"And you think *I* do?"

Mac searched her face for a long minute before he answered. "All right. Let's go to the museum and see what we can find out." He shut off the ignition. "Let's walk."

Kyra and Mac walked side by side onto the sidewalk lining Main Street. Their feet sank into a few inches of muddy snow with the consistency of mashed potatoes.

"Let me know if you want to stop anywhere to shop," Mac teased.

"Cute, Mac. You started this nightmare when you insisted we come here. Let's just get it over with."

"Relax."

"That's easy for you to say. You're not the one going crazy."

"I wouldn't say that."

Kyra ignored his cryptic comment, ignored the undeniably caring light in his eyes, ignored her own urge to play with the danger he offered. Fearing her eyesight would once again trick her into seeing something that wasn't there, she couldn't even enjoy the historic preservation that had been made along Main Street.

She barely noticed the red ribbons twisted around the green street lamps, the poinsettia banners hanging from the posts, or the wreaths and green garlands decorating most of the storefronts. Her thoughts kept returning to Mac and what he might be thinking.

His face revealed nothing at all. Was he regretting having become involved with her again? Not that they had the kind of relationship they'd once shared. Truth be told, they had no relationship at all. But he'd slipped so easily back into her life. Getting used to his presence had required no effort at all. She wasn't accustomed to depending on anybody, yet leaning on Mac seemed so natural.

And foolish, she reminded herself, very foolish.

Nonetheless, she edged closer to him until the

swish of his black sleeve against her lime green one created a calming rhythm.

Mac informed her that City Hall had once occupied the space where the visitors' center now stood. As they entered the building through the pine green door, an overly bright white-haired lady greeted them. Stacks of tourist information littered two walls, but Kyra had no interest in those. As this morning's waking nightmare loomed foremost in her mind, her usual adroitness for small talk slipped out the door.

"Excuse me," Kyra said to the lady behind the counter. "Could you tell me if there ever was a livery stable where the Kimball Art Center is now located?"

"Why, yes." The lady seemed pleased to be of assistance. "The Kimball brothers operated a livery stable and stagecoach on that spot. Let me see, in the late 1800s. Then, in 1929, the barn was torn down so a garage could be built. Horses kind of lost their appeal when the car came into use by most folks. Gotta change with the times." She laughed cheerily. "I believe it was in the forties that Fred Eley took over. He added a dealership and operated the place until 1972. It's interesting that William Kimball, who started the art center, was no relation at all to the original Kimballs in that location."

"That is interesting," Kyra said, trying to keep her impatience out of her voice. Mac's intent gaze on her and his silent questions did nothing to abate the tension. "What railroad company ran the trains into Park City in the late 1800s or early 1900s?"

As if this wasn't the type of questions she was used to answering, the lady's brown eyes twinkled with curiosity. "Let me see . . . the depot was Union Pacific, but the Denver and the Rio Grande also stopped here, I believe. I'm sure we have pictures in the museum that would confirm my memory."

Sylvie Kurtz

Kyra forced a bright smile. "Thank you for your help."

"Don't forget to take a peek at the territorial jail in the basement before you leave," the lady called after them.

Kyra and Mac walked slowly through the dimly lit museum, stopping at each glass display case to examine its content. Picture after picture confirmed what her mind had seen. She'd somehow witnessed Park City in the early 1900s, at the height of the silver mining days.

While part of her marveled at the impossibility of what had happened to her, another remained highly aware of Mac watching her every movement. She wished she could keep her face as impassive as he kept his, but she knew her mask slipped with each feeling and reflected her every thought. Did he see a crazed lunatic or the woman she'd once been?

She felt like neither.

And both.

And she didn't want him seeing her like this, so close to losing control, so far from the strong, successful woman she'd become since he'd disappeared.

"I can hear the wheels turning," Mac said, stopping behind her at a display. His breath fanned her ear with a warmth lacking in their dim surroundings. "What's going on in that head of yours?"

Kyra shrugged and moved on to the next lighted case.

Mac followed. "You're making this hard on yourself. I thought we'd agreed you could trust me."

"Habit, I guess." Her gaze never left the display, but the photographs blurred. "I don't understand why I saw the early days of Park City. It doesn't make sense. I've never been here. I've never seen any movies or read any books about Park City. But everything's the same." As she pointed to a picture of old Main Street, her vision refocused. "I can even tell you

70

what color those buildings and signs were." She stopped and turned to Mac, silently pleading for an answer that made sense. "Why is this happening to me?"

She sensed he wanted to hold her. She wanted him to. But neither of them moved. "Can't help you with that one."

"No, I don't suppose anyone can." She walked to the next panel. When her gaze lit on the photograph she took a step back and gasped. She knew that face.

"Mac!" She fumbled for his hand. "See that picture?"

He peered over her shoulder, reading the accompanying tag. "Hallie Hennesey Eaton Barrett Stern, the Silver Sovereign. She's quite a legend around here."

"That's the woman I become in my nightmares." As her voice scraped through her throat, it felt tight and raw. Was there a connection between them? Was this woman part of her mysterious past?

Mac calmly looked from Kyra to the picture and back. The silver of his eyes glittered and made her catch her breath. He saw it; he saw the likeness. It wasn't all in her head. "There is a resemblance."

"I've got to find out more about her." She squeezed his hand in an unconscious plea.

"All right." Mac loosened her hold on his hand, flexing his fingers to get the blood circulating. "The library's got a microfilm copy of every edition of the *Park Record* ever printed. Let's go see what we can find."

"How far's the library?" Not that it mattered. She would walk a hundred miles to get there, but her need for answers made her impatient.

"Six or seven blocks. Another walk'll do us both some good."

His long strides ate the sidewalk rapidly. Undiluted energy vibrated from him, taking Kyra along for the ride. She held on to Mac's hand tightly so she wouldn't be left behind, wondering what he'd seen to cause his excitement.

"You know," Mac said, slowing down almost as an afterthought, "people might get the idea we're lovers the way you're desperately hanging on to my hand."

"And they'll think you're in an awful hurry to get me into bed the way you're walking so fast," Kyra puffed.

Mac laughed. "You could've asked me to slow down."

"I learned young you don't mess with hurricanes. You seemed intent on your destination."

"Is that how you see me? A hurricane?"

"I try not to see you at all."

He eyed her quizzically.

"It's simpler that way." She deliberately kept her gaze straight ahead.

Mac nodded, pleased. "That's a good sign."

"What is?"

"If you didn't care for me, you wouldn't be fighting so hard to keep me out of your mind."

"Don't sound so full of yourself. I may not have a mind much longer if these nightmares continue."

When he wrapped an arm around her shoulders Kyra didn't protest. "There's a logical explanation for everything. We'll find one for this, too."

In a steep and narrow alleyway between two shops, a movement startled Kyra to a halt. Mac dragged her a full step before he stopped. In the blue shadows Kyra saw a darker silver shape halfway up the incline. Like mercury from a broken thermometer, the shape rolled and changed until the outline showed a wolf with no physical presence to explain the shiny silver shadow. Once again Kyra felt its penetrating gaze bore into her. As patches of previous nightmares blotched into her mind unannounced, she shivered. Evil tainted the images, painted new ones. Silver jaws on snow-white skin. Red blood darkening hospital green sheets.

Kyra.

Her name reverberated through her brain in a deep, raspy voice, sending the cold chill of death pounding through her veins.

Come to me, Kyra.

A metallic bitterness filled her mouth. Her palms grew damp inside her gloves. Her heart raced.

I'll show you everything you want to know.

Standing between the dark shadows of the buildings and the bright sunshine of the street, Kyra felt torn between the promise of answers to the questions destroying her life and the firm tug of Mac's hand calling her back.

Chapter Five

"Kyra?" Mac's voice penetrated the fog in Kyra's mind.

"What's the matter?" he asked, tugging at her hand. His fingers felt warm and reassuring even through her gloves. The shadow's lure faded. Her mind cleared.

"Nothing," she mumbled.

She turned to Mac, then immediately back to the strange shadow. It was gone. The snow lay undisturbed in the blue shadows cast by the buildings.

Nightmares came with sleep. What could she label dreams without sleep? Hallucinations? *Madness?* She shivered, tightening her fingers around Mac's hand, seeking his quiet strength. "I'm fine."

Mac resumed his break-neck pace up the narrow sidewalk along Main Street. Everything was as it should be.

People dressed for the ski slopes sloshed through the snow on the sidewalk. Cars passed up and down the street, staining the snowbanks with muddy slush. Shop doors tinkled their welcome. The scent of the festive pine boughs decorating the storefronts mingled with that of coffee from the deli, yeast from the brewery up the hill, and food from the various restaurants.

Utterly normal.

By the time they made their way to the old Miners' Hospital, which housed the library, Kyra was winded and feeling calmer. Once inside, Mac broke their contact to take off his coat. Kyra shut her eyes to catch her breath and thought she heard moans of pain drifting down from above, thought she smelled the stench of ether. *No, please, no.* Her eyes popped open.

"Are you sure you're okay?" Mac asked.

"I'm fine, honestly. Just a little tired, that's all." She smiled weakly. "You set a mean pace." She didn't want to admit how close to the edge of sanity she felt.

"Here." Mac reached for the zipper on her jacket and slipped it down. As he helped her take her coat off, she was momentarily nestled against him. The comforting feel of him rallied mixed emotions. Part of her feared his easy hold on her heart. Another desperately wanted to believe in the safety she felt in his arms, in his power to make the terror of her odd visions fade and disappear.

She folded the coat he handed her over her arm and smiled tentatively at him. "Thanks."

Stacks of books were shelved in a cozy room. A gray-haired lady worked busily behind the circulation desk. Nothing sinister or out of time shrouded her vision. She sighed her relief.

Everything was fine. She was all right.

Mac gave her a quizzical look, then turned to the librarian. "We'd like to look at the *Park Record* microfilm."

"Third floor," the librarian said. "Let me get you started."

The carpeted wood stairs creaked under their weights. As they climbed, the librarian entertained them with a bit of history on the building. "The hospital building was moved to this location in nineteen seventy-nine, refurbished, and opened as the library in nineteen eighty-two. These stairs and all of the interior wood have been restored to their original detail . . ."

Ordinarily, Kyra would have found this information fascinating, but today she couldn't care less. Restoring her sanity had become more important for the moment than her love for restoring old buildings.

"How far back do you want to go?" the librarian asked.

"Nineteen hundred," Kyra said quietly.

The librarian returned with the rolls of film. "Are you doing research on something specific?"

Mac gave the old woman a killer smile. "Yes, as a matter of fact, we are. My friend is looking for information on Hallie Stern for an article she's planning to write."

"That's right," Kyra piped in. "Anything you could point to that has any information on her would be helpful."

"The Silver Sovereign. She was quite an interesting character. Long-lived, too. She was eighty-three when she died. On the first day she set foot in Park City in over twenty years."

"What happened to her?" Kyra asked. A thread of dread wound slowly around her windpipe, drying her mouth.

"Some say it was suicide. Some say it was murder. Others say it was just plain old age. She was found in her hotel room. Her fortune had dwindled down to nothing and a collection had to be taken up to bury her."

"How did she die?"

"The coroner's report says asphyxiation, but there were no signs of a struggle, no marks on her neck to suggest foul play. It's as if someone stole the breath from her."

"What else can you tell me about her?"

The librarian waved away the question. "I could spend a whole day talking about the adventures of the Silver Sovereign." She shuffled to a book shelf and took down several volumes. "These should give you the information you need." She quickly threaded the microfilm in the viewing machine. "I've got to go back downstairs. Let me know if there's anything else I can do for you." She hurried away before they could ask her anything else.

"Ready?" Mac asked.

He sat down in front of the machine. Kyra sat next to him on the padded bench, piling her coat down beside her to create space between them. He grabbed the lime-green mound and dumped it on the floor on top of his coat. Grasping her chin, he turned her face toward his.

"I won't hurt you, Kyra. I promise. Will you give me the benefit of the doubt?"

"It's not that simple."

Letting go of her chin, Mac's free hand started the machine. "It's not that complicated. I want you. You still want me."

She opened her mouth to deny his claim, but he rested a finger against her lips.

"You can deny it to yourself as much as you want, but you can't lie to me."

He took away his finger and replaced it with his mouth. His lips captured hers with insistence. Kyra started to pull away, then decided against it. She would prove him wrong.

Too late she realized she was proving him right. The taste of him, the touch of him had a drugging effect on her. An effect nothing else had come close to in the last seven years. An effect she'd unconsciously waited to relive. Her left arm rose to encircle his neck. Her fingers traced the hard outline of bones and muscles, relearning their familiar landscape. Her mouth opened to the remembered wild honey sweetness of him. He responded with a deep groan of desire, filling her with a feminine thrill.

As his hand roamed possessively up her thigh to the edge of her sweater, volcanic heat poured through her, enlivening all of her senses. She didn't stop him when his fingertips edged beneath all of the layers of her clothes to find the skin at her waist, but melted into him. His hand explored every rib with an excruciating slowness, then came to rest on the lace of her bra. Enthralled, she moaned at the need his thumb brushing against her breast resonated deep inside her. She definitely shouldn't have allowed him to kiss her, the sensible side of her reprimanded. But the tiny voice of caution was lost in the storm of passion Mac's touch created. One kiss couldn't hurt. What did it prove, anyway? Only that she was alive—which was a good sign. One kiss . . .

Footsteps creaked on the stairs.

"Oops, sorry," a strange voice said.

Kyra startled and jerked out of Mac's embrace. Her cheeks burning, she smoothed her sweater back into place and sidled away from him.

"I just need to get a book." The young man pointed to the shelf behind them and hedged clumsily past them. He bent over, running his fingers along the spines of the books until he found the one he was looking for. "I'll, uh, take this downstairs." Moving backwards, he nearly tripped down the narrow stairwell.

Kyra reached for the pile of books the librarian had given her, throwing Mac a sidelong glance. His eyes blazed with the molten intensity of flowing lava.

78

Hot. Dangerous. Intensely mesmerizing. She cleared her throat and flipped open the first book's cover.

"The way you kiss me doesn't lie." His voice was a low caress for her ears only. The hoarse sensuality of it possessed a quality as disturbing as the kiss they'd just shared. "You still want me." He straightened and fiddled with the focusing knob on the microfilm machine. His voice returned to normal. "But I know it's too soon for us. Your dreams and the mountain are in the way. We'll take care of them; then we'll be free."

The faint echo of old panic rippled through her, making her want to spring up and run. Would the mountain come between them, as that unnamed threat had seven years ago?

She glanced at him, perplexed. "What do you mean, the mountain?"

"Never mind." He wrapped an arm around her waist and pulled her closer until they sat thigh to thigh. His touch had lost its urgency but retained its warmth. "Looks like we'll be here for a while."

Looking at Mac showed her a calm man whose mind was concentrated on the film whirring in the viewer. She'd lost all objectivity when it came to him. There were no sinister plots, no hidden agendas, only the workings of her overactive imagination and bruised heart. She was the one with the problem here, not Mac. Time to get a grip on reality.

"Let's split the work." Kyra searched her pockets and brought out a small pad of paper and a pen. "I'll go through the books while you look through the microfilm." She ripped a few sheets of paper from the pad and handed them to Mac. With a little space between them, maybe she could reactivate her objectivity. "Got a pen?"

"I think so." He picked up his down jacket, patted the pockets, and came out with a stubby golf pencil. "What am I looking for?"

"I really don't know." Kyra opened the first book and fingered the index until she found the page numbers she'd need. "Write down any fact you can discover about Hallie."

Kyra focused on her search, praying all the while that she'd find the answers she needed. Between books, she surreptitiously glanced in Mac's direction. She admired the way he systematically attacked his chore, writing down notes once in a while with an impatient hand. His face could have been carved in stone for all the emotion she saw there. Yet, in this world gone mad, she'd found an island of solace in Mac. He'd said he wanted her; his kiss had made it plain. But how much could she depend on him or on her resurging feelings for him?

Not even the boyish grin he gave her when he caught her staring at him gave away any of the inner workings of his brain or his heart. Kyra wished they could have met under different circumstances, taken more time to get to know each other, been sure of the strength of their friendship before rushing into the hot fires of passion. Fires that still burned strong despite his betrayal. Fires that burned strongly enough to make her want to chance another sudden departure.

She shook her head, disgusted with herself. If they'd waited, then maybe things would have ended differently all those years ago. The thought weighed heavy on her heart and moistened her eyes. She forced her attention back to the next book before she dissolved into tears, trying her best to ignore the man who sat so close to her.

After what seemed an eternity Mac turned off the microfilm viewer and Kyra shut the last book. He stretched his arms and arched his back to ease the visible tension of his body. Then he rubbed his forehead. From the creases Kyra saw there, she knew he had a headache.

"What did you find?" Kyra asked.

He rolled his head and shoulders. "Not much."

"I think I've got some aspirin in my jacket."

"I'm fine." He glanced down at his notes. Without thinking, Kyra got up and stood behind him. Hands resting on his shoulders, she kneaded the tight muscles and tried to decipher his notes. "Ah, that feels good."

After turning the paper right side up, Mac continued. "The lady didn't have much luck hanging on to her family. For all her riches, she must've been awfully lonely. She was born in 1882 in Missouri. She was the daughter of a physician and a school teacher. Married Emory Eaton in 1902. Had a son, Matthew, in 1903. Her husband died in a mining accident that year, and there was a fight over his estate. She won the court case and managed the mine herself. In 1904 she married John Barrett, and in 1905 she had one daughter, Sarah. John also died in a mining accident—something about a coal truck. Let's see . . ."

Mac flipped his page of notes over. "Matthew disappeared in 1921. Sarah had a daughter, Elizabeth, out of wedlock the same year. Sarah died soon after from complications of childbirth, and Hallie raised Elizabeth. In 1922 Hallie married Otto Stern. He owned a sawmill and died there in a freak accident a few years later. She moved to California after the accident and her various social activities and world travels are reported until her death in 1968. Not much here. What did you find?"

"Pretty much the same thing." Kyra reached over his shoulders to pick up her pad and riffled through her notes.

"Anything click?"

"Just one thing." She dropped her pad back on the table. Mac turned to face her. "My birthday is October 23, 1968. The same day Hallie died."

"So?"

"Maybe that's why I feel connected to her." The nascent bud of an idea formed. She pointed to the machine. "Put up the October 1968 film and look at the birth announcements."

With a sigh, Mac did as Kyra requested. "Nothing. No births on that day."

As she peered at the screen, her hands rested lightly on his shoulders. "How about deaths?"

"Only one other than Hallie's." He pointed at the obituary. "Rebecca Carleson Brennan, age twenty-two."

"They don't mention what she died of."

"No."

Bits and pieces that didn't make sense swirled in Kyra's mind, sending it spinning out of control. Hallie Stern died on the day Kyra was born. Rebecca Brennan died the same day. Both in Park City. No births were recorded for that day, but her adoption papers had told her she'd been born in Park City on that date. The day before the Kirtlands moved to Florida, taking her with them.

Was Rebecca Brennan her biological mother? Was Rebecca related to Hallie in some way? Were their deaths somehow related to her strange dreams?

"Did you see a picture of Rebecca Brennan?" she asked.

"No."

Kyra plopped down next to Mac. "At least we know Hallie is a real person and not just a figment of my imagination."

Mac squeezed her thigh reassuringly. "We'll figure it out." He busied himself rewinding the film and returning it to its container.

The nightmare she'd had last night—had it really happened? Had Hallie murdered somebody? If she had, why had they found no mention of it in the papers? If she hadn't, why was she dreaming of it?

All this on top of today's time warp. And Mac seemed to be the only thing between her and a sharp fall into the dark realm of insanity. Or part of the madness. Nothing made sense—not the situation, not the dreams, not her mixed emotions. It was all too much. She needed to let all this information sink in and sort itself into some sort of semblance of order—preferably into two neat columns; one marked DREAMS, the other MAC.

She jumped up. Her fingers dragged along the spines of the books on the shelf labeled LOCAL INTEREST. Her nail caught on the edge of one. She turned to look at it. *The Legend of the Eaton Peak Mine.*

The creak of the stairs announced an arrival.

"How are we doing up here?" the librarian asked. "Oh, I see you've found our local ghost story."

Kyra stared at the book in her hand. "This?"

"Yes. They say that Eaton Peak is haunted."

"Haunted?" Kyra's mind flashed to her encounter with the shadow at the house that morning. Was this the answer she was looking for? She licked her dry lips. "That sounds interesting."

"A miner had a fight with the owner of the Eaton Peak Mine. No one is quite sure what it was about, but there's a pretty good chance it was about the working conditions of the mine." The librarian shook her head sadly. "So many people died or were crippled. Anyway, it's said that when this miner fell into the shaft he cursed the mountain and the man who owned the mine."

Kyra flipped through the pages, seeing only blurrs. "And did the curse work?"

"Yes!" The librarian walked to the window, her gaze directed toward Eaton Peak. "I told them not to build there, but who listens to a little old lady with gray hair these days? No one. I told the contractors they were asking for trouble. They just laughed at me." Her gaze shifted to Kyra and Mac. "But mark my words, that mountain is a disaster waiting to happen. He doesn't want anyone on his mountain."

"Who?" Kyra asked, instinctively moving toward Mac.

"The miner who cursed the mountain, that's who."

Kyra sat next to Mac, seeking his grounding solidity. "Do you know his name?"

"No one knows for sure who he is, but he's killed every single one of the owner's descendants. He swore to when he died. With no one left, he's bound to start on the people who've invaded his home."

The gold lettering on the book's gray cover seemed to gleam. A chill of apprehension shot through Kyra, rendering her mute.

"What makes you say that?" Mac asked.

Something about the tone of his voice made Kyra turn to look at him. Despite his relaxed appearance, lines of tension stiffened his face.

The librarian's gaze speared him. *"It's coming alive again."* An award-winning storyteller couldn't have said the words with more spooky conviction. "I've heard it myself. Every time someone died before, the mountain came alive."

"Avalanches are common this time of year," Mac said calmly.

"Oh, no." She shook her head vigorously. "This has nothing to do with avalanches. It comes from the heart of the mountain. Like a dying man's shaking breath."

Kyra recalled the mountain's odd rumble and the sense of terrible presentiment she'd felt. Her uneasiness returned.

As if she realized she had trespassed on some unwritten rule of propriety, the librarian straightened, took the book from Kyra's hand, and replaced it on the shelf. "Legends are, after all, steeped with seeds of truth."

She gathered the microfilms and took back

into the small room where they were stored.

Mac grabbed their coats from the floor and handed hers to her. He'd turned into an impenetrable stone fortress once again. As she donned her coat, Kyra couldn't help the contrary wish that his earlier warmth would return. As dangerous as it was, it made her feel protected, too.

"We've done all we can for today," he said.

"Yes." Kyra stuffed her notes and Mac's into her pocket.

They walked back to Mac's truck in silence, separated by their unvoiced thoughts. As disturbing as this stony silence was, as alone as it made her feel, Kyra was loathe to ruffle it with pointless chatter—or worse, pointed questions. It was best to remember this solid wall of a man had once disappeared like a puff of smoke.

The brilliant morning sun had faded in a haze of clouds, lending a perfect reflection to Kyra's gloomy mood. They'd found little to help her with her problem. Yet Kyra knew that the key was there somewhere in the information they'd gathered—the right key mixed with a dozen other keys on a huge brass ring.

"Where else could I get more information on Hallie?" Kyra asked out loud before she realized she had.

Mac shot her a quick glance, then turned on Landmark Drive. They thundered past the Wal-Mart before he answered. "There's always the Family Library in Salt Lake. It's world-renowned for its genealogical records. We'll go on Monday. I have business there anyway."

"Great," Kyra said, with resignation rather than enthusiasm.

With the next step charted, she found the puzzle of her nightmares didn't dominate her mind, but the enigma of the man who sat beside her did. And she couldn't decide which notion was the more unsettling.

Chapter Six

Mac turned into the plowed parking lot at Mountain Swift. "I'm going to stop at the lodge for a minute. Smells like it might snow again, and the snowmobile we use for grooming the trails has been cranky lately. I just want to be sure Debbie doesn't have any problems."

"Sure," Kyra answered noncommittally.

She looked drained and tired, and Mac hated to make this stop, but as much as he trusted Debbie, the business was his to worry about. It was a concrete reminder he could live a life outside the Institute. As he parked by the door, he felt like a juggler with too many balls in the air.

And he couldn't afford to drop any of them.

As they walked in, Debbie, dressed in black ski pants and a pink Polar Fleece top, waved to him from the rental ski rack. She politely excused herself from her clients before she trotted over.

"Hi!" Debbie said with a smile that encompassed them both.

"Kyra, this is Debbie Forrester. She manages the store for me. Debbie, meet Kyra Kirtland, a friend."

"Nice to meet you, Kyra. Mac, there's someone waiting in your office. I tried to tell him you wouldn't be in today, but he insisted on waiting."

"Who is it?"

"Don't know." Her eyebrows scrunched over her light brown eyes. "I've never seen him before. But I'll tell you, I don't like the looks of him."

"What do you mean?"

As she leaned forward to whisper, her brown ponytail slipped forward over her shoulder. "He looks a little nuts. I was going to call the cops as soon as I got this batch of skiers on their way."

Mac's jaw twitched. Another complication? "I'll take care of him. How's the snowmobile running?"

"So far, so good. John seems to have the knack to make it start when it doesn't want to, so I promoted him to head trail groomer."

He nodded distractedly, watching Kyra's gaze roaming the room, taking in the carefully organized stock, the coffeepot and plate of cookies Debbie insisted they needed, and the bright Christmas decorations Debbie had hung all over the room. "If it snows tonight, close the pond trail until we can mark the boundaries. I don't want anyone falling in the stream that feeds the lake."

"Will do."

"Busy today?" Mac asked.

"A madhouse! Isn't it great?" Debbie turned to Kyra. "We've had the best snow in ten years this year. Gotta take advantage of the good times when they come."

"Debbie?" a voice called from the counter.

"Coming." Debbie turned to Mac. "Let me know if I can do anything for you."

Mac strode purposefully to his office in the back of the chalet. Preoccupied, he didn't notice Kyra following him.

The office held a massive, utilitarian metal desk on which the stranger had propped his feet. The blond man's muddy boots splotched dirty drips onto papers carefully arranged on the desktop. He sat in the chair, leaning back in a pose of utter comfort, with his hands laced behind his head. After a cursory glance in Kyra's direction the man's cold blue gaze settled on Mac.

The man had changed since Mac had last seen him, but Mac would recognize those icy eyes anywhere. They held the kind of look that could chill a man to the bone. Their dullness reflected no soul, no conscience.

The last time he'd seen Alek Vermer, he'd left the man in the safe care of a hospital psychiatric ward. It didn't look as if the stay had helped.

No good could come of this.

Would Alek remember the picture he'd seen of Kyra all those years ago? If he did, then Mac knew he had just walked himself into a live mine field.

"The Ram finally comes back to his home base," Alek said. His smile, as Debbie had noticed, bordered on the crazed. "I was starting to think I'd have to hunt you down."

"Alek," Mac acknowledged without emotion. "What brings the Vermin out of its hole?"

Alek sidled away from the swivel chair and slithered sideways to stand beside the skis hanging on the south wall. He stood mere inches away from Mac.

"Find the shaft yet?" A crooked grin cracked Alek's tight, leathered features.

Alertness washed over Mac. Something was wrong. No one but him should know about the buried mine shaft. But then, Alek hadn't earned his nickname of Vermin for nothing. His ability to dig out information rivaled that of a rat's for finding garbage. With grim effort Mac maintained outward aloofness. "Think I'd tell you if I had?"

Alek gave Kyra an avuncular glance, dismissing her with hearty laughter. "It looks as if you've been otherwise engaged." He paused, cocking his head to one side, pinning Mac with his arctic gaze. "Do you think that's wise?"

"As usual, you're seeing monsters where there aren't any." Mac's stomach tightened. He didn't need this now. How much did Alek remember? How much did he see with those half-dead eyes? Was Kyra in danger?

"Why don't you wait for me in the lobby, Kyra?" Though Mac phrased it as a question, his voice left no room for argument.

She looked curiously from one man to the other, then started toward the door. "Sure."

"This won't take long."

Mac waited until Kyra was safe in the lobby before he spoke again. "What do you want?"

"You know, the good thing about being on my end of the company is that the burnout rate is very low." Alek smiled crookedly. "What does that say for your sainted Institute?" He examined Mac's face. "You are burnt out, aren't you? It's almost a letdown. I was hoping for one of our famous invigorating skirmishes."

"Sorry to disappoint you. I've retired." Not a muscle moved outwardly, but Mac's insides roiled.

"So I'd heard." Alek's eyes twinkled with knowledge. "What brought you out of retirement?" he goaded. "It couldn't be just little old me. Could it be that the Ram has more than one Achilles heel?"

Alek leaned back, one arm across his chest, the other folded up with the hand tucked under his chin, like an artist studying a subject he was about to paint. "I heard you sent the family away. That's cheating."

"And what would you know about playing fair?" Mac asked.

Alek threw his hands up, then slapped his thighs as he bellowed a laugh. "Fair play? Don't make me laugh. Neither of us plays by any rules. Never have. The only thing that's ever mattered is winning. By any means."

Alek ambled next to the door and peeked out into the lobby. Mac had no doubt Kyra was the object of his gaze. He stood motionless, knowing that showing any sign of caring would doom him.

"It's quite a disappointment to find that the Ram has a heart," Alek said. "I rather fancied you were more like me than you'd care to admit. But I see now I was mistaken. It's just as well that this will be our last encounter."

Alek reached for his coat, where he had left it on the chair. "Watch your back, Mac." He tossed a coin on the desk. "By the way, I've already got a buyer lined up for the Pandora proton data." He threaded on his coat. "See you in the snow, old man."

He stopped by the door and turned back toward Mac. "You always did like sunshine-colored hair." He shook his head. "You've made it too easy this time."

Mac set his back teeth. "Leave her out of this. It has nothing to do with her."

"It never does, Mac. That's why it hurts so much."

With one swift move, Mac grabbed the front of Alek's sweater. "Touch her and I'll kill you."

Alek grabbed Mac's fist and squeezed until Mac let go. "You better than anyone else should realize that death means nothing to me."

"I'll make your life a living hell."

Raucous laughter exploded from Alek. "Is that supposed to be a threat?"

The door closed with a loudness that resonated long after Alek had gone, the echoes warning of impending danger.

And his selfishness had put Kyra right in the middle of it.

Kyra opened the door to Mac's office and peeked around it. In the room's heavy air she could still smell the lingering tension between the two men, hear the ringing resentment, feel the exertion of muscles restrained against action. Mac and the mysterious Alek had faced each other like two mountain sheep ready to butt heads. While she'd warmed her hands by the fireplace, she'd almost expected to hear the grating of hooves on the floor, followed by the concussion of head against hard head.

As Mac reached for tissues, wiped the mud from the papers on his desk, then slowly filed them away, she watched him with open curiosity.

"What was that all about?" she asked lightly as she sat in the padded chair before the desk.

Mac glanced up from his filing but didn't answer.

"It's your turn to trust," Kyra insisted.

He closed one file drawer and reached for the next. "I've stayed alive this long by not trusting anyone but myself."

One, two, three, Kyra counted slowly, in an effort to keep her rising temper in check. Elbows on the chair's arms, fingers laced on her lap, she consciously forced herself to relax. It didn't work. She tried clenching her teeth and biting her tongue. When this failed she looked for a distraction and picked up the strange metal object from the desk. The crudely minted coin had a bold *V* fashioned from two raised railroad spikes on one side and a blindfolded Lady Liberty on the other.

She rubbed the coin between her fingers, enjoying the feel of the raised shapes. "This shaft you're supposed to find—is that what you meant when you said the mountain stood between us?"

He shoved papers into a file. "Stay out of it, Kyra."

"I don't even know what it is you want me to stay out of."

"Keep it that way. You'll live longer." Mac slammed shut the file cabinet, then paced the room like a caged animal.

"What kind of coin is this?" Kyra asked, trying to change the subject.

Mac stopped his pacing and snatched the coin from her fingers. He looked at it with disgust. "This is a warning."

"I don't understand."

"Alek calls himself 'the Judge.' " Mac scoffed. "The railroad spikes represent his twisted version of bringing east and west together." He turned over the coin, exposing the blinded Liberty. "He thinks he's balancing the world's scales." He flung the coin across the room. It pinged against a metal filing cabinet, then dropped with a thud on the ice-blue industrial carpet. "And I'm in his way."

"I thought the cold war was over."

"There are people everywhere who want what others have."

That he'd known Alek had been clear from the way they'd greeted each other—like old enemies who respected each other's abilities. But Kyra sensed something deeper to his relationship with Alek.

"Was he in Hawaii when we were?" she asked on impulse. "Is that why you left me?"

They stared at each other over the desk. The raging storm of anger blustered unguarded in his eyes. Was he angry at her or at Alek? She shivered involuntarily. This man could kill, and with a sharp blip of intuition on the radar of her mind, Kyra knew he'd killed before and would kill again if he had to. She sucked in her breath at the realization and shivered again.

Emotions tumbled through her, crashing unnamed before falling again and again. This hard, unyielding man in no way resembled the one who'd loved her seven years ago, who'd held her so gently after her nightmare last night, who'd patiently helped her sort through nearly a century of newspapers today.

Deep inside, she refused to believe he could ever harm her without a reason, and for the first time since she'd stared at the chapel door, waiting for him to appear, she was forced to acknowledge the fact that he must have had a reason to hurt her then.

"Is that why you left?" she repeated.

"To protect you," Mac said, "I had to hurt you."

He turned away to stare at the map on the wall. Kyra rose slowly from her chair and went to him, putting a hand gently on his arm. "Today—"

"Was a mistake," Mac interrupted. "Easily rectified. As soon as we get back, I want you to pack and leave."

"Leave?" She blinked, dazed. "I can't do that. Not now."

"I'm afraid you have no say in the matter." Mac whirled away from her, picked up a piece of paper from the desk, and jotted down some notes.

As he turned from her, for a fleeting moment she thought she saw regret melt the hard silver ore of his eyes. It was all the encouragement she needed.

"Excuse me, but I don't believe the house belongs to you." She crossed her arms stubbornly under her chest and felt like a six-year-old, but she didn't care. She wouldn't let him push her away without an explanation. Not this time.

"You don't want to argue with me right now." His voice was low, even, holding an undeniable warning.

"Well, that's where you're wrong. Your Tarzan

attitude has me spoiling for a fight."

The blazing intensity of his look made her want to take a step back. She stiffened her spine, resisting the urge.

He reached her in one long predatory step. They stood toe-to-toe. His gaze pinned her like a butterfly in a collector's box. "You have no idea—"

"Exactly," she interrupted and swallowed dryly while fear thrummed unchecked through her. "You expect me to spill my guts without reservation, and when I ask you for one tiny drop of trust you build a dam of rocks so thick, I'm not sure you're behind there anymore."

"That's quite enough."

"No, dammit, it isn't." Her balled fists rose to her hips and she unflinchingly returned his gaze. Suddenly her fear of him vanished and she pressed on. He owed her answers. "You said you wanted me. You expect me to fall into your arms all pliable and willing like I did before, but here you are treating me like yesterday's newspaper. I'm not asking for the world here, just a little enlightenment. You asked for the benefit of the doubt. I'm giving it to you."

Swearing, he paced away from her, then whirled back to face her again. "You want enlightenment; here it is in twenty-five words or less. I care for you. I don't want to see you get hurt. The best way for me to take care of you is to send you away."

The fight gone out of her, Kyra plopped back down into the chair. "That's more than twenty-five words, and I'll have you know I don't need you to take care of me. I've done just fine on my own."

He blew out a breath and raked a hand through his hair. "You've grown into an impossible woman."

"And you've been acting like your shorts are in a knot ever since the librarian mentioned the Eaton mine's ghost. What's wrong with you?"

"Nothing's wrong." He strode to the desk and riffled through the pink message slips next to the phone. "It's been a long day, I've got a headache, and I'd like to get back to the house."

"Okay, let's go."

He shoved the pink slips into his jacket pocket and stepped toward her. "Fine."

As she started for the door, Mac grasped her wrist and yanked her to face him. "I'm asking you to leave the mountain for your own good."

"Or for yours?" she challenged. "I'm too close to answers to leave."

"Are they worth your life?"

A knot of emotion lodged in her throat. "Without them I have no life."

With a muttered oath he let her go and strode toward the door.

Watching his retreating back, a sudden panic seized her.

"Are you going to disappear on me again?" The words spilled out before she could squelch them.

He stopped dead in his tracks. His hands grabbed both sides of the doorjamb. His head fell forward in a helpless motion. "No. This time I can't protect you by leaving."

He would stay. The unexpected relief she felt nearly buckled her knees.

Mac didn't like the feeling of weakness Kyra's presence imbued in him. Pandora protons meant possible danger for all the families living on Eaton Peak, but for him, having Kyra nearby complicated their rescue immensely. He'd been stupid to think he could keep her by his side while he dealt with the mountain. He couldn't afford a weakness, especially not one Alek could exploit. And now her own stubbornness proved an unexpected obstacle.

He had to think, and he thought best while moving. As soon as they reached the house, Mac quickly changed into his red sweat suit and laced on his snow joggers.

Misty danced around him in the hallway as he put on a lightweight jacket. "Can she come jogging with me?" Mac called to Kyra in the kitchen.

She looked up from the tea she was preparing. "How far and how fast do you run?"

"Tell you what: If she gets tired, I'll carry her."

Kyra studied him for a minute, then flashed him a devastating grin that lit her eyes like green stars and took his breath away. Did she know what power that simple smile of hers held?

"She could probably use the exercise after being cooped up all day." Kyra disappeared into her room and came back with a purple leash that matched Misty's collar. "Keep her on the leash."

Mac attached the leash to the collar and hurried out the door. Damn the woman, he thought as he warmed up in a slow jog. Damn her smile. Damn her eyes. And damn her stubbornness.

From day one he'd handled everything wrong. Now he was holding a stick of dynamite with a fuse lit at both ends. When this whole thing blew up it wouldn't be pretty.

"I wish you could talk," Mac said to Misty as they headed up toward the mountain's peak. "Maybe you could tell me how to reason with that mistress of yours."

Misty barked an answer. Mac laughed. "That's what I thought. There is no reasoning with her. She may be the death of me yet."

As he realized with a sinking feeling that the words were more than just an expression, Mac almost stumbled. "Alek is another ghost dredged up from the past, another complication I hadn't anticipated. I should've realized he was the one. It comes with two soft years as a civilian."

For two years he'd managed to bury his past and

live a reasonably normal life. He should have known better. Commitment. Responsibility. Obligation. Words drilled into him. Words he'd once believed in with blind faith. Words that were now dragging him back to a life he'd tried to escape. And because of them he stood to lose Mountain Swift . . . and Kyra.

He wanted her more than he'd ever wanted anything in his life, but to keep her out of Alek's savage clutches he'd have to send her away. He couldn't see any other way to keep her safe.

An odd feeling of failure niggled at him. He dismissed it quickly. He hadn't failed Kyra; he'd protected her. And he would do so again. Even at the risk of losing her.

How long did he have to convince her before Alek struck?

Mac pressed his pace, not liking the direction in which his thoughts strayed. Danger. Caring for Kyra at this moment in time was lethal. In the physical sense. In the mental sense. In every way imaginable. Even his careful training hadn't been enough to mask his feelings for her from Alek. But then, they'd had the same teachers—a fact that was both a blessing and a curse.

The fact that Alek had shown up meant he hadn't located the shaft yet. Alek always tried the easy way first. A trip to Salt Lake tomorrow would give him a head start over Alek. Even if Alek followed them there, Kyra would be safe in the city's crowds. Alek would wait until she was alone at the house. His madness had a certain predictability to it. And if everything went right in Salt Lake, then Kyra would find her answers and be safely on her way home before he and Alek battled for the mountain's secrets.

Mac slowed his pace a little to give his eyes time to search the snow-covered mountainside. According to his research, the shaft should be somewhere along the ridge by his side. With all the snow, it would be next to impossible to find. The package he'd made sure waited for him in Salt Lake should help him pinpoint the exact spot with more accuracy.

Nevertheless, looking for the shaft was a foolhardy enterprise. Between the rotting supports and the threat of avalanche, only a desperate man would attempt the feat.

A man like him.

"Your family's in danger," Jerrold, his ex-mentor, had said three days ago over the secured long-distance line crackling between them. "It's a one-man job and you're the only person who can do it without attracting any undue attention." He'd paused, as was his custom, to let each word sink in. "It could be a matter of national security."

Mac hadn't answered.

"Ever heard of the Pandora Project?" Jerrold asked.

"What about it?"

"We left a monitoring device behind and now we need the data retrieved."

"So?"

Jerrold hesitated. "It came alive a month ago."

"How does that affect me?"

"We think the dormant protons have mutated."

"And?"

"We're not sure. We need to analyze the data to know exactly what we're up against."

Mac silently cursed his government's negligence. The Pandora Project should have been sealed before civilian construction had been allowed to start. When he'd voiced his opinion to Jerrold he'd been told that budget cuts had forced a hasty shutdown, and Pandora's mutation, ten years after the fact, now threatened the mountain's stability and his family.

"Why not evacuate?" Mac had asked.

Once more Jerrold let the silence stretch.

"You can't admit you made a mistake, can you?" Mac hadn't bothered to hide his anger. "That's right; I forgot. That's why you have your little toy soldiers."

"Mac—"

"Can't it wait till spring?" Mac asked, trying to gauge the danger to his family.

"Could have. Intelligence has it someone else is after the data."

Now he knew that someone was Alek. Alek with the dead heart and the implacable soul.

Mac ran faster. His seven-year-old mistakes were coming back to haunt him with a vengeance. Alek would make sure the irony of the situation wouldn't be lost on Mac. And Mac had handed Alek the trump card on a silver platter when he'd stopped at the lodge with Kyra.

A glitter from above shone into Mac's eyes, stopping him in mid-thought and mid-stride. As he puffed smoky breaths, he searched the mountainside. An unnatural quiet permeated nature's usual restful symphony. Even Misty stood on alert, with her nose sniffing the air and her shoulder ruff puffed up.

There it was again: a flash of light. This time there was no mistaking the reflection of the dying sun on a mirror.

Alek was here. And he wanted Mac to know the race had begun.

Mac scooped up Misty, spun, and headed back down the mountain road to Kyra.

Chapter Seven

In the dead of night his victim lay unaware in soft slumber. The silver shadow hung in a corner and watched, looking for Hallie in Kyra, fueling his hatred. It would be so easy to slip down and crush the life from her. He imagined how sweet her life's essence would taste, reveled in the horror that would animate her face when she realized she was lost, and exalted in the knowledge of the power of release as revenge was finally his.

He contained his impatience and slunk across the room to her bedside. He breathed in deeply and exhaled on Kyra's face, ruffling the hair on her forehead.

Dream, liebliche *Kyra*. He melted through the window. *Dream*.

Mac snapped awake abruptly, listening, watching for the danger that had dragged him from a deep sleep. He heard nothing, saw nothing, felt nothing except an urgent need to check on Kyra.

With a lunge he came off the bed, reached for the nine-millimeter Beretta he'd placed on the night table, then made his way across the room.

He didn't understand the pressing compulsion that propelled him from the warm sheets to Kyra's room, or the anxiety that gripped him as he opened the door. He knew only that he had to protect her.

It was quiet in her room; too quiet. And cold, much colder than in his room. His gaze went to the window. Closed. Nothing seemed out of place. No dark intruder loomed in the corners. A careful look around the rest of the house showed him no reason for the gnawing feeling that something was wrong. Alek wasn't here; of that he was sure.

He returned to Kyra's room. She lay sleeping on her bed. Her red-gold hair framed her delicate face like a halo. The sheets and quilt were twisted haphazardly around her. One foot peeked out from beneath the bedclothes.

Watching her filled him with a wild longing. He remembered what was beneath the shapeless tent of flannel and cotton: the fragile bones, the long legs, the body with gentle curves in all the right places. He wanted her, had always wanted her with a fervor he didn't understand, and knew he would want her forever. And to protect her, he would have to risk never having her again.

She slept but, he noticed, it was not an easy sleep. Deep shadows marked the white skin beneath her eyes. A frown crinkled her forehead. Was she dreaming? Should he wake her?

He could deal with the mountain. He could deal with a known threat like Alek. But he found it hard to deal with the invisible monsters populating Kyra's nightmares.

I've failed you. The words echoed through his mind, seemed to fill the silence of the room and to

101

infuse his heart with profound regret. Where had the words come from? the feelings too strong for the situation?

He hadn't failed her. Not yet. *And I won't*, he silently promised her, promised himself.

He tucked her foot back underneath the covers, gently rearranged the quilt around her, and added an afghan for extra warmth. Her mouth opened as if to talk, but no sound came from it. She needed caring. He needed to do the caring. But he couldn't crawl into bed with her and hold as like he wanted to do. It was too soon. Too much of the past still stood between them.

Though the compelling feeling at the pit of his stomach urged him to stay, he could find no logical reason to do so. Kyra was sleeping. Misty the wonder dog snored peacefully on his bed in the other room. There were no signs of danger anywhere. Kyra was safe. He forced himself to turn from her and leave, closing the door gently behind him.

He hesitated, then soundlessly opened her door halfway and left the door to his room ajar, too.

An icy sprinkle tingled on Kyra's skin. She knew she was awake, but she couldn't open her eyes. Her eyelids glowed eerily and numbers like an old reel of film played on the screen of her mind. Five—four—three—two—one. A moment of blackness, followed by a waking scene out of place and out of time.

Mac! No sound came out.

She tried to move her head, but invisible hands held her in a viselike grip. Panic raced through her, compressing her chest under a ton of bricks. She couldn't breathe. Her heart exploded. A thousand ants gnawed at her limbs. Her thoughts zoomed by too fast to catch. Except for the unshakable knowledge of death. She was powerless to ward it off.

She struggled gamely, but the whirlpool of her

thoughts swirled her faster and faster, higher and higher. Her body shook from exertion. She fought each twist and turn with all of her will until the tumbling madness became too much.

Then, *pouf!* Instantly, the whole world calmed. The eye of the hurricane, Kyra thought, as she floated freely in the blessed darkness surrounding her. She tried to move her limbs, to no avail. A dim awareness that Mac stood by her bed filtered through the odd sensation possessing her body. She called to him and got no answer. When she heard the door softly creak shut Kyra resigned herself to her hapless fate.

Sehr gut. The gruff voice resounded in the empty chambers of her mind. *It is useless to fight me.*

The film whirred into action. A single tear slid down Kyra's cheek, onto her pillow. She couldn't do anything, except watch the movie playing before her.

Mac! He tossed and turned in his bed, Kyra's unvoiced plea echoing in his mind. He strained to hear anything out of the ordinary. Nothing came to him except the click of the furnace cycling, the hum of the refrigerator in the kitchen, and the ticks of the clock on his nightstand. Misty cocked an inquisitive eye at him. She stretched, shifted position, and went back to sleep.

He fought his urge to rush to Kyra once more. Turning his back to the door, he forced his eyes closed and ordered himself to sleep.

Kyra's silent plea thundered against his brain. He shifted in the bed until his eyes picked out her quiet form across their opened doors. *I'm here, Kyra. I'm here.*

The scene on the screen of her eyelids opened on a street Kyra couldn't identify. The woman she now recognized as Hallie walked down a wooden sidewalk, each footstep echoing hollowly in Kyra's mind.

A triumphant smile curled the corners of Hallie's mouth in a becoming way. Her hair, knotted at the nape of her neck, was topped with a straw hat trimmed with shrimp-colored silk flowers. She wore a long, tailored brown skirt and a lace-accented blouse that matched the color of the flowers on her hat. Her hands were protected by gloves and her feet by high-buttoned shoes. She swung a long-handled parasol in time to her footsteps.

I did it, Emory, my love. I saved our mine. Oh, how I wish you were here with me. I'd give up a hundred mines, a thousand fortunes to have you back.

Slowly, Kyra felt her essence drifting into the woman's body. Her blood pounded a joyous race in her veins, her spirits were both heavy and light at the same time, and the feeling of enduring love permeated her body. Hallie nodded to an acquaintance across the street. Ed Parker trundled by, barely in control of his new Cadillac. Hallie turned down an alleyway, dark despite the afternoon sun, to a shortcut that would take her directly behind her home.

Out of nowhere a hand jerked Hallie savagely back. "You may have won in the courthouse, Mrs. Eaton, but the case is not over."

Kyra recognized the man with the lupine features as the one who had hit Hallie in a previous vision. His distinctive yellow-green eyes, pointy ears, long straight nose, and graying beard weren't easily forgotten. He stood before her now with a murderous expression on his face—made more fearsome by the dark shadows in which they stood. Kyra wanted to be afraid, but Hallie's body didn't respond with fear; it responded with anger. Slow tremors erupted in the region of Hallie's stomach and rose, making small popping sounds in Hallie's head.

Hallie shrugged the offending hand off her arm. "Get your hands off me, sir."

"Not until you give back to me what is mine." The man seized both her arms in a bruising grasp.

Hallie struggled to free herself, her anger building even as the skin beneath her sleeve throbbed with pain. She took a deep breath and kept her voice even and flat. "Mr. Schreck, please, the court case is over. The judge's decision is final. If you'll excuse me, I have a business to attend to."

Schreck's steel grasp tightened. "Half of this business rightly belongs to me."

His voice held a maniacal tone, warning Hallie that she needed to stay calm. She stopped struggling and stared squarely at the man before her, determined not to bow down to his threats. "The court didn't agree with you. All of the mine was in my husband's name. All of it now belongs to *me*."

A derisive sneer twisted his features into a sinister caricature. "*Ach!* I grubstaked your husband in exchange for half the shares. Without my investment there would have been no mine."

Hallie, already bored with the tiresome argument, sighed heavily. "Then why didn't you tell the court so? When you were asked whether you held any stock in my husband's mine you answered no."

Schreck pushed her roughly against the wall. Her hatpin loosened and her hat fell to the ground. The material of her skirt scratched noisily against the brick, and Hallie felt some of her hair stick to the masonry. Schreck's eyes burned fanatically, mere inches from her own.

"I could not jeopardize my other holdings," Schreck said, anger flaring his nostrils. "Your husband agreed to my silent partnership."

Hallie reached behind her head and gingerly pulled her hair from the bricks, ignoring the steely grasp that bruised the flesh of her shoulders. "I'm afraid he never imparted that information to me. I can only go by what the papers he left behind told me. The Eaton mine belonged entirely to him."

"I invested four thousand dollars in grubstake money. My fifteen hundred shares are now worth millions."

Knowing all the hard work Emory had put into starting and operating his mine, Schreck's audacity infuriated Hallie. This mine was all she had left of the man she had loved with all her heart. She would see his dream come true, no matter what the cost.

"I refuse to be a target for an opportunist such as you," Hallie said. "You may think that females are only good to warm your bed and launder your shirts, but I assure you, Mr. Schreck, that my parents saw fit to raise me with no blinders." She slammed both her hands at his chest to push him away.

Schreck pressed her shoulders against the wall once more with rough hands. His animal-like features were sharpened ferociously by the long shadows of the buildings. "I just want what is rightfully mine."

Hallie refused to acknowledge her discomfort at his heavy-handed behavior. "According to the law, Mr. Schreck, that is *nothing.*"

"My investment—" Schreck hissed between clenched teeth.

"Does not exist."

"You can't run the business by yourself. Women are not allowed in the mines. You know miners are a superstitious lot and won't accept your command."

The bubbles of anger in Hallie's head popped at a feverish pace. As she squared her five-foot-five-inch frame to its full height, her hands unconsciously went to her hips. "I've been privileged to a good education. My husband shared his daily operations with me. We were partners in every sense of the word. I understand how the business is run and I am entirely capable of taking care of the mine myself. We are no longer in the Dark Ages, Mr. Schreck.

Women have held the vote in this state since 1896. Furthermore, I am not looking for an overseer. I am not planning on having a manager rob me blind. I will take care of my business myself—just as my husband would have."

Hallie shoved Schreck away with all her might. He stumbled back, surprised. Taking advantage of Schreck's momentary astonishment, Hallie harnessed her anger and flung it full force at him.

"As for the miners," Hallie said, jabbing the pointed end of her parasol repeatedly into his chest, pushing him out of the shadows of the alley into the light of the street, "I have no fear that they will accept me when they see their livelihoods depend on me and that nothing will change in the mine's operation. I have a young son to raise on my own. I will do *everything* to make sure he lacks for nothing."

As a passerby gave him a wary look, Schreck plastered a polite smile on his face. He bowed like a gentleman. But when his gaze returned to stab Hallie's the first flutter of fear rippled through her.

"I damn you," Schreck said, as if it was the greatest of compliments. "And I curse your son and all of your descendants. You have cheated me of my rightful riches." He turned to leave, then pinned her with his gaze once more. "You have not seen the last of me, Mrs. Eaton. Rolf Schreck never gives up."

Kyra's fear mixed with Hallie's, separating them. *Mac!* Kyra called, but no sound came out of her dry throat. She hung on to Mac's image to keep herself in the present.

The reel of film ripped unexpectedly, as if someone had snatched the running movie from its projector. Kyra found herself stumbling backward into space. She jerked up to a sitting position just as she was about to crash—into what, she couldn't remember. Her heart pounded furiously against her chest and the sound of her blood whooshing past her ears blocked out everything else.

One thought dominated her mind: She had to get away from this room. Now. She had to find Mac.

As he watched through the window, the silver shadow cursed. What had gone wrong?

Suddenly he felt the strong energy linking Kyra to the man across the hall.

Him!

The silver shadow wavered like a wind-maddened weathervane. No! This was unacceptable. He'd waited too long for his release to have it jeopardized by an unknown faction.

He funneled his anger and transported himself to his resting place. He flowed past the murky entrance of the cave, past the slimy shaft, down into the heat to the bubbling pit filled with the bleached remains of human misery. As he eased himself into the boiling sump, the dark waters glowed an eerie green. He fed on the despair, gorged himself on the tortured souls of hundreds of dead miners. His strength grew, and with it came the answer to his problem.

As a new plan formed, his thunderous laughter echoed through the mountain. The perfect plan. He'd bring Kyra here, where the wretched influence of this man couldn't reach her. Kyra would be his, and he'd finally be free from his hellish prison.

All he needed was a helping hand, and he knew just where to get it.

The ominous rumble of the mountain had Kyra sprinting from her room to Mac's. Reason caught up with her at the door, and she halted with both hands gripping the wooden frame.

This was crazy. She couldn't let a dream make a fool out of her again. But it hadn't been a dream, had it? She'd been awake. She'd known exactly what was happening, if not why or how. So why had she fled to find Mac as soon as she'd been freed from the evil bond? Because he was her link with reality, a source of safety.

She remembered how she used to sneak into her parents' room with her pillow and blanket when she got scared as a child, to make herself a nest beside their bed. Her father's relaxed snores would comfort her and lull her back to sleep. But she wasn't eight years old anymore, and Mac didn't snore. Slipping between the sheets with him would be a dangerous proposition, one she wasn't yet prepared to deal with. She'd come to him because she needed his groundedness. Then she realized with a sudden pang that she wanted *him,* too.

She watched him sleep with the traitorous Misty curled at his feet. His features were soft in the moonlight, making him seem approachable. She wanted to feel his lips on hers, his hands touching her flesh—arousing her, creating within her an undeniable awareness that she was very much alive and on the earth plane, not caught in some time-warped vision. Heat swirled from her center upward, sending her pulse racing, warming her skin as she remembered how Mac's naked body felt pressed against hers. She imagined all of his boundless energy channeled into pleasuring her and breathed a sigh of desire at the sight of the images that came to mind.

Kyra shook her head, tearing the pleasant daydream apart like soap bubbles from a child's wand. Thinking of Mac that way would only set her up for another disappointment. He wasn't the staying kind of man, and she didn't want a one-night stand. She'd be better off seeking comfort elsewhere tonight.

"Did you want something?" Mac's husky voice roused her from her wandering thoughts. The silver of his eyes shone in the darkness and a new tension snaked low in her belly.

"I-I was looking for Misty."

Misty cocked an eye open at the sound of her name and then closed it again.

"Looks like she's settled in for the night," Mac said. "Did you have another dream?"

"Yes." Kyra swallowed hard, trying to put the episode behind her.

"Are you all right?"

The note of concern in his voice almost made her believe he cared. "Yes. Fine."

"Do you want to talk about it?"

"No." Kyra hesitated. "I guess I should let you go back to sleep."

Mac smiled and raised the quilt covering him. "There's room for one more."

She couldn't tell from his expression whether he was teasing or testing. Either way, she didn't have the strength to spar with him tonight. She felt too vulnerable. "Uh, no, thank you."

Kyra backed away and shut the door as she left. She padded back to her room. The cold terror that still clung to the air made her shiver. She grabbed the quilt and afghan off her bed, headed for the living room, nestled her body into the comfortable sofa, and closed her eyes. Sleep wouldn't come. She reached out to pet Misty's head and found only empty air. She imagined the heat of Mac's body curled against hers and the warm comfort she'd drawn from it only last night and tightened the quilt around her shoulders. She bit her lower lip to keep her strangled sob from coming out.

Never before had she felt so lonely.

Chapter Eight

The twenty-three miles between the house and Salt Lake City seemed like a hundred. Mac's stony silence made Kyra edgy. He'd barely said two words to her since they'd gotten up that morning, and he looked as tired as she felt.

This was the second day of Mac's silent treatment. He'd spent all of Sunday away from the house. She should have been relieved to have time by herself, but instead Kyra found herself listening for his returning truck all day.

In between the restless pacing and waiting for Mac's return, she'd rummaged through the bookshelves in the basement and read all she could about Park City and Utah in general. She'd wanted to make the trip to Salt Lake by herself today, but Mac insisted it was silly to drive in two cars when he needed to go there, too.

So far the scenery had remained in the present. Kyra was relieved. She was too tired to deal with a screwed up perception today—especially after two sleepless nights filled with erotic fantasies of Mac, calculated to keep her nightmares away. They'd done that, all right; the problem was, they'd also gotten her incredibly aroused, and just being near Mac made her tense with anticipation. She craved his touch in a way she'd never hungered for food. Only the memory of his unexplained departure and the pain of her broken heart kept her from making a fool of herself by seeking a physical connection with him.

Mac parked near Temple Square. He walked her to the Family History Library at a pace that made it impossible to enjoy any of the sights.

"I'll meet you here at four," Mac said. "Are you going to be all right?"

"It's been a while since I've needed a baby-sitter."

Mac nodded, ignoring her sarcasm, then took off at his break-neck pace down West Temple—destination unknown. It left her wondering what she'd done wrong. With a shrug, she decided the problem was his, not hers. He'd been in an unreadable mood since his meeting with Alek. With a little determination, she'd soon sort out the maze of her nightmares and get back to her normal life. Whatever that was.

One thing was certain: it wouldn't include Mac.

Life offered no guarantees, but knowing Mac, he'd leave sooner than later, and the last thing she needed was to get involved with a man who didn't understand the meaning of permanent. She squared her shoulders and turned toward the building. She hadn't come here to brood over Mac's dark moods or his wandering feet. She had other more pressing business on her mind. Ignoring him, she decided, was the best policy for the moment.

Kyra was surprised by the modern exterior of the Family History Library. She'd expected something that held so much personal information to have a more homey look, not stark white, modern lines. She opted for one of the library's familiarization classes, then got down to work, alternating between searching the computer files and browsing through the millions of records kept in books and catalogs.

By three her eyes burned, the base of her neck was stiff, and the pile of information she'd gathered would make any soap opera seem dull. Murder, incest, suicide, and a myriad of strange deaths had her wondering if Rolf Schreck's curse on Hallie had indeed come to pass. She stuffed all her notes in her shoulder bag and went out into the lengthening afternoon shadows.

After a quick bite of soup and salad in a nearby deli Kyra decided to explore the surrounding area. At four she was waiting for Mac by the library door. When he hadn't shown up by four thirty she decided to go to the Mormon handicraft store on the other side of Temple Square.

Her mother had enjoyed quilts of all kinds, and Kyra found herself admiring the colorful patterns she saw. She remembered the afternoon Mac had helped her pick out the perfect Hawaiian quilt to add to her mother's collection. The afternoon had ended with their purchases forgotten in the car and a passionate interlude in the living room.

Kyra moved on to the next rack of quilts. A particularly well-made pinwheel lap quilt caught her eye, and before she knew it, Kyra was walking to the cashier with her treasure. Only then did she remember that her mother was dead, and her mother hadn't even been her mother. A wave of sadness swept through her. She pushed the quilt away.

"I'm sorry," Kyra said to the confused-looking woman behind the counter. "I've changed my mind."

She rushed blindly out of the store, thankful for the birdlike chirp at the light telling her it was safe to cross the street; her tear-filled eyes had blurred everything around her. She slowed her pace, dried her tears, and forced herself to admire the millions of Christmas lights shining on Temple Square. By the time she reached the library again she'd recovered her composure.

Mac paced impatiently in front of the glass doors, a long, fat cardboard mailing tube protruding from under one arm, and more than once he narrowly missed hitting a passerby with it.

"Where were you?" Mac asked in a bark that would have cowered a pitbull.

"*You're* an hour and a half late. *I* was here on time." Obviously his day out alone hadn't improved his disposition.

"Only an hour." His lightened tone dampened her rising anger. "I've been looking for you since five."

"Sorry," Kyra said. "I got tired of waiting for you and went to look at the lights on Temple Square."

"I guess I should apologize."

"Don't put yourself out on my account."

He reached for her elbow with his free hand and started guiding her down the sidewalk. "Are you hungry? Let's find a place to eat before we head back."

It was as close to an apology as she was likely to get, Kyra realized. At least he had the good sense to look as if he was sorry for speaking harshly to her. She wasn't really hungry after her late lunch, and she wasn't sure she could handle Mac's conciliatory gesture. She was afraid her feelings would show and his wouldn't, and her quota for throwing herself against stone walls was getting pretty close to full. "Misty's been cooped up inside all day. I should get back to her."

For a fleeting moment disappointment flickered across Mac's face, and Kyra felt its echo in the hollow of her stomach. He'd extended her a peace offering and she'd turned it down.

"All right," Mac said, his features returning to their stony set. "Let's go home."

Home. Kyra sighed heavily. Home used to be Florida. It should have been Utah. By rights of inheritance, Eaton Peak should've been hers. But she had no family left in Florida, and Utah was proving a torture of the soul.

Home. After her findings today Kyra wasn't sure where that was anymore.

Mac had convinced Kyra that stopping to bring home a pizza wouldn't add unduly to Misty's imprisonment. He'd ordered a half pepperoni and sausage and half mushroom and green pepper pie while Kyra waited in the truck. Mac hadn't eaten all day, and the pizza parlor's aroma nearly drove him crazy. He leaned his elbows on the counter and cradled his head in his hands, trying to make sense of all he'd found out.

Sunday had been a real bust. He hadn't been able to reach anyone he'd needed. Jerrold couldn't be found even at his private number. No one answered at the Hadleys' home.

"You'd have thought this was a national holiday," he muttered into his hands. Unless he was mistaken, Christmas was still a week away.

Today had gone more smoothly. He hadn't headed straight to his contact after he'd left Kyra at the library; he'd wanted to do some research of his own first. If you knew where to dig, Mac thought, the whole world was an open book. From a safe phone he'd called Jerrold and updated him on the situation and Alek's presence. He'd also asked for extra information. Jerrold had promised him an answer and made a date to call him back later that afternoon.

Mac had placed several more calls, the most disturbing one to Dr. Shana Merit, a psychologist friend who lived in California. If Shana was right, then

Kyra was in deep trouble, and he might not be able to help her at all.

Shana had outlined several possibilities for Kyra's disturbing nightmares, but her last suggestion set off internal alarm bells that wouldn't quit.

"Possession? As in evil spirits?" Mac had asked with a sneer of disbelief. "Come on, get real."

"Actually, it sounds more like obsession. It sounds as if he's influencing her mind from outside and not inside of her. I know it's an unusual diagnosis, and it's considered outside the accepted normal realm of psychology. I hesitate to even bring it up, but the symptoms you've described . . . well, they fit."

Mac raked a hand through his hair and kneaded the back of his neck. "Let's say for the sake of argument that I'll even consider that this is possible, if she is being possessed by some sort of spirit, then why is this thing only bothering her in her sleep? Why not all the time?"

"From what you've described he's bothered her while she's awake, too. Possession takes energy, and the entity might not have enough to take over completely. He may not even want to."

This was nuts. Why was he even listening to Shana's outlandish suggestions? "But why is this happening to her now?"

"It sounds as if she's in a vulnerable state, with the recent loss of her mother, the possible loss of her job, and your unexpected reappearance in her life. This offers a perfect window for spirit influences to enter."

It was enough to stress anybody, but to the point of *possession?* Not Kyra. She was stronger than that. But she was also very sensitive, he acknowledged. He'd witnessed how she could tune into his moods, his desires, his very soul. "Why in Park City? Why not in Florida, where she lives?"

"Often spirits are bound to their place of death—"

116

Mac straightened his stance with sudden insight. "You think it's the man in her dreams that's bothering her."

"He's a likely candidate." There was a pause. "Mac . . ." Shana's voice gentled. "Possession, obsession, can't occur without the consent of the victim."

"Then you're wrong." Mac shook his head. "I've seen how these nightmares affect Kyra. I can assure you she's not consenting."

"It may be a subliminal consent," Shana insisted.

"Really, Shana, do you hear how implausible what you're saying sounds? You're a psychologist, for heaven's sake, not one of those New Age weirdos. You don't really believe it's possible, do you?"

"I do, Mac." He heard the eraser end of a pencil drumming on her desktop. "I've dealt with half a dozen genuine cases myself."

"With success?" Her admission surprised him.

Shana hesitated. The drumming stopped. "Yes and no."

"Explain."

"It all depends on whether or not the subject is strong enough to resist the entity."

Kyra was strong, of that Mac was sure, but the lack of sleep was wearing her down. He saw it in the pale skin, the bruised eyes, the lack of energy. He frowned. "If you're right, is she in any danger?"

"It all depends on the entity's purpose."

Frustration had him pacing in a tight arc around the corner of the desk where the phone sat. "How do we find out?"

"You should get in touch with someone experienced in helping a spirit cross over to its proper plane. A medium. I can see if there's anyone in your area avail—"

"There isn't enough time."

"I suggest you make the time, my friend, because if you don't, you may be in a heap of trouble. Trouble even you won't be able to get yourself out of."

The conversation had left him frustrated, and the knowledge that time and circumstances were against him did nothing to relieve the pressure. He flipped impatiently through a stack of plastic-coated menus stuck between a napkin holder and a sugar shaker. Now, hours later, the tension still permeating his body made him restless and uneasy in a way he knew worked against him.

His expected calls had been returned, his package retrieved, and Mac had a picture that didn't match his expectations. He *was* making progress—with understanding the mountain's problem, if not with Kyra's.

His future depended on his ability to protect Kyra. If he lost her, would he end up as mad as Alek?

A disturbing thought.

Mac swiveled the red vinyl stool around and looked at Kyra's outline in the truck's darkened interior. He longed for the carefree days they'd shared in Hawaii. He tormented himself with memories of making love to her, of losing himself in the warmth of her body, in the sweet release of their passions. He tortured himself with his aching need to possess her again.

He snapped the stool resolutely away from the outside view.

The future of the people living on Eaton Peak depended on his ability to reach the mine's heart before Alek. If he failed, he would only add to Alek's madness. And his conscience wouldn't allow him to enjoy the civilian life he'd carved out for himself over the past few years. The Institute would own him.

A sobering thought.

When his number was called he paid for the pizza and grabbed the box handed to him.

He turned too sharply out of the parking lot and the pizza box slid across the backseat. Kyra reached back just in time to keep it from crashing to the floor.

"There's no need to speed, you know," Kyra said. "Misty'll be all right for another few minutes. And we can always warm the pizza up in the microwave if it gets too cold."

Mac didn't answer. Somehow he had to find a way to make Kyra leave before Alek decided to use her against him, before, if Shana was right, an evil spirit possessed her completely.

As he drove, he watched her out of the corner of his eye. The dark circles under her eyes marred her pretty face. He knew she'd spent the last two nights sleepless on the living-room sofa. He'd spent those same two nights just as awake as she had.

He'd sensed her nightmare the first night. He'd sensed her fear the second. And he'd wondered where all this sensitivity had come from. He'd settled on his training in the subtleties of human nature as an explanation, but the answer had left him feeling vaguely troubled. He'd felt compelled to get away from her on Sunday. He'd needed the distance to put his feelings for her in perspective, only to discover that when it came to Kyra there could be no perspective.

He'd spent half the day looking for Alek's camp and, after luring Alek into following him to ensure Kyra's safety, he'd spent the other half checking on the progress in his condo, catching up on the paperwork at Mountain Swift, and trying to reach people who didn't want to be found—dropping just enough tidbits of information in Alek's direction to keep him interested.

"What did you find out about Hallie today?" he asked. The rumbling noise of the engine usually pleased him, but against Kyra's silence it roared in his ears. The feeling was disquieting.

"A lot," she said but didn't elaborate.

"Like what?" He tried to make his tone light, in

sharp contrast to the tension of his muscles. The starless night didn't help. It made him feel as if he was on the edge of a black hole, ready to be sucked in at any minute.

"Hallie was my great-great-grandmother."

The words spoken so quietly had the impact of a prize-fighter's punch to his gut. *The woman who haunted Kyra's dreams was her great-great-grandmother.* He glanced worriedly at her. Her pale face shone like polished alabaster in the moon's pale light. How had this discovery affected her? Why hadn't he thought she might need him today?

"Talk to me," he said.

Kyra stared silently out the darkened window, and Mac couldn't help grinding his teeth.

"I'm trying to help you, remember?" He forced a smile.

"You asked me to leave, remember?" She turned to study him. "Look, I'm not sure what your agenda is, but I can handle this problem without you."

She had to leave. It was better that way. Involuntarily, he remembered how she'd clung to him for comfort only a few days ago, the feeling of her soft body spooned against his, the scent of passion flowers that had lulled him to sleep. He cursed Jerrold and damned Alek. But most of all he blasted himself for putting Kyra in danger.

"You should see someone about those nightmares," Mac said. The name of the medium Shana had given him burned in his breast pocket.

"They'll stop." The lack of life in her voice tugged on his softened heartstrings. "Once I understand them, they'll stop."

"Tell me," he cajoled, wanting to lessen the distance between them. "I really want to know what you found out. The Silver Sovereign had quite a fascinating life."

"You don't seem like the type of guy who'd enjoy soap operas."

"That bad?"

"Yes."

Kyra stared up at him. He knew he had to keep her talking; every moment of silence felt like a deepening chasm, one he soon wouldn't be able to bridge. But nothing came to mind.

"I feel lost," she said finally, and turned her attention back to the bleak darkness outside the truck window.

With anyone else he would've known exactly what to say, but not with Kyra. He weighed words and rejected them. His answer seemed pathetic even to him. "Don't worry. We'll find you again."

They wound their way up Eaton Peak in an uncomfortable silence. As soon as they neared the house, he sensed something was amiss. Misty's furious barks, muffled through the closed garage doors, could be heard from outside.

"Stay here," he ordered.

As Kyra scrambled out of the truck before he'd even turned off the ignition and raced for the door, he swore. She dropped her keys twice before he reached the door and took them away from her.

"Something's wrong," Kyra said in a shaky voice.

"Stay out here. Let me check it out."

He slinked along the hall wall, making himself as small a target as possible. As he crept his way to the laundry room, his senses were on high alert. Misty shot out past him and sped directly to the back door, growling all the way. Mac followed her. He tried the back door and found it unlocked. He traced the barely noticeable footprints to the edge of the balcony. Misty sniffed at the trail, then stared into the woods.

Alek, emboldened by thoughts of superior skill, no doubt, had trespassed and left his mark as a taunt.

The time for action had come.

Kyra's gasp of outrage brought Mac back inside the house. He found her bent over a broken piece of pottery.

"I thought I told you to stay outside until I came for you," Mac said.

"He broke one of Lynn's best ceramic pots. Look; it was signed by the artist. It's irreplaceable. Why would he do such a thing?" She picked through the broken shards of pottery with one hand and kept Misty away with the other.

"Who?" Mac asked as he watched her sort through the mess.

Kyra lifted a large chunk of broken clay to reveal the coin Alek used as a calling card. "Your friend Alek. Why would he do that?"

"He's not a friend." Mac bent down to Kyra and picked up the coin. He grasped it in one hand with a ferocity that turned his knuckles white. "To him this is all a game."

"I don't understand."

Mac looked deep into Kyra's spring green eyes, willing her to see the danger in which he had placed her. "He's warning me that something precious can be broken easily." She gave him a quizzical look. "Your life means nothing to him. If it'll help him get what he wants, he'll use you without a second thought." He wanted her to stay close to him more than anything in the world. He feared that if he let her go, he'd never see her again. But for her own safety she needed to go. "It means that you need to leave."

"I can't." She rose and turned away from him, rubbing her arms as if she was suddenly cold. "There's a reason the past is speaking to me. I don't know why, but I need to be here to figure it out."

He shot up, gripping both her shoulders and shaking her. "Don't you understand the danger?"

"No, frankly, I don't." Kyra glared angrily at him, her hands on her hips. "You've skulked around like a boar with a chip on his shoulder for the past few days. I have no idea what kind of game you and Alek are playing, or why both of you insist on involving me in it. You've treated me with only slightly more regard than you would a potted plant. So why don't you enlighten me, Mac, and tell me what's going on?"

He tried to find the right words to convey his worry without jeopardizing his mission. He couldn't tell her about Jerrold or Pandora. He couldn't tell her the reason for Alek's hatred. And he certainly couldn't tell her about Shana's diagnosis—not before he looked into it more carefully.

Her anger and her wariness afforded her a measure of safety—albeit a small one. And her safekeeping was his first priority. If only she'd agree to leave, then he could stop worrying about her.

"Fine," Kyra said, then stalked off. "You can play the stone wall all you want. Until you give me some concrete reasons why I need to leave, I'm staying exactly where I am."

Kyra slammed her bedroom door, leaving him standing in the middle of the living room with Misty staring up at him accusingly.

Chapter Nine

Look for the positive, Kyra admonished herself as anger roiled through her. She unwound her braid and brushed her hair with punishing strokes. There had to be something she and Mac could agree on in this crazy situation. She slammed her brush onto the dresser top, then flopped onto the bed.

She'd picked up the habit of looking for the silver lining in every storm cloud from her mother. For every ruined sand castle her mother had found a lesson in structural stability. Every sorrow had lent her mother an opportunity to teach a lesson in optimism. Even when Mac had left her at the altar her mother had made her realize she'd avoided marrying the wrong man.

But Kyra feared all her mother's optimism wasn't going to help her this time. She rolled onto her stomach, cradling her chin in her hands, and looked out the window at the gibbous moon shining down on the mountain. Its light cast silver shadows on the white snow, rendering a kind of unearthly beauty to the scenery. The wind suddenly stirred the pines and set the shadows into motion, destroying the solemn serenity of the picture. Even Mother Nature seemed to be mired in defeatism tonight.

Shadows. She shivered. Shadows like the ones in her mind were destroying her life. Shadows, she now realized, that had been haunting her long before she arrived in Utah. A flicker of fear sparked inside her. She resolutely blanketed it away.

Kyra turned back to stare at the ceiling. What held her here? Why shouldn't she just pack her bags, as Mac wanted, and leave? Chances were she'd never be back in Utah. She could always make up an excuse not to go back to Summit Station in the spring, when the Utah Historical Restoration Society started their restoration project. George would understand. He'd probably be angry for a while, but if she applied herself even harder at her other projects, he'd soon forgive her. She scratched a line in the reasons-to-leave column on her mental list. Away from Utah she could go back to her old life.

Unfortunately, things weren't that black and white anymore. She wanted to find out why Hallie and Schreck's relationship haunted her. *Scratch one in the reasons-to-stay column.*

She needed to find out what had prompted her biological mother to give her up, and why she'd died that night. Kyra had wondered what had happened twenty-nine years ago ever since her adoptive mother's confession. If she didn't stay, she'd have to come back and put the mystery to rest. So why not do it now and end the torture?

As she thought back to her precious childhood, tears slipped unchecked down her cheeks. Lincoln Logs, popsicle sticks, sand, pots and pans, toothpicks, nothing had been immune to her need to touch and construct. She'd had an instinctive eye for line and color and an innate feel for space and texture. She'd created spectacular environments for her dolls. Her parents had encouraged her talents by making materials available, taking pictures of her masterpieces, and bragging to anyone who would listen that their little girl was a genius. She still remembered the embarrassing thrill of hearing her parents' effusive comments about her creations.

When in college George had given her a way to use her architectural talents she'd found heaven. The last thing she wanted to do was jeopardize the job she loved so much.

Kyra rolled over restlessly once more. A partnership. George had offered her half his company. But only if he could count on her. The only way she could put her all back into her work was to find out Hallie's secrets. Another mark in the *stay* column.

Pictures of Mac's smiling face crept into her mind. Remembrance of his touch set a slow fire burning inside, warming her skin. Then the rain of reality set in, dousing the fire.

She knew she should run away from him. She'd never felt for anyone the reactions he incited in her. Never had anyone completely taken over her senses the way Mac did. Her relationships with other men had been ones of quiet comfort. With Mac there was a promise of depth that thrilled and frightened her. And the strong possibility of finding herself alone again. She wanted to let go of her doubt but found she couldn't. Not yet.

Who are you trying to kid? Kyra thought as she rolled over once again and buried her head in the pillow. She'd fallen head over heels in love all over again with a man who couldn't wait for her to leave. The situation was impossible. As surely as night followed day, if she stayed, Mac would hurt her. She put two marks in the *leave* column in her mind.

The scales were even. Usually the thought would

have pleased her, but today she'd hoped the scales would tip heavily to one side or the other, making the decision for her.

On the other hand, Mac had no reason to lie about her safety here. But which column did his concern fall under?

Right now she didn't feel secure anywhere. There were too many loose ends, and they were all tangled into one knot of Gordian proportion. Up and down the seesaw in her mind went, leading her nowhere.

Her sleepless nights and her draining day of research finally caught up with her. The thoughts zooming in her mind slowed and settled on Hallie. She yanked her heavy sweater over her head, then pulled off her boots and socks. With a yawn, she wrapped the quilt around her and let sleep envelop her.

Kyra vaguely heard the sighing of her door opening. She felt the specter of Mac's presence looming over her, but she hadn't decided how to deal with him yet, so she let her drowsy mind carry her deeper into the folds of sleep.

When the icy sprinkles melted on her face she didn't fight back. She knew she'd dream about Hallie, and dreaming about Hallie held the key to her nightmares. This dream might put her one step closer to understanding why her life had been turned upside down since she'd arrived in Utah. She relaxed and welcomed the vision, praying it would hold answers.

Sehr gut, Liebchen, the voice she'd come to recognize as Rolf Schreck's echoed in her mind. *Understand why you are cursed.*

Kyra heard an unfamiliar hum even before the black screen of her lids changed into a moving picture.

Hallie stood tapping her foot by an open, wood-braced double elevator shaft. She wore a black riding skirt, topped by a tailored jacket over her high-necked robin's-egg-blue blouse, and a stiff hat covered her hair. The elevator clattered to a halt, and Hallie looked irritably out the shack's small window.

Kyra's spirit drifted into Hallie's body, allowing her to share Hallie's thoughts and feelings.

Hallie usually worked in her office in town, but she liked to surprise her crew once in a while by visiting the mine herself. Today she had an appointment with Arthur Jennings to visit the new lode recently unearthed on the five-hundred-foot level. Jennings had glowed about the vein of rich ore, and Hallie could hardly wait to see it.

Her husband's find two years ago had proved to be a veritable treasure. A pleased smile curled the corners of her mouth at the thought of Emory and the way he'd lifted her and twirled her around him when he'd told her of his find. The mine still earned her a monthly income that averaged around fifty thousand dollars—with no end in sight. Her business acumen had surprised all the critics who had predicted failure, but it wouldn't have surprised Emory at all. Her heart gave a small lurch and resonated with emptiness.

In the year since Emory's death Hallie had missed him terribly. He'd always appreciated her intelligence and told her often that in his eyes her beauty had been her second most desirable asset, after her mind. He'd shared his business dealings with her and marveled at her insightful questions.

In the past few months John Barrett had started courting her openly. He owned the White Rock mine, which ran next to the Eaton mine. Marriage to him could provide an easy solution to Schreck's constant harassment. It could prove to be a very profitable merger, too—provided an amenable financial agreement could be reached. But still Hallie hesitated. She knew she could never love anyone the way she loved Emory. And John would want more than a merger on paper. She wasn't sure she had anything to give him.

She enjoyed her social standing to its full extent and jealously guarded her fortune—it was all she had left of Emory. She could comfortably remain a widow for the rest of her life, if it wasn't for the trouble Schreck was giving her.

Hallie paced the floor impatiently. The swish of her skirt and the drumming of her heels on the wooden floor could barely be heard over the sighing of steam, the creaking of cables, and the reverberating reports of drills working deep in the mine.

As she paced, Hallie noted the deterioration of the aging structure. She'd already ordered plans for a larger building with lofty ceilings, lots of windows, and room for a second set of elevators. But for now this gloomy wooden shack would have to do. It protected the shaft head and housed the machinery that kept the mine alive with action.

Two naked bulbs, one on either side of the room, hung unlit from electric cords. A small barrel-like stove heated the room in colder weather, and miners' clothes, on pegs, lined one wall, waiting for the shift change. Cool steam, used in the lowest portions of the mine to counteract the heat below, rushed up from several openings on the floor. Hallie was careful to skirt them. She extracted a handkerchief from her pocket and daintily wiped away the moisture beading on her face.

One half of the room was occupied by an enormous spool on which steel cables wound and unwound to operate the steam-driven hoist that raised and lowered the elevator cages. Jack Tarr, the operator, kept his eyes firmly on the dial that told him the location of the cages. A bell on a pull rope above his head was his only means of communication with the men working below. Jack's skill at this job had saved many lives, and Hallie didn't mind paying him the extra dollar a day, especially when she put her life in his hands.

Hallie turned away and redoubled her pacing. Jennings's tardiness made her positively livid. These days it didn't take much to make her mad. Ever since the court had legally entitled her to all of her husband's mine, Schreck had harassed her daily. Some days he was sweetness personified. On others, his determination took on an evilness that curdled her blood.

He'd even had the gall to hit her during one of his visits. That's when she'd installed a pair of guards at her side. With Jennings late, she wished she hadn't agreed to give them their earned day off. The situation was becoming intolerable, but she didn't know what to do to stop Schreck. If something didn't come to her soon, she was afraid she'd have to resort to more drastic measures.

Only yesterday she'd cabled her uncle in California, asking for his advice. She hadn't wanted to discuss her problem with anyone in Park City. Even though John Barrett was her friend, right now he was still her competitor. She hoped Uncle Ronald wouldn't be long with his answer, allowing her to avoid marriage.

"What's keeping Jennings?" Hallie asked Jack Tarr as she completed another circuit of the room.

"Don't rightly know, Mrs. Eaton," Jack answered in his heavy Cornish accent. "Mabbe 'ee got delayed at the assayer's office."

"I'm tired of waiting for him." Hallie stepped onto the elevator platform. "Who's working the five-oh-one today?"

"Jones and O'Connor, ma'am." Jack handed her a carbide lamp and matches. " 'Ee be careful now, my beautay. They be workin' the widda-maker. Mr. Jennings wants to widen the drift."

The miners often referred to the drills they used to bore holes for dynamite in the hard rock as widow-makers because their kick had cost more than one man his life. Hallie knew the widow-maker was only one of the many ways men lost their lives in the mine. In the last month alone, she'd lost seven men to accidents or silicosis, and several more had become permanently disabled by the loss of limbs. Yet hers was considered the safest mining company in the area.

"When will they blast?" Hallie asked.

"Not till next shift."

"I'll be careful. Take me to five-oh-one."

Jack nodded and set the contraption into motion with the help of two levers. The cage had barely moved a few feet, when Schreck jumped into the moving elevator, startling Hallie.

"Jack! Stop the cage!"

Hallie's cry was lost in the inhuman cacophony of the working machinery. He must have snuck by while Jack was busy concentrating on his dials. How dare he! She grabbed for the bell hanging on the cage's iron frame, but Schreck pulled her savagely away.

Hallie struggled, then stopped suddenly when she felt the pointed end of a hunting knife pressed below her breast at an angle that would pierce her heart should she move.

The whirring groan of cables slowed as they reached the 501 drift. Schreck shoved Hallie off the platform into the bored tunnel and rang the "All Clear" signal on the bell. The elevator clanked away to answer another call.

"Finally a chance to talk alone." Schreck pushed Hallie to a sitting position on a rock outcropping. "I do not appreciate your scarcity these past few weeks, Mrs. Eaton."

The smell of wet dust permeated the air and the

hammering of drills reported in spurts down the length of the tunnel. Already the mine's hot, humid air had Hallie's clothing sticking uncomfortably to her skin. Schreck lowered himself next to Hallie and brought his mouth to Hallie's ear, making his voice audible above the mine's din. Hallie moved her head away .from the uncomfortable caress, only to be jerked back into position by Schreck's rough hand.

"Time has run out," Schreck said, breathing heavily into Hallie's ear. "I want what is mine."

"Nothing I have belongs to you."

"*Ach*, Hallie. I have tried to win your respect and your love."

Hallie flinched at the feel of Schreck's callused finger on the contours of her cheek.

"But it seems you prefer another. I have heard John Barrett has proposed. That is not an acceptable marriage. If you are looking for a partner, I will fill the spot. I urge you to accept my proposal, my dearest Mrs. Eaton."

"I'm afraid that is simply out of the question. I won't bend to your brutal tactics. Mr. Barrett's proposal has nothing to do with my mine. It is a merger of two loving hearts, not one of assets."

As he howled mockingly, Schreck's head bent back. "Do not make me laugh. You have no heart. You have proven that to me this past year as I have tried to court you like a gentleman."

Schreck twisted around so that he kneeled before Hallie, the hunting knife poised again at her heart. With his free hand he pried the carbide lamp from her hands and placed it on the rocky floor.

"Hallie Eaton, will you be my wife?"

His lupine eyes shone eerily in the yellowed light of the lamp. A stab of fear pierced through Hallie. She couldn't say yes, and it was obvious that Schreck wouldn't take no for an answer. She dropped her gaze to her lap and smoothed her skirt, stalling. Uncle Ronald's answer would come too late. So would marriage to John Barrett. The time for drastic measures had come.

I've failed you, my darling. I've failed you. Emory's last words echoed in her mind. And for the first time since his death, she feared he might have.

"Your answer, *liebliche* Hallie." Schreck poked the knife into a buttonhole on her jacket and deftly sent a button flying down the shaft a few feet from where they stood.

Hallie stared blankly at the shaft's gaping hole. She'd have to kill him. It was the only way to get out of the situation.

Schreck heaved himself up, grabbing Hallie by the collar and raising her to a standing position with him. As he walked her to the timbered supports lining the shaft, her feet barely touched the ground. He leaned her slightly forward so she could see the blackness of the hole. She knew it dropped at least a thousand more feet down into the heart of the mountain. The macabre pinging of water against the wall announced morbidly the painful death such a fall would incur.

Hallie swallowed hard. "I would be delighted to be your wife, Mr. Schreck."

"The honor will be mine."

As he smiled his approval, his beard prickled the skin of her neck. Hallie gasped when Schreck jerked her around and crushed her against his chest. His eyes glittered feverishly, setting fear thrumming through her veins. His mouth descended toward hers. He paused, his lips brushing hers as he spoke. "Now that we are officially partners, I will seal our engagement with a kiss."

His stale breath made Hallie's stomach lurch. She closed her eyes and braced herself for his touch. But when he tried to insert his whiskey-tainted tongue into her mouth, Hallie lost her composure, bit the offending piece of flesh, and ran blindly into the darkened tunnel toward the noise of the hammering drill.

She heard Schreck wail his pain and quickened her pace. As she sped with all her might into the blackness, her heart beat wildly. She tried to remember how far into the tunnel Jennings had said the new vein had been found. When she ran into an unexpected curve, the sleeve of her jacket tore. She forced her feet to keep moving.

"Help!" Hallie cried at the top of her lungs when she saw a pinpoint of light straight ahead. But the pounding drill drowned her voice.

Schreck caught up with her and hauled her back savagely toward the shaft, knife pressed into her side. His voice hissed into her ear. "You will pay for all your sins."

She couldn't give in to this madman. Life would be hell. Even death was preferable to living with this monster. She had to fight. Without analyzing her chances of success, Hallie dove into action.

She pretended to trip. Schreck's grip loosened to allow her to regain her balance. She turned as she fell and landed on her bottom. As Schreck reached down for her, Hallie hooked one of his legs with her foot, sending him sprawling to the floor. When his armed hand hit the rock his fingers let go of the handle, and the knife skittered away from him. Hallie scrambled up, reaching the knife before Schreck could regain his mobility.

Hallie ran once more toward the sound of the drill deep in the tunnel, but her long skirt hindered her progress, and Schreck's cruel hands on her shoulders put an end to her flight.

He whipped her around, and Hallie watched in morbid fascination as her hand drove the blade of his knife toward his side. The sharp steel plunged forcefully under the last rib into his liver. As he crumpled to the ground, Schreck's face contorted in surprise. A profusion of bright red blood soaked his white shirt and drenched his gray pants. As shock set in, his skin turned a pasty white.

His murderous gaze pinned her. He pushed himself up and stumbled toward her, pulling the blade from his side. The knife fell with a clang to the ground. Schreck tried to stanch the renewed flow of blood with his hand.

"Ich schwöre meine Rache," Schreck said, advancing awkwardly toward her.

Hallie backed away reflexively, feeling blindly with one hand for the rocky wall. She laughed dryly to gain a measure of courage. "Swear vengeance all you want, Mr. Schreck. Your threats don't scare me. You're on your way to hell, where you belong."

Schreck lunged at Hallie, his bloody hands seeking her throat. The sticky slipperiness of his fingers against her skin revolted her. As she gulped for air, she grasped his wrists and tried to push them away from her throat. But her hands kept slipping on his blood-slicked skin. His fingers squeezed her neck with surprising strength.

"I will . . . take you . . . with me," Schreck gasped raggedly.

"Never."

Beads of sweat poured from his ashen forehead and melted the clownish smear of blood on one side of his face. At that instant he looked like the devil personified, and Hallie feared she had made a dreadful mistake.

Suddenly the pressure of his hands on her neck diminished. Schreck's arms fell limply to his sides. She shoved him.

"I damn you to eternity in hell," she said to regain courage.

He stumbled back one step. "I'll be back . . . for you . . . and all of yours . . . until there are none left."

He stumbled back two more steps. He teetered. His eyes widened. Then he pitched out of sight into the black hole. "I'll be back for . . . you."

As he plummeted down the shaft to his death, his last words echoed and re-echoed against the walls.

Breathing hard with fear and shock, Hallie scurried back to find the lamp. The light caught the spot from which Schreck had fallen. As if his shadow had become separated from his form, the imprint of his body remained etched in eerie silver white on the rocky floor.

Clutching the lamp with both hands, Hallie saw the blood. It was everywhere. It dripped from her hands, stained her shirt, and pooled at her boots. She dropped the lamp.

"Go away!" Rivulets of red were drying on her fingers. She wiped the offending sticky mess back and forth across the front of her skirt. "Leave me alone."

But even as she yelled for help Schreck's silver shadow stared up at her from the ground, and she knew without a doubt that he would haunt her all her life.

I've failed you, my darling. I've failed you. Emory's final words mingled with Schreck's curse, reverberating through Hallie's mind until she could stand it no more. She fainted.

The movie in Kyra's mind disappeared like a film strip burning on a projector light. A flash of light blinded her. Then a stygian darkness enveloped her.

She bolted straight up in her bed. Gasping, she stared numbly at her hands, fully expecting them to be covered with blood, but she could see only black. The sounds of Schreck's body hitting the shaft walls rang in her ears.

Go to the mountain, liebliche *Kyra. There you will find the answers you need.*

Kyra quickly cast aside the quilt. Heart racing, she

darted into the hall. Still caught in the grips of her nightmare, she couldn't seem to escape the deep black around her. She ran along dark corridors that curved around her like heavy mist.

She was trapped. Panic washed over her.

"Mac! Where are you?"

His touch had brought her out of her time-warped vision before. She needed him now.

She bounced off an unseen wall, feeling a clammy stickiness seep through the arm of her turtleneck.

Go to the mountain, Schreck's voice commanded.

She ran faster. "Mac! I need you."

I've failed you, my darling. I'll be back for you-ou-ou. I've failed you. Her mind resounded with Emory and Schreck's last words, chasing her down the tunnels of her dream. She ran as fast as she could, but her progress got slower and slower, as if the mist had turned into heavy snow, accumulating fast. Halting, she squinted through the darkness for signs of light.

The sound of heavy breathing bounced all around her. She wasn't alone. Fear galloped through her. Danger. If he caught her, she would die. The overwhelming fear wouldn't leave her. Swallowing her terror, she concentrated on the sound. Someone was waiting. Just around the corner. She swiveled on her heels and raced heedlessly across the dark, away from the unknown stranger.

"I'm lost, Mac. I'm lost."

Follow my voice. Come to me, Kyra. Schreck's voice intruded into her mind. She pushed herself faster.

"Wake up, Kyra. Wake up!"

Mac! He'd heard her. She turned toward his voice. "Help me!"

Her lungs burned from her effort. She gasped for air. Afraid to stop, she drove herself on.

Come back to me, Kyra. You need me, Schreck whispered, the strong pull of his voice luring her. She stumbled and fell, breaking the thin thread joining her to Schreck. Gathering herself back up, she sped ahead.

Shadows swirled around her, taking the shapes of people whose skeletal arms reached out to her. They crowded around her, tighter and tighter, calling her name. *Kyra, come to us, Kyra.* A dozen voices, a hundred voices pecked at her brain.

She came to a sudden halt, turning in helpless circles. "Stop!"

What's happening to me? Where am I? Closing her eyes, she clamped her hands to her ears and drowned at the voices with her own desperate cry.

"Mac!"

The mountain shook beneath her feet. Blindly, she reached forward into the dark with her arms and ran. She became aware of Mac's presence, aware of his voice among the cacophony of the others.

"It's me, Kyra. It's Mac. Don't run from me."

Like a needle in a compass, she focused on Mac's voice, moving surely toward it.

Then she saw him. He stood, coming in and out of the shifting mist. She skidded to a halt. Between them gaped a deep chasm.

His hands, his voice beckoned her. "It's all right. You're safe."

Glancing at the black abyss between them, she hesitated. "Help me."

"You're safe now."

A quiet calm replaced the frantic panic. A blinding light cut across the deep black. Somewhere behind her a horn blared. Keeping her gaze focused on Mac's face, she hurled herself across the swirling mist separating them and landed hard against his chest. He brought his arms around her roughly, holding her in a tight embrace.

"You almost got yourself killed. What were you thinking of, running in the middle of the street at night?"

She heard Mac's voice, but the words didn't make sense. As he held her, the mist and the shadows vanished, but the dark remained. Kyra became aware of the cold wind cutting through the thin layer of her turtleneck, of the snow beneath her bare feet, of the night all around her. She was outside. How had she gotten here?

As if he might disappear, she held on to Mac's waist in an almost savage embrace. He buried his face in her hair and kissed her, holding on to her just as fiercely.

"Are you all right?" Mac asked gruffly.

She wanted to cry out her frustration. She wanted to laugh her relief. *All right* was the last thing she felt. She feared she might never be *all right* again. What had happened to her? Was it possible to get lost in a dream? And what would have happened to her if Mac hadn't reached for her across the dark mist of her nightmare? She raised her gaze to trap his.

"Hold me, Mac. Don't let go."

He didn't release her. The sounds of her heaving breaths rasped against his chest.

"Shh. It's all right now. It's all right."

She snuggled against him. "I feel like I'm going crazy. I was stuck in there. Stuck in my dream. If you hadn't pulled me out of it, I—"

"You'd have found your way back just fine."

His expression grew taut. She held her breath, fearing he would push her away. As he lifted her into his arms, his brilliant gaze never left hers. Silently, he carried her across the asphalt road, up the driveway, and into the house.

A myriad of emotions flowed through her, pressing intolerably against her, igniting a reckless need for release. When he set her down in the foyer to close the door she twisted in the gentle hold of his arms to face him. Her hands locked around his neck. She pulled herself up on her toes and dropped urgent kisses onto his mouth, his cheeks, along the tensing column of his neck, and felt the cold horror of her nightmare fading.

"Hold me, Mac. I need you to touch me. I need to feel alive."

The heat of him covered her like a living quilt. She reveled in the warmth, in the solid flesh beneath her hands, pressing herself closer to him.

A muffled groan escaped him. He caught hold of her wrists and pushed her away from him. Every inch of him vibrated with tension. The gray of his eyes flickered with the banked fires of desire.

"Mac?"

"Not like this, Kyra." The sound of his hoarse voice broke through her dazed excitement.

"Not like what?"

"Kyra . . ."

Her trembling fingertips reached for his cheeks and stroked them in a mixture of reassurance and need. "Mac . . ."

He closed his eyes and broke their contact. The tension of his body, the clenching of his fist showed her the rigid control he exerted.

Kyra shivered in the sudden coldness surrounding her and rubbed her arms against the chill. She waited quietly, for what she wasn't sure. Reassurance? No, it ran deeper than that. She wanted the wall around him to crumble. She wanted to know he'd never leave her again.

There was only silence. Her sense of comfort and security withered and vanished. She felt cold all the way down to her soul.

Gentle regret filled his eyes. "Not here. Not now. Not with all these ghosts around us." Even the softness in his voice didn't counteract the icy ache growing deep inside her.

He wasn't hers. Not then. Not now.

Don't leave me alone, she wanted to say, willing

him to understand her fear. But she didn't. She couldn't. "It's okay. I'm fine. Go back to whatever you were doing."

"We need to talk about what happened tonight."

"Not now. I need to think."

"Don't take too long." With a tightening of his jaw, he slid the deadbolt on the front door into the locked position and brushed past her, disappearing through the basement door.

Alone. She was alone. Again.

Chapter Ten

An angry growl rumbled like an earthquake deep in the silver shadow's center. He'd had her trapped where he wanted. A minute more and she would have been his willing victim, following him wherever he led. Once again he'd miscalculated the power McKane held over Kyra. McKane had reached for her across the space of dreams and plucked her out of his grasp.

As his own energy had waned, he'd felt the bond growing stronger between Kyra and this man. If he couldn't avoid McKane's influence on Kyra, he'd have to eliminate him.

The shadow paced the length of the house. Fear would weaken the bond. Yes, fear; that was the answer. Once the bond was broken, suffocating McKane would be child's play. It always was. Alone, their bonds cut, the strongest of men wet their pants with fright. And their terror sapped their strength, building his own. Then he barely had to touch them before they crumpled like rag dolls, begging for mercy, then for a quick death.

Once McKane was out of the way, Kyra wouldn't be able to resist him any longer.

What did this man fear most?

An idea formed. Yes, of course. The solution had stared at him so plainly, he'd missed it.

Joy gave him a spurt of energy. He used this energy to locate his mark. His plan set into action, he flowed to his home deep in the bowels of the mine.

He had to rest. He had to rebuild his energy. Triumph. Its sweetness filled him with anticipation. Soon his wait would be over.

In the basement Mac reached across the pool table for the package he'd brought back from Salt Lake City. The image of a terrified Kyra popped unbidden into his mind. She'd run past him, calling his name, not even seeing him standing by her. She'd recoiled from him when he'd shaken her shoulders. The terror he'd seen in her eyes had frightened him as no mission ever had. Her already pale complexion had paled even more, giving him the impression she was no more than a ghost when she'd raced out into the night.

Never had he felt more ineffectual than as he'd watched her run blindly into the road, watching a car miss her by inches. Never had the feeling of failure weighed on him more than as he'd helplessly tried to shake her out of her dream-induced spell.

What had happened to her? Could Shana possibly be right? Could Kyra have been possessed by Schreck's spirit? Could such a phenomenon actually take place? He fished out the piece of paper with the phone number Shana had given him, stared at it, then shoved it back into his pocket. There had to be a logical explanation. There always was.

Mac examined the cardboard tube in his hands,

but as much as he looked, he didn't see the container, only Kyra. Why didn't he just haul her off to the airport and send her flying out of danger?

Because Kyra had to make her own decisions. As much as the Institute had taught him to play God for them, he'd never mistaken himself for Him. And because he owed his family a debt for all the heartaches he'd caused them as a teenager, he couldn't simply drag Kyra off to safety and go with her.

It was as simple and as complicated as that.

Mac drove Kyra's distracting image out of his mind, but it kept easing back in. What was she doing? Was she all right? He curbed his urge to go check on her.

The last thing he'd wanted to do was leave her alone, but if he'd stayed, reassurance wasn't all he'd have given her. It would have been so easy to accept her invitation, to assure her that making love was the natural thing for them to do. But she would be defending herself against her fears, and he wanted her to come to him for himself, not as insulation. And if he'd accepted her invitation, he'd have wound up hating himself; or worse, she would have wound up regretting her impulsive actions.

"It was just a dream," Kyra assured herself. Mac's retreat had brought her nightmare back in vivid colors, leaving her feeling cold and alone. "It wasn't real. It was just a dream."

She repeated the phrases like a mantra all the way to the kitchen. How could a dream be real? Weren't dreams the mind's way of analyzing the events of a life? The events in her life had been bizarre lately. Wouldn't it follow that her dreams would be, too?

She gulped down a glass of water. When that didn't help ease the tremors rippling through her body she splashed her face with the ice cold spray.

As she dried her face with the green-and-white

kitchen towel, Kyra knew with certainty that she couldn't leave. Hallie had faced her fears; so would she.

The bizarreness of her life since she'd come to Utah was Schreck's vengeful shadow at work. The dream had showed her as much. And he wouldn't let her leave. If the curse was real, he'd already killed four generations of Hallie's descendants, as well as Hallie herself, and he wouldn't settle for anything less than total annihilation of Hallie's blood.

He wouldn't let her leave. In his twisted mind, he couldn't. But what did he have to gain? If she knew the answer to that question, the scales wouldn't be tilted so heavily in the silver shadow's favor. Could a spirit shadow transcend death and come back to life? Was that what he sought? She shook her head in disbelief. If Mac could hear her thoughts, he'd really think she was crazy.

Needing comfort, she looked into the living room, expecting to see Misty curled in the recliner. The chair was empty. Towel in hand, Kyra walked to Mac's room to see whether her beast had decided to nap there and found that room empty, too. She reached the breakfast bar before her attention fell on the crescent of light eking from beneath the basement door.

Mac.

What was he doing down there? What was he thinking? She'd made a fool of herself yet again by throwing herself at him. When would she learn? Probably never, she realized. Her heart would always belong to him, even if she barely registered a scratch on his. She shook her head. Now was not the time to become mired in futile thoughts.

Mac was right about one thing, Kyra decided. She couldn't live morassed in a bog of indecision. She had to act. She had to make quicker decisions.

Right! Kyra strode purposefully to the stove and

put the towel back in its place with a precision that would have pleased her strict father. She leaned her backside against the counter and crossed her arms under her breasts.

Decision number one: She'd stay. All she could count on in the future was her job. Her job depended on her mental well-being, and she'd only get that if she put a stop to Schreck's curse. For that she'd have to go to the mountain and risk losing herself in another shadow-induced nightmare, risk losing . . . everything.

She shivered but forced her spine to stand ramrod straight.

Decision number two: She'd find a way to mend the rift between herself and Mac. Though they might never share the relationship she'd once envisioned, she needed his ability to draw her out of her dreams. It could mean the difference between life and death when she encountered the shadow in his own territory.

She needed Mac's friendship. Other than Misty, he was her only company here, and she couldn't stand those unbearable silences between them. She'd deal with the empty spot he'd leave in her heart later.

"Here goes nothing," Kyra said as she pushed herself off the counter and headed toward the basement. She hesitated for a second at the door, then swallowed the leaden ball that was stuck in her throat.

Mac forced himself to concentrate on the task at hand and ripped the top off the tubular package. The tube contained two maps. The first pinpointed the route to the Eaton mine shaft—three hundred feet to the right of the position indicated on the public maps and a hundred feet higher. Not much of a problem in the summer, but with several feet of snow covering the evidence, it definitely would have taken him longer to find the shaft head.

The second map showed a transverse section of the mountain, with its circuitous maze of tunnels and chambers. His goal—the eighteen-hundred-foot level of the mine, drift number 1806 in stope number 1801. It was a hole in the ground, buried deep in the twisty intestines of the mountain. This particular chamber had been renamed Pandora's Box by the physicists who had once worked there.

The tube also contained instructions indicating the location of the recording equipment left behind. It had stopped sending signals a month ago. Before the malfunction there had been a peak of activity that hadn't been felt since the start of the experiment in 1968. For years they had tried to recreate their early success. Since the experiment had been canceled there had been no more than a blip of activity. By retrieving the dead recorder the Institute scientists expected to find, buried in the data, the reasons for the activity and the sudden death of the equipment.

Mac brought out several padded sample collection vials from the tube and placed them alongside the maps.

The last items in the tube were a series of palm-sized red boxes. Mac arranged each one in a line on the pool table's green felt. They looked like innocent Christmas packages. Mac sneered. Looks were deceiving.

Jerrold had told him that after activating the mechanism, one on each level, he'd have only two minutes to clear the area and move on to the next. The contents of the box would expand a thousand-fold into a foam that would harden into rock, forming an impenetrable, permanent seal that would run the length of the shaft. The scientists hoped this would neutralize the Pandora protons' spontaneous decay and stabilize the mountain once more, making it safe for the mountain's residents to continue living there.

"Why can't I use a remote detonating system?" Mac had asked Jerrold.

"We simply don't know what we're dealing with and can't take any chances."

Yeah, right, except for all the ones I'll be taking.

And, thanks to the Institute, not a single resident would realize they'd ever been in danger.

Mac couldn't believe he'd once rationalized his actions with that thought. But then, never before had his family been directly involved. While he carried out his missions without emotion, he'd acted more like a machine than a man, he realized. People had a right to know their government had goofed. Especially when the mistakes placed their lives in jeopardy.

When had the Institute's accent changed from peaceable confrontations to guerilla tactics to accomplish their goals? And why hadn't he noticed the shift? Mac tried to pin down when his attitude toward the Institute had changed and didn't like the answer.

At twenty-one everything had seemed so clear-cut. He wished for his lost youthful idealism, regretting the cynicism that now colored his life.

Mac reached down at his feet and picked up a white padded backpack. He set it on the pool table and carefully packed the red boxes.

He sensed Kyra's presence before he heard the doorknob turn, keenly aware that his pulse had picked up tempo despite his centered thoughts. With each step closer she took, his muscles tightened as he vainly tried to build a fortress strong enough to deflect Kyra's powerful effect on him.

"Where's Misty?" she asked, a shaky smile on her lips.

At the sound of Kyra's voice the dog hopped off

the comfortable chair by the floor-to-ceiling windows of the basement and trotted toward her mistress. She launched herself into Kyra's arms and demanded to be petted. Kyra laughed softly, cooing to the dog.

"What's all this?" she asked, walking toward him. She stopped beside him and looked at the items spread over the pool table.

Mac rolled up the maps and stuffed them back into the tube. She was too close. He felt his pulse pound at his temple. The room seemed uncomfortably warm. As her hair softly tickled his arms even through the material of his long-sleeved shirt, desire stirred low in his belly.

He shifted his weight, putting a slight distance between them. The scent of passion flowers she wore brought vivid images of sunshine and sea . . . of paradise. Would he never be allowed even a slice of happiness? He swallowed his bitterness. This would be his last mission. Jerrold would have to find someone else next time he needed a clean-up job done. Better still, he'd make sure no one else got caught in the Institute's clutches.

When Kyra reached for one of the red boxes, Mac covered her hand with his and pulled it away.

"Don't touch," he said more gruffly than he'd planned. How could anyone's skin be so soft? He dropped her hand, as if it were a piece of hot lava.

"What's in the boxes?" She snapped the hand Mac had touched back to stroke Misty's coat.

"Repairs to a mistake," Mac said in as neutral a voice as he could manage.

"Your mistake?" Kyra pretended to examine the vials still displayed on the table, but Mac caught her sideways glance at him.

"No." He methodically packed the boxes into his backpack.

"What exactly is it that you do? It's become obvious in the last few days that your resort is only part of your business."

Kyra sat on the table, swinging her long legs over the edge. Misty rolled over on the green felt to have her belly scratched.

Mac didn't know how to answer her question. The resort had been his only job for the past two years. He'd responded to the Institute's call only because it involved Brad and Lynn. He wanted to confide in Kyra, but years of secrecy weren't easily overcome.

"What is it? Some sort of Secret Service job you can't talk about?" Kyra chuckled, but it seemed forced.

"Something like that."

Her smile froze, then melted, but her voice remained soft. "I was kidding."

"I'm not."

She looked at him for a long minute. "It can't be easy to live a life alone like that, just you and your secrets."

Surprised, Mac jerked his gaze away from hers. "I'm not alone."

"Aren't you, though? How many women have you dated since you left me at the altar? How many close friends do you have now?"

The questions sent uncomfortable jitters jumping through his body. He could count his relationships with women with the fingers of one hand. None of them had lasted long. None of them had compared to Kyra. As for friends, the resort and his various activities had kept him too busy to forge bonds.

He hadn't felt lonely . . . except when he'd thought of Kyra. And whenever he did, he'd felt a deep need to keep moving, to keep searching, and this driving need had leaked through even the relentless activity required to rebuild his resort and keep it afloat. Kyra was right. Despite all the people who passed through his resort door, he was alone.

As if it were a live bomb ready to explode, Mac concentrated on the placement of the next box into his backpack. When the last box was safely packed he zipped the backpack closed.

The seconds ticked loudly between them. Kyra waited patiently for him to say something, petting a thoroughly entranced Misty. What he wouldn't give to be in the dog's place!

Mac wanted Kyra. Not just for a night, but forever. This need ran deeper than the physical desire crackling between them. She had once brimmed with life. She had once dared him to dream. She had once unknowingly made him believe there could be a future without the Institute. With Kyra around he could imagine permanent roots—he could imagine being content in them.

Would it be so wrong to start a bridge of trust?

"I was an environmental engineer," Mac said.

"What's so secret about that?"

Mac sneered silently. That's exactly what he'd thought when he'd accepted the position at the Institute. "I worked for a company called the Condor Institute. They hired me fresh out of college. Looking back, I can see it was more than my engineering degree that attracted them."

"What else was there?"

"The trouble I got out of."

"What kind of trouble?"

Mac shrugged. "Normal kids' stuff."

"I still don't see where the hush-hush comes from."

"The Condor Institute is a front. Most of the cases they handle are straightforward environmental clean-ups. That's all an outsider would see. There's one department that doesn't exist on paper. It consists of special field agents who do the clean-ups no one else will." He paused. "I was one of those agents."

Her forehead wrinkled in concentration. "Those

clean-ups—that's what you referred to earlier as a mistake?"

"That's right." Mac tested the backpack's load for stability. "I loved my job. It was exciting. Never the same. I was good at it, too. And I thought I was making a real difference."

"I still don't understand. What mistakes did they make?"

Kyra's fingers stroked Misty's ears, and Mac had to look away to stifle his envy. "Not *their* mistakes; other people's mistakes. People who don't always want their mistakes fixed."

"If it's a mistake, why wouldn't they want it fixed? That doesn't make sense."

"No, it doesn't, does it?"

"It sounds like a dangerous job."

"Sometimes it was."

Her eyes shone bright. They warmed him like green sunshine. But in their centers he saw her vulnerability, saw the pain he had caused her bleed anew.

"That's why you left me, wasn't it?" she whispered.

"Yes." His jaw twitched painfully with the admission.

Her head bent forward and she concentrated on petting Misty. He could only guess at the conclusions her fertile imagination conjured, and he knew that before the evening ended he would have to tell her what had happened to rip him from her side all those years ago.

"Alek—is he one of those people you're talking about?" she asked after a long, too thoughtful silence.

He gritted his teeth at the mention of Alek's name.

Kyra's hand stilled on the dog's hair. "Mac, who exactly is Alek Vermer?"

He answered on one long, regretful breath. "I once called him brother."

Chapter Eleven

Kyra's leg stopped swinging abruptly, and her mouth dropped open while question after question whirled through her mind. "Brother? As in sibling? But I thought you and Alek were enemies."

"As in close friend. And love and hate aren't that far apart, are they?"

"You know, you amaze me sometimes." Kyra fingered Misty's ear and the little dog grunted with pleasure.

"Me?" Mac slid the backpack from his shoulders and placed it carefully on the table. He unzipped it and rearranged the load. "How's that?"

"Sometimes you seem as if nothing can touch you, and then, when I least expect it, you come up with something sentimental like 'Love and hate aren't that far apart.' What do you know about love?"

His mechanical movements made her want to scream, *Talk to me. Look at me.* But she didn't. She forced herself to stay calm and quiet.

There was that unbearable silence again. Kyra swallowed the anger threatening to erupt unchecked. She realized Mac was trying, but some sort of macho training had taught him to keep his feelings under lock and key, trapping them inside beneath the steel of his heart. It left her with the distinct impression she was drilling through the tough metal with a dull bit.

As he rezipped the pack, his jaw flinched, and she saw the almost imperceptible movement of teeth grinding together. He tested the load once more, his face an unbreachable wall.

She longed to see him relax, as he had when they'd shared the pancakes—was it only four days ago? It seemed like a lifetime. She wanted to fade the harsh lines of stress on his forehead and cheeks with soft kisses, fill her senses with his earthy scent, lose herself in the exploration of the taut body beneath the red shirt and age-softened blue jeans. She wanted to have what they'd once shared and turned their backs on.

Letting her thoughts stray this way would get her in trouble.

Forcing her attention back to Misty, Kyra cleared her throat. "What happened between you and Alek?"

Mac shrugged. "It's a matter of perception."

"I don't understand."

He sat on a corner of the pool table, dangling the backpack between his legs, his gaze directed toward the floor.

Kyra swallowed her impatience and managed to keep her voice light. "Please, Mac, talk to me."

He looked up at her. The silver of his eyes was a tornado of emotions, swirling with such savageness that she wanted to run to him, hold him, and comfort him—as he'd done for her that first night. But the stiffness of his body language kept her rooted to the spot.

With a sigh, she put Misty down and shooed her away. Ignoring Misty's begging noises, she tried to think of a way to get through Mac's thick protective wall.

Kyra slid along the edge of the pool table until she was close enough to reach for Mac's hand. She touched him tentatively. "What happened between the two of you?"

Mac hesitated, then got up. With the backpack in hand he headed for one of the two offices off the game room.

Frustration tensed every muscle in her body. She bit her tongue to keep from yelling at him, instinctively knowing this would drive him farther away. Before she could formulate an alternate plan to draw him out, he came back out of the office empty-handed. He sat once again beside her on the pool table.

"The people in our department at the Institute were as close as family," he said. "Alek and I started working there on the same day. We hit it off right away and worked so well together, we became a special team. We could almost read each other's minds. That got us out of more than one sticky situation."

She reached for his hand once more, trying to ignore the strange rhythm her heart played against her ribs. His fingers tightened comfortingly through hers.

"Eight years ago Alek met someone special," Mac continued in a dispassionate voice she knew he used to mask his emotions. "He knew the danger. We'd all been warned against it. But he loved Anna so much he married her anyway. He wanted to quit. His contract still had a month to go. They made him honor it. One last mission; then he'd settle down for a plain, ordinary life. We all kidded him about it because he worked with such zest."

She wished she could join him in the faraway

place his memories had taken him. Instead, she squeezed his hand reassuringly. Her heart fluttered when he squeezed back.

"It was supposed to be my mission, but I declined it." He paused, lifting his gaze to hers. "I was determined to use up all the vacation time I had coming to me."

He was with me. She almost choked on the realization. She recalled the phone call he'd had the first night they'd spent together. Even though he'd taken the call in the other room, she remembered his harsh insistence that he was owed the time and would take it.

"Alek struck a deal. For an early release, he'd go in my place." Mac's gaze fell away to the floor once more. "When he got home Anna was dead. She'd been murdered—her throat slit from ear to ear. A warning note had come in the mail that morning, but it came too late for Alek to find. The mission had already been accomplished." He paused. His grip on her hand increased. "She was three months pregnant."

Kyra gasped. "That's awful."

"I got a call at dawn the morning of our wedding. It was Alek. . . ." His voice trailed away. "I had no choice but to leave you, Kyra. Not just because Alek needed me, but because I knew if I stayed, if we got married, one day the same thing could happen to you. I couldn't take that risk. I figured a clean break would be less painful in the long run."

"You were wrong."

"You got over me."

"No, I never did."

He stared at her. The molten silver of his eyes swirled with regret. Then the falling veil of his dark lashes hid his soul from her view.

"What happened to Alek wasn't your fault," she said.

Mac shook his head. "He cracked. He retaliated by taking three lives. He went crazy, and I couldn't stop him."

"It's not your fault."

"I knew him as well as I knew myself. I should have realized—"

"There's no way you could have."

"If I'd gone, Anna would still be alive."

"Oh, Mac." She wanted to take away all the pain and all the guilt he'd suffered through the years, but she was too choked up to manage anything else.

His gaze settled on their intertwined hands. His thumb rubbed the side of her hand in a needy caress, taking as much comfort as he was giving.

"I went to visit Alek after the funeral. He told me this had to be good-bye. I thought he was going to kill himself. He assured me he wouldn't. He said that from now on we'd be enemies. He told me what we were doing was wrong. He asked me if I was sure I was fighting on the right side. I didn't know how to answer him. But I don't think it would have mattered what I told him. He wasn't listening. His pain was too great."

As if burdened by an invisible load, Mac's shoulders rounded. "He figured that if everyone knew everyone else's secrets, there'd be no reason for the Institute's special department to exist. No reason for innocent people like Anna to die."

Mac closed his eyes. She wanted to say something—anything—to make him feel better, but the stone on her heart weighed her down too much, and no words came out.

"Somewhere along the way the lines got blurred," Mac said. "He became obsessed with the idea of equality. I don't think he knows who or what he's fighting anymore. The taste for blood, for revenge, took over whatever lofty goal he once had."

He opened his eyes and turned his gaze to her.

Kyra's eyes swelled with tears of compassion at the haunted look he gave her.

"We've met a few times since," he said. "It's never been pleasant. Two years ago a new recruit got killed because he was partnered with me. When I started questioning my work I got transferred to a desk job. Can you imagine me behind a desk?"

She smiled and shook her head. The possibility was rather hard to imagine. Mac definitely wouldn't have been happy.

"I decided I'd had enough of playing games, so I quit. I've been running Mountain Swift ever since."

In the space of a heartbeat a question swelled and surged, crashing into the open before she could recall it. "Why didn't you come for me then?"

Mac let go of her hand. She twisted it in her lap to keep the empty feeling at bay.

"I'd hurt you," he said after a long, heavy pause.

The bruised part of her heart agreed. Had he come back for her, she would have sent him away. But after his explanation, the part of her heart that had never forgotten to love him wanted to argue. She did neither. The faraway look in his eyes told her he was retreating. She had to bring him back before the distance between them got too wide.

"What brought you out of retirement?" she asked.

Mac got up and tugged on her arm to follow. He went to the tube and spread the transverse map on the table. She was secretly pleased when he laced his fingers through hers as he pointed to a spot near the bottom of the map with his free hand.

"After Eaton Peak's silver mine was abandoned in the early sixties the government used it for experiments," he said. "They studied cosmic rays and their by-products—neutrinos and muons—on the two-thousand-foot level in a three-mile tunnel that had been bored there. They constructed a trap—a mini supercollider, if you will. They uncovered the existence of a subatomic particle they thought would give them a better understanding of the forces of the universe, but their equipment was too primitive to catch the elusive particle, so the experiment was terminated in the early seventies."

His finger moved up an inch on the map. She snuggled closer, enjoying his warmth against her body.

"At the same time, on the eighteen-hundred-foot level, physicists conducted an experiment dealing with the spontaneous decay of protons. I can't go into any details, but they had a promising start. Then nothing. Twelve years ago they stopped the experiment but left a monitoring device there.

"A few months ago the equipment started showing signs of activity once more; then it just died. Residents in the area started complaining about strange rumblings. The scientists are afraid the Pandora protons they created have somehow mutated and the mountain is in danger of collapsing."

"And since Lynn and Brad live here the Institute used them to lure you back."

"You got it."

Mac turned Kyra around to face him. With one finger he traced the contours of her jaw. She leaned into his touch, enjoying the trail of fire it left behind. She held her breath in anticipation, her gaze fixed on his lips.

"Alek has no conscience anymore," he said hoarsely. "That makes him a very dangerous man. He wouldn't hesitate to hurt you."

Kyra's gaze moved to his eyes. "Why? I've no connection to you or your mission."

"Because you're here, and he knows I wouldn't let him hurt an innocent by-stander. If he thinks I care for you even a little bit, it makes his job that much easier."

"Do you?"

"Do I what?"

"Care for me." She found she was holding her breath, waiting for his answer.

He regarded her thoughtfully. "Would I be trying so hard to keep you safe if I didn't?"

Her heart beat in a joyful race. He still cared. She contained the thrill the knowledge gave her and swam back into their conversation before he decided to dam up again. "How would it make Alek's job easier?"

"He'll use you to make me do all the work. Then he'll kill us both."

"If Alek is as demented as you make him out to be, what is it he wants from the mine?"

"The recorder." He winced. "He can sell the information on it overseas and embarrass the U.S. Government all at once."

Mac gripped her shoulders, and with a determined shake he silently demanded that she look at him. "You wanted a concrete reason to leave. I've just given you one."

She reached helplessly to his cheek with her hand, feeling the rough stubble of his beard under the pads of her fingers. "I can't, Mac."

He removed her hand from his face and brought it to his lips. His dark lashes lowered as he kissed her palm, sending a tremor of desire rolling through her. When his eyes opened she saw the molten silver liquefy and darken. She found it hard to swallow with her throat so dry.

"You have to," Mac said.

She rested her head against his heart. Its rapid race sent pleasing waves of warmth through her. She loved the feel of his hand tangled in her hair. To keep this communication flowing between them, she had to be as open with him as he'd been with her.

"I can't turn my back on the truth when I know where the answers are," she said softly. "I've done it for much too long."

"Kyra—"

"When I was a kid I knew there was something wrong, but Mom and Dad would always pretend there wasn't. They loved me, I know that. But there was something unnatural about the way they kept me corralled."

Whenever a stranger had looked at her, they'd whipped her out of sight. They insisted she account for her whereabouts every minute of her life. She'd felt smothered. And no matter how she complained, on this one point they had never given in.

"My friends' parents weren't like that. I never got to go on sleepovers. I never got to go to camp. I escaped to college only because I accepted a scholarship without my mother's permission. She cried when she found out. Begged me not to go." And Kyra had almost given in.

"But she wouldn't explain why." That had been the clincher. If her mother had given her one good reason, she would have stayed, but she hadn't, and her "I know what's best for you," had made Kyra more determined to leave.

"Then I found out I was adopted, and I thought maybe they'd stolen me. Their lawyer assured me they hadn't, but I knew there was more to it."

She turned her gaze to Mac's face. "The answers are all in the mountain."

He pushed her away and held her at arm's length. "No! That's out of the question. With Alek around it's too dangerous. Even the scientist aren't sure what's waiting inside that mine."

"So we might as well work together rather than against each other." She searched the closing circles of his soul, hoping against hope that she'd reach him before he shut her out completely. "I need you. You're my lifeline. You can take me out of the nightmares. With you, I can get my life back."

He let her go. "I can't risk your life when staying

away from this mountain could save it so easily."

"That's the problem, Mac: He won't let me leave. Not until I'm dead or he's free."

"Who won't?"

"The silver shadow."

Mac paced away and back, rubbing his neck as if he had a crick in it. "Do you hear what you're saying?"

"I know it sounds crazy, but—"

"Okay, I'll look for whatever it is you're searching for while I'm down there." He increased the tempo of his pacing. "There's no need for both of us to risk our lives."

Frustration, anger, desire, and longing all rolled into one. She had to make him understand. Her hand reached out for his arm. He stopped and turned his gaze to hers. The storm she'd seen earlier raged in his eyes once more. He wanted her to leave because he cared. The knowledge touched her deeply. But she had to stay. Without her freedom from the past, she could have no future—with or without him. She had to find the truth, no matter what the cost. Too much was happening to turn back.

"It's me he wants, not you."

The evil had to be stopped. And if she understood the dream correctly, she was the only one who could stop it. She wasn't sure how, but she knew she had to try. She could die trying. The thought sent an icy shiver rippling down her spine. But if she won, the prize of freedom would be worth it.

"In my dream tonight," Kyra said, "there were people there. I could feel all their emotions as if they were trying to transfer them to me to get rid of them. Sticky, bleak emotions. So much death, Mac, so much pain. And I could feel them all like punches that leave bruises. I wasn't in control of the dream. It took me where it wanted. It was almost as if I was possessed."

He whipped around to face her, giving her an astonished look.

"I know it sounds crazy, but it was like I was losing myself . . . my soul. I need you to keep me from getting lost in those dreams. I'll help you. We can help each other."

He drew her down and they sat on the edge of the pool table once more. "I know I pushed you into finding your own strength to resolve your problems, but searching for a mine entrance in the middle of winter is a dangerous proposition."

"You're doing it."

"I'm trained for it."

"I'll be with you, so I'll be safe."

"Kyra." There was a note of exasperation in his voice, and he was coming darned close to being patronizing. Kyra stiffened defensively. "There's a logical explanation for what's happening to you—"

"There is. It's called a curse." Her inborn ability to reach people seemed to desert her when it came to Mac.

He rolled his eyes to the ceiling.

"Why is this concept so unbelievable to you?" Kyra demanded.

In the pause that followed she could see him searching for words.

"Because I can't see it or touch it or hear it or even smell it or taste it. I've been trained to rely on my senses for survival."

"What about your instincts? What do you think those are? What about the silent communication you and Alek shared to get you out of tight situations?"

"There's nothing paranormal about that. It's simply common sense."

"If you say so." Kyra shrugged. "What about your ability to sense when I'm about to enter into one of the shadow dreams?"

"I have no idea what you're talking about." He

hopped off the table and paced the length of it.

"I feel you checking on me. You think I'm sleeping peacefully, so you leave. But you sense something isn't right. What is it you feel, Mac? The cold? The dark? The evil?"

He brought his hands down on both sides of her, caging her with his arms, trapping her with his gaze. "I don't believe in ESP. I don't believe in ghosts. I don't believe in curses. If you wanted me to snag the moon from the sky, I'd do it in a heartbeat. If you wanted me to battle a giant, a dragon, I'd get my sword and cut them down for you. But what I will not do is risk your life for no reason."

"I've waited for answers for so long, Mac. Not just this past month. I realize now I've been looking for them all my life. I'm too close to quit. With or without you."

He swore softly and jerked away from her.

"Okay." He raised his hands in resignation. "I'll help you."

A vast sense of relief welled up inside her. With Mac helping her, she wouldn't get lost in the twisted fabric of shadow-induced dreams. The feeling of being anchored grew, giving her new strength to face whatever lay ahead.

"Thank you," she said. A thought suddenly formed. "Do you think your mission and my dreams are connected somehow?"

Mac dismissed the notion with a sharp shake of his head. "I don't see how."

"Then how come we both ended up here on this mountain at the same time? How come we're both being called to deal with its heart?"

A sad expression crossed his features. "Bad timing. It seems to be a recurring pattern with us."

On impulse she threw her arms around his neck and drew his face to hers. At her touch, Mac groaned with a mixture of need and exasperation. One arm circled her shoulders, the other her waist. He pulled her closer, letting her feel his hardened desire. He answered her kiss with a power that reduced her to heated liquid. If his arms hadn't been holding her up, she was sure she'd have fallen helplessly to the floor. Her heartbeat thundered in perfect rhythm with his. The taste of his mouth, more heady than any wine, sent her mind in a spin, unbalancing her. She lost herself in the moment.

He pulled away from her. As if he'd just run a marathon, his breaths came in rapid succession. "I want to get one thing straight: I'll be making the rules for this expedition."

"I'm very good with rules," she said just as breathily.

Misty growled. Still holding on to each other, they both turned in her direction. The hair on Misty's shoulders stood straight up. As if she was going to pounce right through the windows, she sat half-crouched.

A flashlight came on, illuminating Alek's face with grotesque shadows. Kyra gasped. He tipped his head back and laughed uproariously. She cowered against Mac. As suddenly as it had come on, the light disappeared.

A thunderlike roll quaked through the mountain, rattling the windows. The light over the pool table flickered, then died. The joy she'd felt at Mac's kiss was eclipsed in a second. In the dark, the rumblings of the mountain taunted her with the knowledge that if Mac was right, by being in his arms, she'd just shown Alek the chink in Mac's armor, imperiling both their lives.

Chapter Twelve

The next morning Kyra woke to the smell of bacon frying. She wrinkled her nose as she stretched and yawned. Wrapping the blue-and-white quilt around her shoulders, she got up from the living-room sofa and headed for her room.

"Good morning," Mac called to her from the kitchen. Misty sat on a stool, eyeing his every move.

His tone was light and carefree, and Kyra couldn't help wondering if he'd forgotten last night's incident in the basement. The electricity had come back on half an hour after it had failed, but Mac had refused all her attempts at conversation. When she'd tried to touch him, he'd pushed her gently yet firmly away. The sudden switch from warm openness to cool distance had left her feeling like Ali Baba's greedy brother, trapped inside a cave of treasures because he'd forgotten the magic phrase. She didn't want to surrender this new kind of intimacy when she'd just discovered it.

After a while, she'd given up. He'd triple-checked the lock on each window and door. And she surmised he'd spent as restless a night as she had, judging from his middle-of-the-night prowling. At least, she hoped he had. He deserved it. He liked concrete things, and their kiss had been concrete enough. So why had he pushed her away after promising they would act as partners? If she lived to be a hundred, she'd never understand this man.

"Good morning," Kyra said, not sure yet how civil she wanted to be.

"I've got a vegetable omelet ready to go for you. Should I cook it now?"

"Sure."

Kyra stared at him for a minute. His shower-damp hair curled around the collar of his white turtleneck. In his gray sweatshirt, with MOUNTAIN SWIFT emblazoned in navy on the front, he looked suspiciously relaxed. He's cooking, she reminded herself. He's always relaxed when he's cooking. A closer inspection of the handsome planes of his face revealed a tension under the facade of calm.

He placed a skillet on the stove, then smiled at her. "You have time for a shower."

Don't, a voice whispered in her mind. Kyra shook her head. You're being silly, she chastised herself. The nightmares and last night's episode with Alek had her on edge. She had to wake up, and a cold shower would be the fastest way. There were so many things to go over with Mac; she wanted to be alert.

While they planned their trip into the mountain, she hoped to recapture the closeness they'd shared last night. Alek's knowledge of their involvement couldn't be as dire as Mac had predicted. They were forewarned, and if they stuck together, Alek couldn't separate them, using one against the other.

Her work in architecture had taught her the basic

principle of supportive strength. If it worked for steel and timber, why not with people?

She hurried through her shower and dressed methodically, donning an emerald sweater over her cream-colored turtleneck and pants. Then she quickly pulled her damp hair into a ponytail, holding it in place with an ivory barrette. Her hair would frizz if she didn't dry it, but she didn't care. Mac was up to something, and she had to find out what it was.

When she reached the kitchen, a steaming omelet waited for her, but Mac was nowhere in sight, and neither was Misty. Kyra heard noises coming from Mac's room and decided they must be there. She sat on the stool and downed the glass of orange juice Mac had placed next to her plate. She cut into the omelet. Cheese and a variety of vegetables spilled from its middle onto the plate. She hadn't realized how hungry she was until she started eating.

As she cut herself another bite, her fork resounded noisily against the plate. Her brain crackled with nervous thoughts. Something was wrong. But what? Each tick of the sunflower-shaped kitchen clock sounded like a bomb. Kyra's eyes darted about, searching for the source of her apprehension.

Then it hit her.

She bounced from the stool, knocking it backward. She raced into Mac's room and crashed against the door when her hand couldn't turn the knob fast enough.

"Mac!" Kyra called in a high-pitched voice. She fumbled twice more before the knob gave and the door opened. Misty came bounding out.

The room was empty.

It didn't take a genius to figure out that he'd gone out to the mine and left her behind.

"Damn you, Mac McKane! You can't get rid of me that easily. Not this time."

If he thought leaving her behind was going to stop

her, he didn't know her half as well as he thought. Playing the sacrificing knight had worked seven years ago, but she wasn't as naive as she'd been then, and she refused to be cast as the lady-in-waiting.

She ran to the front closet and grabbed her coat, hat, and gloves. She jammed her feet into her hiking boots. Thinking they were going out for a walk, Misty danced around Kyra. As Kyra laced her boots with more energy than necessary, she took several large, cleansing breaths. She couldn't go tearing about like a madwoman. She needed a plan.

Misty at her heels, she sped down the basement stairs and looked for the maps Mac had shown her last night. They weren't on the pool table or in either of the offices. She found the empty tube and the backpack with the red boxes stowed at the bottom of an empty file drawer. Why had he taken the maps but not the boxes?

What should she do next? She leaned her elbows on the table, spread her hands on the green felt, and closed her eyes. If she could only picture the map, she could figure out where he had gone.

A dim image formed. She didn't know exactly where Mac was, but the markings she remembered on the map gave her a good idea. She hurried up the stairs to catch up with him. Without ceremony, she left Misty in the laundry room and rushed outside.

His truck was gone.

After five days of inactivity in the driveway, Sully's frozen engine refused to start. With a curse that would surely have made her father threaten to wash her mouth out with soap, Kyra slammed the Del Sol's door and started jogging up the mountain road.

By the time she reached Mac's truck, she couldn't catch her breath. She rested against the truck's side and scoured the mountainside for signs of him. He seemed to have disappeared. The ponderosa pine and gambel oaks didn't betray his position.

With her lungs still burning, she pushed herself off the truck and examined the area for tracks. She found a light trail of footsteps and decided to follow them. As she stepped into the first set, she sank to her knees. She struggled to the next set. The same thing happened. How in the world had Mac managed to walk on top of the snow? She trudged her way along the trail, resting every few steps to catch her breath. She vowed to get into shape once she returned home. In the meantime, she had to keep going. She shook her head to fight off the light-headed feeling the altitude and her physical effort gave her.

It didn't take her long to figure out that there was no way she'd be able to sneak up on Mac. In the quiet of the mountain, each of her steps, falling through the snow, sounded like a herd of thundering elk.

She'd have to ask him his secret for walking without being heard. Not that he'd share that particular tidbit with her. Sharing information wasn't his strong suit. And neither, it seemed, was keeping promises. Hadn't she learned her lesson on that point? *Temper, temper. Save your energy and your anger for when you catch up with Mac.*

Looking up ahead for signs of life, she wished she'd remembered her sunglasses. Even with her eyes squinted to slits, the brightness of the snow hurt.

Kyra stopped suddenly. Her heart thundered against her chest from her exertion, her leg muscles throbbed, and her breath came out in smoky puffs. She looked around. Nothing had changed, but she sensed someone watching her, waiting for her.

"Mac?"

No, not Mac. She closed her eyes and, like a radio antenna, moved her body until she'd focused on the strongest pull of energy. When she opened her eyes she saw a wolf-shaped silver shadow sitting at the base of a pine.

It stared at her. A picture of Rolf Schreck flashed into her mind. Last night's nightmare jumped back to life like a video stuck in fast forward. She faltered several steps back, landing on her rear.

It was just a dream. But it had felt so real. Like a prelude to death. She shook her head. She wasn't ready to die. With Mac's help, she would break the curse before it broke her.

"What do you want?" she called to the shadow.

You are mine. His dark voice whispered in her mind.

"I belong to no one."

She stared at the silver shadow. It separated itself from the tree and stood alone with no concrete reason for its existence. Her cheek tingled. She reached up to touch it. Through her thin gloves she felt the double wavy line that had appeared after her first nightmare in the house. It throbbed like a fresh burn.

An eerie sensation prickled through her. The air seemed to grow thicker, to take on substance, to darken. Reality seemed to fade. The scenery shimmered like heat waves off hot asphalt, curving around her like the walls of her nightmares.

No! This time she wouldn't let herself be drawn into the shadow's vision. But the pull was irresistible.

She found herself standing in complete darkness, but this time she was able to squelch the panic.

Think, think! How had the visions ended before? With Mac pulling her out. But this time Mac wasn't anywhere around.

Broken pictures flitted in and out of her mind, but none stayed in place. She fought them by planting an image of Mac firmly in her mind, anchoring herself in the present.

The pull weakened. The dark walls thinned. Once more she could view her real-time surroundings through a filmy haze.

"What do you want from me?" she demanded.

I want what belongs to me. The voice, low and baleful, sounded in her mind.

"I don't have anything that belongs to you. What could I possibly give you?"

Retribution.

"For what?"

For everything.

She could see this conversation was going nowhere fast. Fear tightened her stomach into a knot. "Just how would I accomplish that?"

Come with me, Kyra. We both want this conclusion.

She swallowed hard. Going into the mountain without Mac close by to help her wasn't something she relished. She had to stall. "How do I know you're telling me the truth?"

The chain at your neck.

Kyra's hand unconsciously sought the antique silver chain around her neck, fingering the moonstone trapped in the filigreed head of a key. "What about it?"

Rebecca Brennan gave it to her daughter on the day of her birth.

Before she could say anything, the silver shadow shimmered and disappeared.

"Wait!" Kyra yelled in the wolf shadow's direction. She scrambled up and hurried to the spot where she'd last seen the shadow. When she reached the pine under which he'd sat, there wasn't a single mark on the snow.

Had she imagined it? No, she couldn't have made up the bizarre conversation they'd shared.

A wave of dread made her shiver. She decided to get moving again; she needed to find Mac.

Each dark pine and naked oak seemed to shake its limbs at her like giant fingers admonishing her to turn back. A raven shrieked at her from a snowy ponderosa bough, prophesying doom. A squirrel crossed her path. He stopped to chastise her, wringing his tail all the while. Then he bounded away, leaving her to the mournful sound of the wind on the snow.

"Stop it!" She was letting her imagination get the better of her. Those were just trees. That bird was just protecting its nest. The squirrel was defending his lunch. As for the shadow . . . well, he was just a figment of her imagination, brought to life because of her vivid nightmare.

There. Problem solved.

Kyra resumed her trek. If she spent her time jumping at every moving shadow, she'd never find Mac. And that was, after all, priority number one. He'd made her a promise, and she intended to make him stick to it.

Ten minutes later, she looked back at her trail. The view was breathtaking so high up. She could see forever. Highway 80 was a thin black thread below. The mountainside, dotted with houses and illuminated by the sun, looked picture-postcard perfect.

Safety waited for her down there.

But a pull from her soul drew her gaze upward once more. The sun had shifted, throwing the top of the mountain into shadow. She shivered, unraveling a thread of fear deep inside her. She had no choice. If she wanted to live freely, she had to find Mac and she had to find a way to destroy Schreck's curse.

He had wasted precious energy dealing with Kyra during daylight. He should have known it was too early. He should have known his strength hadn't been rejuvenated enough. But when he'd sensed her nearing his home, he'd thought she'd come to him.

Like a raging bull he smashed his anger against the sides of the shaft.

She hadn't come for him, but for her companion. To add insult to injury, she'd used McKane to ground herself. And McKane had heard her despite the distance separating them.

McKane had to be eliminated, and he could not waste any more energy doing it himself. Counting on others always carried a risk.

Once more he threw himself against the shaft to vent his anger.

Too late he realized his fit of temper might jeopardize his prize.

"What are you doing here?"

Mac's voice startled Kyra out of her thoughts. As she gasped, she put a hand over her heart. "You scared me."

"What are you doing here?" Mac repeated. He was barely visible in his white suit against the backdrop of snow.

"I told you I'd find the mine with or without your help. You're the one who's being so pig-headed about the whole thing."

His expression hardened. "It's for your own safety."

"And who elected you judge of what's good for me?" Anger stirred enough energy for her to fight back, even though every muscle in her body hurt. "You promised to take me with you."

"No, I promised to help you. And you promised to let me set the rules."

"Because I thought I'd be included."

"You will be. As soon as I've judged it's safe. Reconnaissance is done alone."

Her resentment flickered and died. Right or wrong, guilt had been eating away at him for years. Though he chose the wrong way to express it, she realized he had her welfare at heart. "You could have explained."

"I wasn't in the mood for a scene like this one."

"I'm a reasonable woman, Mac, not a child. All it would have taken is a word or two. Don't shut me out."

They glared at each other for a minute. "Did you find the shaft?" Kyra asked finally, breaking their deadlock.

"Yes."

Kyra sighed. It was back to one-word answers. At this rate she'd soon have to make the answers as well as the questions. Why couldn't they talk as openly as they had last night? She much preferred his kisses over his silences.

"Have you seen Alek?" she asked.

"He's here."

She swiveled her head in either direction but saw nothing. "Where?"

"Around." Mac gave a sardonic smile. "Why do the dirty work when someone else'll do it for you?"

"He's a real charmer, isn't he?"

"Remember that."

"You *are* grumpy when you don't get your beauty sleep, aren't you?"

Mac raised an eyebrow but said nothing.

"Well? Are you going to show me what you found or am I going to have to keep following your tracks when you're not looking? How, by the way, did you manage to walk on top of the snow when you're heavier than I am?"

"It's all in the distribution of weight."

Mac's eyes were hidden by his dark sunglasses, but she sensed the computer in his brain sifting through his options. A moment later, he motioned for her to follow, and silently led her to a hole in the snow on the side of the mountain.

"That's it? That's the shaft?" Kyra couldn't believe what she saw.

"What did you expect? A front door?"

She ignored the sarcasm in his voice. "Well, yes. In my dream, there was a shack over the shaft head, and an elevator to go down into the mine." Her hands gestured the approximate location.

"The mine shack is long gone. And the scientists took their office down when they left." He removed a utility tool from his backpack and started prying at the wood boards covering the shaft.

"How are we going to get down there?"

"*We* aren't going anywhere." As he removed the nails, they groaned their protest. He piled the planks neatly to one side and pocketed the nails.

"But I have to—"

"Do you know how to rappel?" Mac interrupted. He leaned into a particularly stubborn nail and the board cracked beneath him. He jumped clear before gravity took him down with the broken plank.

"No, but you could teach me."

"I don't have time." He poked his head into the opening. After reaching for a flashlight, he surveyed the inside. Satisfied, he put the light away and attacked the boards once more.

"It can't be that hard."

He dropped another board on the pile, then walked over to her. "What exactly is it you're looking for, Kyra?"

She let his anger bounce right off her. She knew she couldn't give him the definitive answer he sought. "I don't know."

She only had feelings to go on, and speaking of feelings wouldn't assuage his heated temper. "I just know the answers are down there. That's where the curse started, and that's where it has to end."

"Why?"

His dark, unyielding features frightened her until she remembered it was his way of showing concern.

"Because even if you seal the mine so solidly no one can ever enter it again, the evil will still be there. The shadow's evil. Schreck's evil. Even Alek's evil. They're all connected. I can feel it. And your family, and all the people living on this mountain, will be in danger until it's put to rest."

176

"This obsession of yours isn't healthy."

Kyra closed the distance between them, eyeing him directly. "You feel it, too. I know a lot more about you than you think, Mac. You know I'm right about the evil; that's why you're so worried about your mission." He flinched, giving Kyra her answer. "It's more than Alek. It's alive in the mountain."

As if to prove her point, a low rumble started deep in the mountain. It escalated until the trees shook, shedding the snow from their limbs. A second, more resonant boom joined the subterranean rumblings.

He looked up at the mountain's peak and Kyra followed his gaze. White froth cascaded down the sides at a dazzling speed. Panic paralyzed her body as Mac uttered a single word.

"Avalanche."

Chapter Thirteen

Mac shoved Kyra forcefully toward the black entrance on the side of the mountain, then grabbed his backpack and quickly followed her inside. He pushed Kyra safely away from the entrance and against the side of the cavern, carefully avoiding the space where the shaft should be.

Kyra's fists clung to the back of his snow suit, but the deafening noise of the cascading snow made it impossible to talk. Her sweet fragrance reached him even through the dank smell of the dark cave. Mac held her as close as he dared, hoping his protective posture would be enough to reassure her. He removed his sunglasses and closed his eyes against the strobe light–like effect of the rushing snow on the afternoon sky.

Mac's mind drifted back to Kyra's accusation. She was right. From the very first he'd sensed a clawing darkness about the mountain. Even on a bright day like today, the warmth of the sun never reached the soul—not on this mountain. At least not for him. He'd only had to look away to distant peaks as he'd climbed to feel the difference.

He'd felt this somber shadow when he'd first visited Brad and Lynn's new home. But he'd shoved his abstract feelings aside and looked for a concrete explanation for his uneasiness. When he'd found none, he'd opted for action. It was one of the reasons he'd installed all those locks, and the reason why he visited Brad and Lynn so often.

In a life where he had to question every relationship, his family was precious. And so was Kyra. He didn't want her swallowed by this invisible evil on the mountain anymore than he wanted to lose his family to an experiment gone bad.

As snow chuted in front of the entrance and blocked out all the light, Mac pressed Kyra further against the rocky wall, using his body to shield hers. He wouldn't let an unseen shadow cheat him out of his chance for happiness.

After what seemed an eternity the noise lessened, then subsided. In contrast to the deafening roar, the silence it left in its wake was deathly. In the pitch blackness, neither of them moved, as if even the bat of an eyelash would set off the avalanche again.

Kyra was the first to stir. With a long shuddering breath of relief, she collapsed against his chest and started to shake.

"We're all right," he said to reassure her.

"I thought we were going to die. I was so scared."

"So was I." He tightened his hug, surprised by the truth of his words. He'd been scared he would lose her before he could win her again. "But you didn't hear it from me," he added lightly.

She smiled against his coat and laughed nervously. He felt her head move away and her eyes search the darkness for his. "We're not stuck in here, are we?"

"I don't think so. Don't move." He reached for the

backpack at his feet and fumbled his way inside until he found a flashlight. He turned it on and handed it to Kyra. Next he took out a folding shovel. Action would keep him grounded.

"Point the light over there." Mac directed the beam for her, then started digging.

After a few minutes his shovel poked a hole through the snow, allowing a ray of light into the cave. He continued until he had a hole big enough to fit his head through, then looked around.

"It's not as bad as it looks," he said. "The worst of it went around us."

Mac resumed his task. Refusing to give his fragmented thoughts concrete form, he concentrated on each shovelful until he had cleared a space big enough to fit his body through. He panted slightly from his focused exertion. He was glad that, for once, Kyra hadn't bothered him with dozens of questions. Hopefully, her silence meant she'd reconsidred her foolish trek into the mine—or would at least be willing to stay put while he capped the shaft permanently and sealed the past away.

What if she was right, though, and the foam didn't seal the problem? He folded the shovel, then took the light from Kyra. Evil existed; he could grant her that much. He'd seen enough of it to know. But could it actually live without a vessel? He shook his head. He was letting Kyra's ideas disrupt his clear thinking.

"Let's have a look around, since we're here," he said, his voice echoing against the cave wall as he played the light on the floor.

The rock, wet from the high humidity, glistened black. The smell of moist dust and mildew itched the inside of his nose, but he managed to stifle the coming sneeze. The shaft hole took up more than half the floor space of the small cave. An open-sided, rusty, steel-framed elevator waited above the dark hole. On one side there was a small mound covered with a piece of dirty oilcloth patched with spots of greenish black slime.

Mac whipped off the cloth, revealing a generator that seemed to be hooked up to the elevator. He examined the pulleys, cables, and connections, and smiled. The machinery had remained in remarkably good shape, considering it had sat idle for the past ten years in this musty environment. He kneeled next to the generator and checked the engine.

It was a Briggs and Stratton, and the nice thing about a Briggs and Stratton, he thought, was that it was always fixable. He fiddled around with the engine for a few minutes more, and decided it could be revived easily enough with a good cleaning and a part or two. Add some fresh oil and some gas, and voilà—an operating system.

Having a working elevator would make his job much easier. He could be in and out in no time. A day's delay while he got the parts would be worth it. Besides, it would give him time to convince Kyra he could handle the "evil" she insisted she needed to confront, and that he could bring her back the answers she wanted. Even as the thought passed through his mind, he realized it would be a futile mission, but he'd have a day to try. He could be persuasive when he wanted. He'd been good at it once.

But Kyra had a hold on him no one else had ever had.

As he repacked his tools, Mac faltered. In a moment of lucid understanding, Alek's torment became only too clear. He would have given up his job at the Institute to spend a lifetime with Kyra, as Alek had done for Anna. And like Alek, he had this one last mission to get through before he could consider this happy prospect. Loving Kyra the way he did, he'd have wanted to avenge her death, too.

Suddenly he understood Alek's games. He understood the release his former friend wanted. Alek would wait the extra day. Then he'd have the last confrontation he wanted, and he would make sure Alek got his one last wish.

"Let's go," Mac said. He hoisted his pack on his back.

"We can't go yet!" Kyra pointed the flashlight in Mac's face.

He deftly took the light away from her and shone it on the entrance. "I need to get a few parts to fix the generator and then we can use the elevator. No rappeling."

He eased out of the somber cave into the light of day. Turning his face to the sun, he drank in hope.

Kyra scrambled out after him. *"We?"*

Mac turned back to face her and smiled, glad to see the confusion on her face. Let her believe he'd take her with him when he came back. She'd relax and he could ease in a few persuasive thoughts. He didn't like lying to her, but he'd have a lifetime to make it up to her. "I'd rather keep an eye on you than have you wandering around the mine by yourself."

Kyra looked at the roiled snow around them. He followed her gaze. The picture-perfect landscape had turned into chaos. Snow mounded down the side of the mountain like a mogul course designed by the devil himself. Uprooted trees and snapped branches stuck out of the rough bumps like a giant game of pick up sticks. Evergreen needles dusted the slopes like beard shavings in a sink.

Had someone sheltered like Kyra ever witnessed such a mess? He doubted it, and he noted sadly that, compared to the kinds of devastation he'd seen, this barely registered a blip. Her stunned reaction to the rearranged scenery touched him. He wanted her to keep that sensitivity, and he would do his best to ensure that she would.

"Do you think Alek got hurt in the avalanche?" she asked.

"I doubt it. The man seems to have more lives than a cat." Mac's gaze scanned the mountainside. He saw no signs of life, but he sensed that Alek was still alive, and waiting.

He set his backpack aside, then gathered broken pine boughs to cover the shaft entrance. He didn't like leaving it open, in case kids wandered up and decided to explore, but the wood planks that had originally covered the hole were now buried under snow and probably halfway down the mountain. Silently, Kyra joined him and helped strengthen his protective structure.

"Now that you've uncovered the shaft, won't Alek get whatever it is he wants while you're out getting your parts?" Kyra tucked the last bough in place.

"He'll wait." Mac slipped on his sunglasses, then stood back to examine their camouflage job. He nodded. It would do.

He heaved on his pack and started to walk down the mountain.

Kyra followed in his footsteps. "How can you be so sure?"

"It's not the data he wants."

Kyra stopped in her tracks. "Then what?"

Mac kept walking. Understanding Alek's motivation had given him a whole new perspective on his behavior and hope for the future. But he could do nothing about the future until he took care of the past. Just a few more days and he could leave it behind—forever.

Then he could start dreaming again.

"Mac! Answer me."

"He wants one last favor from a friend."

After a good soak in the hot tub, Kyra's stiff muscles relaxed. When she came back into the house, the delightful odor of tomato, mingled with oregano, permeated the air, and Misty's playful bark echoed against the high ceilings of the living room.

The sight of Mac on the floor playing tug of war with the dog made her smile. Misty let go of the rope when she saw Kyra and rushed toward her with an inane doggy grin on her face. She jumped into Kyra's arms and panted loudly, her tongue lolling out one side.

As Misty nudged her hand to be petted, Kyra laughed. "What have you done to her?"

"We've been getting better acquainted." Mac flowed up from the ground in one smooth movement, making her conscious of his masculine grace. "She's quite a pistol. I've never had a pet. I didn't realize how much fun they could be."

He scratched Misty's ear, and the dog beamed back at him in adoration. "Dinner's almost ready. Are you hungry?"

Kyra's stomach answered for her with a thunderous gurgle.

"I guess you are." He smiled and headed for the kitchen.

"What's on the menu, oh great chef?"

Mac opened the oven and sniffed the tangy aroma. "A beef ravioli casserole. My specialty." As he took out the dish, he glowed with pride. "But have no fear, my little vegetarian, I thought of you, too." He placed the casserole on a wooden cutting board. "I made a meatless version just for you."

"You're spoiling me."

"You haven't seen anything yet."

The fierce possessiveness of his gaze made the fire of a blush creep to her cheeks. "I, uh, need to get changed."

She hurried into her bedroom and changed out of her wet bathing suit and robe into a warm, aqua-colored sweater and jeans.

"Let me make a salad," she said as she entered the kitchen.

"Yeah, I guess we should have a vegetable of some sort. The bowls are in the cupboard next to the sink."

Kyra found a wooden bowl, placed it on the counter, then rummaged through the fridge for salad fixings.

With a knife, Mac ripped thick slices of bread from a crusty loaf, slathered them with butter, then sprinkled them with garlic salt. He changed the grill's height in the oven and turned the knob to broil.

Misty stood on her back legs and batted her forepaws furiously, all the while making funny little begging noises.

"Forget it, Miss Piggy. No handouts for you," Kyra said as she headed for the sink to scrape a cucumber. Her shoulder accidentally brushed Mac's, sending a liquid longing deep inside her.

The whole scene reeked of domestic intimacy, and though a part of Kyra wanted to enjoy this peaceful moment, another waited tensely for something to shatter it, for the silver shadow to creep into the warmth and infect it with its icy evil, destroying the illusion. She looked around the kitchen. Was it just an illusion? When had she become so distrustful? Why couldn't she take what was offered without expecting it to vanish at any given second?

They ate in companiable silence, each on opposite sides of the counter. Kyra thoroughly enjoyed the way the tangy sauce, enhanced by the garlic and spices, swirled around the pasta and slid down her throat.

"This sauce is really good," she said as she poised her fork to take another big bite.

"Thanks; it's my own recipe."

She found herself longing for the sound of his voice, yearning for the kind of intimate conversation they'd shared last night. "What kind of kid were you?"

Mac gave her a rueful smile. "I was the kind of boy

your Daddy would've told you to keep clear of."

She looked at him pensively. There was an air of mischief behind the sculpted features. "I'll bet you gave your parents gray hair."

He chuckled. "They both had a head full by the time I was eighteen."

"And then?"

The smile disappeared. "Then I left and I learned."

Kyra put down her fork and reached for a slice of bread. "I'm sorry about this morning. I should have trusted you."

Her mother had called her "the Equalizer" as she grew up. Finding balance was important to her, and tension of any kind upset the scales as far as she was concerned. Although Mac had been in a good mood since they'd returned from the mine, not even the long soak in the hot tub had removed the feeling of apprehension burning at her solar plexus.

"I should have explained," Mac said.

She tried to change the conversation to Alek and his sudden change of status from enemy to friend. He refused.

Kyra picked apart her piece of bread. She'd already started; she might as well pursue the point. "What happened to change your mind?"

He took a long draft from his mug of dark beer. "A man's got to have a few secrets, or else where would the mystery be?" he teased.

The one thing she did know about Mac was that he could be as obstinate as he could be persistent. He'd decided the subject was closed, and she knew she couldn't change his mind. The matter wasn't important enough to her to pursue further.

After dinner, he took his coffee, and she her tea, to the living room. Misty settled comfortably on the recliner. Mac suggested they play a card game. Eager to keep the light mood going, she agreed. They settled on rummy. They talked about nothing and everything. She was beating him two out of three games and having a wonderful time.

Mac dealt a new game. Picking up her hand, she concentrated on the cards.

"I've been thinking," he said, putting the remainder of the deck between them and turning the top card over to start the discard pile.

"About what?" she asked, shuffling her cards into numerical order. She took a card from the top of the deck, then discarded.

"A friend of mine gave me the number of someone who could help us with your ghost. I think we should call her."

Raising both eyebrows, she cast him a questioning look. "What kind of someone?"

"A medium."

Kyra gaped. "A medium?"

He played his turn, spreading a run of king, queen, jack, and ten on the coffee table. "Although I have my doubts about the whole concept, Shana said this woman's talent is real. I have no reason to believe Shana would lie to me."

Kyra was so dumbfounded that she couldn't think of a single intelligible thing to say.

"She said this woman could help us send the spirit back to its proper plane," he said without lifting his gaze from his cards.

"I don't believe it."

"It's your turn." He nodded toward the hand of cards she now openly displayed. She snapped them back up. "I thought a medium would be right up your alley."

She played her turn. "Not the medium; you. This isn't like you at all."

"If you wanted, we could give it a shot." He picked and discarded.

She rearranged her cards and played her turn. "We're talking about unseen, unproven things here."

"We're talking about your well-being. I may not believe in ghosts and possession, but I believe you believe, and if a medium can help you get rid of this ghost in your mind, then I'll try it."

She eyed him for the longest time, not quite sure how to react to his offer. "Why not? It can't hurt."

With an inordinately pleased smile, he spread his cards, finishing his run of hearts and emptying his hand. "I win."

Though she couldn't think why, she had a feeling she'd just agreed to more than talking to a medium.

Kyra shook out the newspaper and hid behind it. Not that she saw any of the words, but it put up a shield between her and Mac. Her insides quivered in nervous somersaults at his proximity.

He'd been in an inordinately good mood since last night. His relaxed mood had been what she'd hoped for, yet it left her feeling anxious. It was like waiting for the seesaw to come down when you were balanced in the air, not knowing if your partner would jump off and let you slam back to earth. His offer to see a medium had increased the apprehension rather than diminished it. As she turned the newspaper page for show, her silent sigh resounded deep in her soul.

She watched him serve her his version of egg burritos with a generous side order of hash browns. The stress lines on his forehead and around his mouth seemed to have magically faded away, but the sizzle of oil on the hot pan mirrored the tension stretched taut within her.

He leaned across the counter and uncovered a fruit salad. "For you," he said.

His smile took her breath away. A smile reflected in his eyes, along with . . . longing. He expected her to eat after that! She gave it her best try, but it was hard to swallow with her throat so constricted. She'd put up the paper as a barrier, but it wasn't helping. She could still feel Mac's heady gaze on her.

He crumpled the top of her paper with his fork so he could see her face. "Want to go skiing today?"

"What?" she was worried. Whenever Mac was nice, she'd learned, it meant he was up to something. She hated not knowing what.

"Skiing. My place. Today. You and me."

There was that smile again. She'd do anything to see him smile at her like that. Even make a fool out of herself on the slopes.

"Sure," she said, against her better judgment. It was hard to think straight when it felt as if her heart was going to defibrillate at any second. "What about the medium?"

"You've got an appointment at four-thirty." He removed his fork and the paper sprang back into place. "I didn't know you were interested in stocks."

She glanced at the newspaper page. "Sure. Got to keep up with my investments." She couldn't care less, but he wouldn't know that.

He laughed and cleared the dishes to the sink. "Are you ready?"

Skiing might actually be fun. At least they'd be moving, and she wouldn't have to keep seeing the way his eyes shone like polished silver, or wondering about the medium. "As ready as I'll ever be. What about the parts for the generator?"

"Ordered them this morning. I'll get someone from the resort to pick them up for me."

Not knowing what else to say, she nodded.

Mac put on his coat. "Have you ever skied cross-country?"

"No." She shoved her hat and gloves into her purse. Crouching down, she clucked to Misty, then fitted the leash on her collar.

"It's easy. You can start with a lesson; then I'll take you out on the trails." With that, he closed the door behind them. Why did the tumbling lock resound like a warning?

Kyra was glad to have Misty to pet while they drove to Mountain Swift. Mac's happy chatter irritated her, and the irritation bothered her.

Once at the resort, Mac signed her up for a lesson with Debbie, set her up with boots, poles, and skis, and then took Misty to his office. The way he'd had her nerves on edge since yesterday, she should've been glad to have him out of her sight, but to her chagrin, she found she missed him. It was as if his presence was a well from which she drew her energy.

Debbie was a good teacher and made learning to ski fun. In no time at all Kyra had the hang of the movements and felt ready to tackle the trails.

She found Mac in his office. He was on the phone, leaning back in his chair with his feet on the desk and Misty on his lap. He looked good in his bright red sweater and navy ski pants. Too good. And relaxed. Just as she'd wished he would. If only . . . But she wouldn't allow herself to wallow in self-pity. She'd enjoy today and think about the future later.

They shared a pleasant lunch, then left Misty perched on a stool behind the counter, supervising the operations and eyeing the plate of cookies by the register.

"Bet you there won't be a single one left by the time we get back," Kyra said as they stepped into the sunshine.

"I'm sure you're right." He smiled at her again, and all the nervous tension she'd managed to shed during the lesson came back with a thudding whomp.

While he snapped expertly into his skis, she fumbled clumsily into hers. As her boot finally clicked into place, she berated herself for acting like an infatuated schoolgirl. Mac cared for her, but he had a nasty habit of breaking promises to her. Their relationship didn't stand a chance of survival—not without that basic trust. The problem was, though she couldn't have it, she wanted a life with this man, wanted the easy companionship they shared when they weren't arguing over her dreams or her leaving.

Kyra shuffled stiffly in the classical style Debbie had taught her on the paralell tracks in the snow, while Mac glided gracefully in a skating motion on the cleared path beside her. He waved and kidded with members of college ski teams whizzing past them, and he didn't seem to mind her slow pace in the least. They made their way companionably over the hilly course. He didn't laugh when she fell, but encouraged her to get up on her own with helpful hints. He kept up a running commentary on the sights, and gradually she relaxed.

"What do you do when the snow melts away?" she asked on one of her frequent rest stops.

"In the summer we hike. I own a chunk of the land behind the string of condos over there. I also have access to maintained trails on enough adjoining land to make for interesting day trips. It's beautiful here in the summer. You'd like all the pretty flowers."

She loved flowers, but she'd never see Utah in the summer. She'd never set foot in Utah again if she could help it. The sinking feeling at the pit of her stomach told her she'd be missing out on a wonderful experience.

"If you invite me, I might visit." She held her breath. She wasn't sure what she wanted to hear. She knew only that her heart ached with an emptiness she longed to have filled.

"You don't need an invitation. You're welcome at any time."

No requests to stay till summer. No declaration of undying love. No strings attached. Just words that could be taken a thousand different ways. Disappointment bruised her tender ego and she sped off again with a burst of energy. He caught up with her in a few strides.

He shot her a mischievous smile. "Race you to the duck pond."

"Does it have real ducks?"

"Where do you think it gets its name?" He took out a small plastic bag filled with grain from the pocket of his red and black Polar Fleece jacket and dangled it in front of her. "I'll even let you feed them."

"They're still here in winter?" Kyra asked skeptically.

"Sure. There's a mountain stream that flows into the pond and keeps it free of ice. The tourists love to feed the ducks, and Debbie makes sure they have enough nutritious food to keep them nice and fat. We even built them a duck condo."

She couldn't help laughing at the picture her mind conjured up. "What does the winner get?"

He cocked his head sideways, and she saw the smile in his eyes even through his sunglasses. "Loser makes dinner."

"Make sure you lose then, because I'm a terrible cook."

Mac's smile widened. "Winner gets a kiss—graciously served up by the loser."

Kyra blushed, and couldn't decide on which end of the kiss she'd rather be. If she lost, she could make it a short peck on the cheek. If she won, she could enjoy the feel of Mac's arms around her once more.

With her heart pounding against her chest, she sped off toward the last hill before the pond.

"Watch out for the trees," he warned.

She scrunched into a tucked, more aerodynamic position, and poled to gain speed going down the hill. As the strand of pines neared, she put more weight on her left ski to help ease herself around the curve. The stream that fed the pond gurgled to her right and the dark pines loomed to her left. Her goal was the wide bridge between the two.

With a twinge of panic, Kyra realized that she'd built up too much speed for her skill level and started to straighten her frame. As she made the first curve, relief flooded over her. She hopped out of the tracks and brought her skis into a snowplow position to slow her speed. As the next curve neared, Kyra switched her weight to her right ski. A thrill of excitement rippled through her. She'd make it safely to the flat trail beside the pond and the cozy feeding station next to the duck condo.

Suddenly, out of nowhere, the wolf-shadow materialized in the middle of the trail in front of her.

I'm waiting for you, Kyra. His voice vibrated in the tissues of her brain.

Her heart lept to her throat. Her right ski wobbled underneath her. Her balance wavered. A current of fear zapped adrenaline through her veins.

She overcompensated to the left and started to fall in that direction. She overcompensated to the right. Jerking her body up, she tried to move her skis sideways to stop. Her skis crossed. Momentum carried her forward.

Her arms, still holding the poles, flayed before her like windmill blades gone berserk. Looking forward, she gasped in horror. The water loomed dark gray before her. None of her contortions altered her course.

She tumbled head first into the frigid pond.

Chapter Fourteen

Mac paused at the top of the hill, giving Kyra time to make it to the bottom before he zoomed down. It went against his grain to curb his competitive spirit, but in this case he'd make an exception.

He could already taste her sweet lips and feel her body pliantly molding itself to his. That certainly couldn't be called losing. He smiled, then shook his head. If he kept up this train of thought, he wouldn't be able to move. Besides, he didn't want Kyra to win by too much.

Mac jettisoned himself down the hill, building up speed with each jab of the poles. He loved the feeling of the wind on his face, the thrill of seeing the trees blur as he raced by them. He loved the control he had over each muscle and how he'd perfected his skill until each minute movement responded with the desired effect, resulting in a near-perfect performance.

He could thank the Institute for that. They'd taken

a young man brimming with eagerness, but lacking in self-control, and turned him into a man with honed instincts and sharp skills. He wasn't sure who'd won the most by the transformation, but gaining control over his once gangly body had given him a measure of satisfaction he'd always be grateful for. Too bad they'd had to shatter all the other illusions he'd held. All that youthful enthusiasm wasted on a department that didn't really care about anything but the bottom line.

No, that wasn't true. He'd done some good. Most of his missions had helped people and the environment, made them safer. Like in Hawaii. And Alaska. And all the little blips of geographical rescues no one would care to record. But it was the other ones he was thinking of now. The ones that still gave him nightmares in weak moments. The ones where the lines of right and wrong hadn't been carefully delineated. Where the good guys hadn't worn white and the bad guys black. Where he hadn't known which side he was on, and when the mission had been over he hadn't been able to tell what had been won. Those secret missions had eaten at him little by little. And when Alek had gone over the edge, the lines had been blurred beyond recognition.

One last mission—for his family and for the chance of a lifetime with Kyra. Maybe when it was all over he could start his own foundation and go back to doing those salvages that had given him such satisfaction. The resort was fun, but he missed the sense of purpose the Institute had so ingrained in him. Kyra's job kept her on the move, and maybe somehow he could merge this new idea with her movements. The thought brought a wide smile to his lips. This plan had potential.

But the smile died when he rounded the curve and saw Kyra fighting for her balance. His stomach twisted with nausea.

"Kyra!"

He pushed his body into overdrive. But he couldn't reach her in time and had to watch helplessly as her unbalanced slide turned into a sickening plunge into the ice-cold water. The water seemed to explode with the impact of her body. White plumes of spraying water burst upward, hiding her momentarily from his view. Surprised ducks scattered, flapping wings and quacking.

He spiked harder with his poles, launching himself forward faster. He tucked and stretched, trying to draw more speed. He cursed the distance between them.

It seemed like an eternity before he reached the pond. He stopped with a flurry of snow and swiftly popped his boots out of the skis as he evaluated the situation.

Kyra was still under water, struggling wildly for her freedom, but trapped by her skis. There was no time to think. He jumped into action.

He took off his jacket, hat, and gloves and dumped them on the wooden bench. Kyra would need dry clothes.

He splashed thigh-deep into the pond. The cold sucked his breath. He plunged his hand into the murky water, barely noticing the icy sting. He grasped for Kyra's head. Her wild thrashing and his fast numbing fingers made her slip from his grip. His fingers clenched around her jacket's collar, and he pulled her head out of the water.

She sputtered and gasped for breath.

"Hang on."

His free hand probed into the arctic water and fumbled to untangle her arms from the poles and skis. Trying to keep her head up and his torso as dry as possible, he sank his hand once more into the frigid water. Kyra's jerky movements hindered his progress. His fingers slipped in the oily water, groping mud and slippery rocks.

While precious body heat bled into the cold water, he found himself irrationally angry at the pond, as if it were a living entity consciously dueling him for Kyra.

"Stop fighting me!" he ordered.

Finally his fingers found purchase on the skis. He inched them forward until he reached the bindings. Pressing hard on the release, he popped one boot free, and then the other. Then he hauled her out of the pond and onto the bench by the feeding station.

Despite the bright sun shining down on them, the combination of cold winds, low temperature, and wet clothes were prime conditions for hypothermia. Though he was cold, most of his upper body was still dry. Kyra was sopping wet from head to toe. He had to work fast before her core temperature dropped too low. Already she shivered uncontrollably.

"Kyra? How are you doing?" Mac snatched off her dripping hat and crammed his dry one over her wet head.

"C-cold."

"We'll get you warm again." He ripped off her gloves, stripped off her sopping coat, and replaced them with his own dry clothes.

He had to get her warm, and fast. Running to get help would take too long. He couldn't leave her here by herself. The closest place was his condo. He made an instant decision: He'd get her home and warmed; then he'd call for help.

"Can you stand?" Mac asked.

When she nodded he helped her up. "You're going to have to put those skis back on. Do you understand?"

"I c-can't," she said through chattering teeth.

"You have to. You need to stay warm." He turned her around. Through the naked oak branches, he pointed out his condo. "That's where we're going. It's not very far. You need to keep moving to stay warm. I'll help you. Okay?"

She nodded jerkily. He retrieved her skis and poles from the water and helped her into the equipment. "Come on. You can do it."

Another blast of wind whipped at them. Mac watched impotently as Kyra struggled stiffly to keep moving forward between racking shivers. He encouraged her with each shuffle. Never had he felt so vulnerable. He cursed himself for his stupidity, but he'd wanted time alone with her, and the beginners' trails were always so crowded. He should've known better than to take her on the expert trail. He should've realized she couldn't acquire the skills needed her first time out on skis. Now he was paying for his selfishness. Just as he had in Hawaii. No, he corrected himself; Kyra was the one paying for his mistake.

He shivered. The cold was starting to get to him, too. He could barely feel his fingers curled around his poles. The ice forming on his pant legs and his sweater's arms made his movements stiff. Knowing that however bad he felt, Kyra had to be feeling worse, gnawed at his conscience.

A course that should have taken five minutes took them fifteen to travel. He worried more and more about her with each step. Her coordination was lessening. The few words he could get her to utter were slurred.

Finally they reached his condo. Mac dug through the mailbox for his extra key and whipped the door open. He snapped both their skis off and left them strewn at the door. He pried the poles out of her hands and gently lifted her into his arms.

He slammed the door shut with his foot, then proceeded at a fast but smooth pace toward his bedroom, stepping over the mound of construction materials in the living room. He paused at the foot of the stairs to turn the thermostat up as far as it would go. The furnace blasted on, churning warm air out of the vents.

Her eyes were closed, her lashes dark against her blue skin. "Kyra, honey, you've got to stay awake."

"So tired."

Her voice was low and slurred, and he pressed her closer to his heart. "I know, but you've got to stay awake until I can get you warm again."

He set her down on his bed and quickly stripped off her wet clothes. He talked as he worked, asking questions and getting precious few answers. Her skin was too blue and much too cold, and her intense shivers made his task difficult.

Once he'd removed all her wet clothes he guided her under the covers. Then he raced to his guest bedroom, ripped the blankets and comforter from the bed, and layered them on top of the blanket and comforter already covering her. He tucked the mountain of warmth gently around her, removed the pillow so her head wouldn't be higher than her heart, and tenderly pushed aside the strand of hair plastered to her cheek.

"Talk to me, Kyra."

Her eyes fluttered open. "Where am I?"

"You're at my house."

She looked at him quizzically; then fear pierced her spring green eyes. "The wolf-shadow. I fell."

Wolf shadows again. Delirium wasn't a good sign. She needed more warmth. He hurried to the fireplace and quickly started a roaring fire.

"Kyra? I'm going to go downstairs for a minute. I'll be right back."

"Sleepy."

Mac controlled his urge to shake her, knowing a sharp movement at this point could easily jar her into unconsciousness. Instead, he caressed her cheek.

"Kyra, honey, you've got to stay awake. Can you hear me?"

She mumbled and moved away from his touch.

He trapped her chin gently in his hands. "Kyra. Look at me. Come on. I know you can do it."

Her eyes fluttered open again.

"Good girl. I'm going to go downstairs, and you're going to keep your eyes open until I come back."

"Sleepy."

"You can sleep when I get back."

He didn't like the blank look on her face or the way her eyes were unfocused. "I'll be right back."

"Okay."

Mac thundered down the stairs, stripping out of his clothes as he went. He jerked a mug out of the cupboard, filled it with water and plopped a bag of tea into it before stuffing it into the microwave. While the water boiled, he rushed to the laundry room and snagged a clean sweat suit from the dryer.

He cursed as each precious second ticked by. Once or twice he called up to her and thought he heard her mumble answer. When the microwave beeped, he pulled out the tea bag, cursing once more as he burned his finger. He added some cold water to the cup, then two heaping teaspoons of sugar, and stirred as he mounted the steps two by two.

Once back in the bedroom he sat on the edge of the bed and eased Kyra up a little so he could get the warm liquid into her.

"Come on, drink up. It'll make you feel better."

She tried a sip and choked on it. She pushed the mug away, but he insisted that she try again.

"Too sweet." She tried to push the mug away once more.

"This from a woman who considers sugar the most important food group in the pyramid," he said lightly.

He tipped the mug toward her mouth, but the shivering increased, and the liquid dribbled uselessly down her chin.

Time for stronger measures, he thought. He slipped under the covers beside her. He spooned himself against Kyra's cold body, wrapping his arms around her naked flesh and willing his heat to warm her. How could she still be so cold in the uncomfortable warmth of the room?

Without the frenzied activity to keep his thoughts at bay, the feelings he'd suppressed infiltrated his mind like germinating weeds and took root.

He'd never truly felt fear before. Even in the most dangerous situation, he'd known that if he relied on his brain and his well-maintained body, he could get himself out of anything. He couldn't call the adrenaline surge he'd felt on those occasions fear. Not even when death surrounded him. It had been his job, and he'd disconnected himself from it—watched death from a psychic distance. When Martin Patrick had died in his arms, he'd felt regret and anger, but not fear.

Now he feared he would lose Kyra before they'd had a chance to try again. The thought leadened his heart.

Kyra's wracking shivers began to subside. Mac breathed a silent sigh of relief when they weren't replaced by stiffening muscles.

"Kyra? Are you feeling warmer?"

"A lit-tle bit."

"Tell me what it was like growing up in Florida." Mac knew he had to keep her awake, and talking seemed to be the best solution.

"I had a great childhood with devoted parents. H-how about you?"

"You're the one who's supposed to do the talking. How else can I tell if you're awake?"

"I don't want to talk. I want to be warm again."

"That's what I'm trying to do."

She squirmed around until she faced him. The blank, unfocused look he'd seen earlier had been replaced with a feverish blaze of intensity that lit a new trail of fear along his spine.

"The shadow," Kyra said. Her hands reached to grip his shoulders. "He's waiting for me in the mountain."

Mac noticed her touch wasn't ice cold anymore, but her fixation on the shadow worried him.

"He's not real, Kyra. He's part of your dreams." Mac spoke gently as he urged her body closer to his.

"He *is* real."

"Do you hear what you're saying?" Mac shook her slightly, trying to make her see the absurdity of her words.

"Yes, I do. I know it makes no sense to you because you can't see him, but he's real and he was there. With me Hallie's line dies."

"Then what?" Mac didn't think brain damage was a usual effect of hypothermia, but he supposed he couldn't dismiss the possibility.

"He won't have to kill anymore."

Was she planning to offer herself as a sacrifice to this phantom shadow? He chased away the black thought speeding through his mind. No, the idea that the mountain's evil had somehow permeated Kyra's consciousness and possessed her while she was weak was simply too preposterous to accept.

"Kyra, honey, you've just been through an ordeal, and sometimes when people get as cold as you did, they have hallucinations. You're safe here. I won't let anybody hurt you."

"Don't talk to me as if I'm a sick child."

Her still damp hair tickled his hand around her shoulders. Mac noticed the blue tinge to her skin had been replaced by a feverish blush. Maybe he ought to get her to a hospital.

"You can't stop me," she said with frightening intensity.

"Kyra—"

"I don't want to die. I want to feel alive." Her gaze bored into his. The desperate demand he saw there made him suck in his breath.

"You're not going to die," Mac managed to say as he carefully breathed out.

Her hand reached up to his cheek. "I don't care that you think I'm crazy. I don't care that you don't believe in the wolf-shadow. I know you feel the strong current between us. I want to feel that power explode. Like before. I want to feel every fiber of my being alive again."

She paused and pressed her lips suggestively against his, drawing an instant reaction from him. She twined her arms at his nape and her lips brushed his again. "Make me warm again, Mac. Make love to me."

Chapter Fifteen

"No." Every muscle in Mac's body tensed beyond endurance.

When he uttered the word Kyra stared at him in disbelief. The fiery look in her eyes heightened his already simmering desire.

Only a crazy man would refuse such an offer, but he didn't want her this way, when she wasn't herself, when she was using him to drive away her fears. He would control himself. He would be the gentleman he'd once professed to be.

"You want me," she said simply.

She shifted her weight and slid her body up to better reach his mouth with hers. As the movement of her soft skin against his set off explosions of yearning, Mac stifled a groan. She planted a demanding kiss on his lips, but he refused her an answer.

"And I want you," Kyra continued softly. Her breath against his mouth cooled the heat she'd created with her touch. The hunger radiating from her dazed him. "That was enough seven years ago. Why can't it be now?"

Remembering the times Kyra had kissed him in a rush of emotions unleashed by her nightmares, Mac pushed her away with a regret that shook his body.

"You think you want me, but what you want is comfort. I am not going to make love to a woman who's still recovering from hypothermia."

His mother had taught him and Brad early on— even before they understood what she meant—that when a girl said no she meant no, no matter how badly their hormones raged, and that they had to respect that wish. But his mother had never mentioned that there might come a day when the woman he wanted more than his next breath would offer herself up to him and he'd have to turn her down. The tension stringing him tighter than sinew on snowshoes threatened to shatter all his good intentions.

Mac held Kyra at arm's length underneath the unbearably hot covers. "I won't deny that I want you. But I won't take you to soothe your desperation. When we make love it'll be because you want *me* as much as I want you, not to drive away demons. You'll have a clear mind, and you'll know exactly what you're getting into."

He watched her avert the round saucers of her eyes, but not before he saw the hurt. With his index finger, he tilted her chin up.

"You're right," he said softly. "I do feel the power between us. That's why we have to wait."

The shimmer of unshed tears glimmered in her eyes, tearing at his heart. She looked as if she battled an inner war as trying as his own, fighting to hang on to something that was slipping away from her— from both of them.

"We might not get another chance." Kyra's voice was barely above a whisper.

"We'll have a million chances."

He saw doubt cloud her eyes, but he knew nothing he said would chase it away. Her vulnerability in that moment made him feel protective and possessive. He wanted to assure her that everything would be all right, but he knew he couldn't.

Her gaze dropped to his chest. "Mac, out of that busload of women visiting the Halemaumau Crater, why did you pick me out?"

He thought back to the moment his gaze had fallen on Kyra. She'd seemed to materialize from the sulfur steam rising out of the stark volcanic rock—a goddess of his own, with hair of golden fire and eyes that promised spring to the winter already settling in his heart. A deep, unsubstantiated knowledge that she would change his life had overwhelmed him. He had to be near her. He had to feel her. He had to have her. It had seemed as if his very life had depended on it. Even a half hour of logical debate hadn't lessened the feeling. He shook his head to clear the vibrant memory.

"The way the sun haloed you made me think of life," he said. "I had to be with you. Why did you accept?"

She shrugged. "I don't know. There was something about your eyes, about the energy vibrating from you. I wanted to say no, but I couldn't."

She paused, turning her gaze up to him once more. "I don't like the way you did it, but you were right to leave me in Hawaii. We're nothing alike. You like meat; I won't touch it. You like action; I like quiet. You like to wander; I like roots. Marriage would have tied you down. You would have grown unhappy."

"What makes you think I'll go away this time?" he asked tersely. "I've been at Mountain Swift for two years now."

"You're telling me you haven't had itchy feet? After all the movement and excitement of your other job, don't you find this one dull?"

A flare of guilt mixed with the anger. "Not in the way you think."

"It's all right, Mac. I'm not looking for a commitment. I'm not looking for marriage. I've got a wonderful, fulfilling career ahead of me. I just want what we had before. Once more. That's all."

"You need to rest—"

"I don't want to argue. Not now." Her fingertips drew tiny patterns on his chest. Mac swore softly.

He'd already slipped twice in front of Alek because of his strong feelings for Kyra. He knew what Alek wanted, but he also knew Alek would fight with his all. He couldn't expect anything less. That meant a single distraction could easily make him worm meal. And Kyra was a powerful distraction. He had to look beyond desire, beyond the force drawing them together. He had to stay sharp—for a few more days—and he couldn't do that with Kyra around.

Mac started to slide out of the bed. Kyra stopped him with a hand around his biceps. "Don't go. Keep me warm. Please."

When he didn't answer she quickly added, "I promise I won't try to kiss you again."

No, you'll only kill me with your nearness.

"Please, Mac."

If she hadn't said his name in just that tone of voice, if it hadn't echoed so melodically along the cords of his tensed nerves to land with such a pining sigh on his heart, he might have been able to resist and slip some hot water bottles between the sheets to replace the warmth of his body. But she had. And on top of the pleading of her fingers on the wound muscles of his arm and the supplication in the green pools of her eyes, he found he couldn't tell her no yet again. He broke down and crawled back in next to her.

Mac excused his weakness as Kyra snuggled close

to him. He shut his eyes against the golden-red cloud of her hair tickling his cheeks and wished he could somehow close down the olfactory center of his brain. The sweet scent of passion flowers, released by her warming body, tortured him.

His brain, without permission, flooded with images of them, naked on a sandy beach, their bodies entwined, surrounded by the intoxicating odor of tropical flowers and the erotic rhythm of the lapping sea. He forced the picture out of his mind and let his breath out in a long, slow motion, so Kyra couldn't sense his personal torture.

Kyra snuggled deeper into the crook of his neck. As her hand came up to his chest and brushed his nipple before coming to rest just above his racing heart, Mac drew in a sharp breath. Was she doing this intentionally? He wasn't sure how much more of this he could take before the animal in him completely took over the machinelike control he fought to maintain.

"Go to sleep, Kyra," he said in a husky voice.

"You've been telling me to stay awake."

"I know. But for both our sakes I think it'd be best if you went to sleep now."

She shifted restlessly for a few minutes. Mac thought the time would have been easier spent in hell. With each movement she sent shards of desire rasping through his veins. It was getting harder by the second to remain master over his body and his mind.

He struggled to understand what it was about this particular woman that could take thirteen years of training and throw it out the window so easily. There was no rational explanation, and that made it all the harder to accept.

A needle of anger stung him. Kyra shouldn't have the power to make him feel more whole by her mere presence. All those years he'd prized his independence. And this woman, driving him crazy with her touch, had become as vital to him as one of his own limbs.

"I can't sleep," Kyra whispered against his chest.

Mac swallowed the latest wave of tension her breath created on his skin.

"Count sheep," he said gruffly.

"I tried, but the wolf-shadow waiting on the other side always gobbles up the lambs as soon as they jump over the fence."

With a movement containing more coiled tension than comfort, he stroked her shoulder. "I'm not very good at bedtime stories. Why don't you tell me one?"

Kyra was silent for so long, Mac thought she'd drifted off to sleep. He allowed the painful coil of his muscles to relax a bit.

"Why did Alek call you Ram?" she asked.

Surprise jolted his eyes open. God, would the subject never be closed! Mac seized on the anger twisting his gut. Anger was easier to handle than the disturbing sensations of Kyra's silky skin so close and yet so out of reach, she might as well have been halfway across the world.

"Can't you pick a cheerier subject for a bedtime story?" he asked sharply.

"I can't help it. No matter what I try to think about, my mind always comes back to the dreams and Alek. All the things that are keeping us apart." She turned her gaze up to him, melting away his anger. "I want to forget."

She pleaded with her eyes, but he chose to answer her question rather than deal with the emotions warring through every fiber of his being.

"He called me Ram because I never lost my footing no matter how bad the conditions were, and no door was ever an obstacle."

Kyra sighed regretfully, ripping her gaze away from his. "What did you call Alek before he . . . left?"

"He was always Vermin. He could bug anything without being detected, and he had the role of a mole down to an art. That's why it was so hard for the Institute to keep up with him after he turned. He taught his recruits well, and the Institute never found the moles until Alek wanted them to. But you don't want anymore nightmares, do you? Let's talk about something else."

She nodded, torturing him once more with the soft caress of her hair. A moment later she tilted up her head, and her piercing gaze kept him captive. "If you were making love to me right now, what would you be doing?"

So startled was he by her question, for an instant all he could do was stare down at her in amazement. "What?" he finally croaked.

"If you were making love to me, what would you be doing?"

Mac knew he should jump out of bed right then, before there was nothing left of his sanity, but he was mesmerized by the fiery swirls of spring green and deeper emerald in her eyes.

He groaned inwardly. And then, because he hated his weakness, he wanted her to ache with the same need thrumming urgently through his body.

"We'd both be dressed," he said, then swallowed hard, squeezing a breath of space between their bodies. "And I'd be slowly taking off your clothes."

She smiled seductively, making his body ripple with renewed tension. "I was too cold to notice before."

"And I was too worried about you to enjoy it." The words slipped out unchecked, bringing with them a different kind of worry. Admitting vulnerability was asking for an early death. What did it matter? Kyra already knew he cared about her. She already had him on a collision course to an early grave from the second Alek realized she meant anything to him.

"Tell me how you'd take my clothes off," she implored, not moving a muscle.

The Institute should have hired her as a master of torture, he thought. "Very slowly."

Mac watched as his words faded the desperation from her eyes and ignited the slow burning fire of desire. Emboldened by his effect, and to keep from devouring her alive, he slowly pushed her away, resting her head on the ruby, topaz, and hunter green paisley pattern of his flannel sheets. He turned his body sideways until they faced each other and their bodies didn't touch. Warming her from a distance would be safer—for both of them.

He could feel the heat radiating from his flushed body, feel the tightness of his throat as he swallowed, feel the fire low in his belly begging for release.

"If we were making love right now, we'd be standing in the middle of the room. I'd be kissing you softly while my hands were moving slowly down your arms. Then they'd find their way under your sweater. Slowly, they'd explore your body, savoring each curve, each angle, each rib. And then I'd tease your breasts with my thumbs."

He imagined her soft breasts swelling under his touch, their peaks straining toward him. It took everything he had not to reach out and feel whether his words had created the reaction he was sure his hands would have gotten. She licked her dry lips, tempting him to taste the moist trail she'd left behind.

"Then what?" she said on a breathy thread of voice.

"Then I'd slip off your sweater, and your shirt, and your undershirt, and your bra—all those layers you put on between you and the world. Then I'd sample a taste of your cheek, and your ear, and your neck, and your shoulder, until your skin was on fire and I could mold you to me like a second skin."

He saw the spark of desire deepen the color of her

eyes to almost black, heard the soft gasp escape her parted lips. He felt the prickly film of sweat blister his own skin, and the painful pulsing that were his reactions to hers.

"After the clothes, then what?" The pulse at Kyra's throat pounded under the fine silver chain erratically thrown over the crescent-shaped birthmark where her shoulder and neck met.

"Once all our clothes were off I'd give you a look that would have you blushing from head to toe."

When Kyra's pupils widened to impossible size, Mac curled his fingers around the flannel sheet to keep his hand from breaching the span between them and touching the delightful pinkening of her skin.

"I'd invite you to my bed," he continued, not knowing how long he could keep up his seduction and not do something about it, but enjoying the transformation on her face. "And I'd taste you all over again. I'd read you with my hands until my mind could memorize every line of you. I'd touch you and taste you until you begged for me."

Even though they were apart, he felt the rhythm and the heat of her breath increase, and reveled in the knowledge that her heart pounded as hard as his.

"And then?" Her voice was barely a whisper, but with all his nerve endings exposed, he could hear every heartbeat, feel every breath, and her whisper sounded more like a shout.

"And then I'd tease you some more, until you thought you'd die if you didn't have me."

Her sharp intake of breath was followed by a nervous licking of lips, but her smoldering gaze never once wavered.

"And then?"

"And then . . ." He swallowed. "And then I'd watch you fall apart in my arms when I gave you what you wanted."

The image of her body writhing beneath his was so powerfully alive in his mind, he knew he had to leave now or he'd never be able to do what he'd just described to Kyra. He'd take her fast and hard, and he'd hate himself afterward.

He jumped out of bed and strode resolutely toward the bathroom.

"Mac?"

Her strangled question made him falter for half a step.

"Go to sleep, Kyra."

He restrained his urge to slam the bathroom door, closing it firmly behind him and twisting the lock into position. He ripped the shower door open, then turned the knob to cold before he let the punishing spray numb the fire raging like hell through his body.

There was one consolation, Mac thought; if Kyra was half as hot as he was now, she'd be all right.

He turned his face to the freezing water and cursed hotly. The icy shower was having no effect on his desire to make Kyra his own once more, or on the feeling that his weakness for her would be his undoing.

Kyra's whole body throbbed from Mac's seduction. He hadn't touched her, yet she felt as if his hands and his mouth had left not an inch of her skin unsampled. She burned with a feverlike heat. Her pulse thudded at her temples, her neck, her wrists, and her ankles. And her soul cried bloody tears as Mac locked the bathroom door behind him. Knowing she might never have the chance to have him fulfill the erotic fantasy he'd woven for her left a gaping hole where her heart should have been.

She heard the spray of water coming from the bathroom and knew without a doubt that the water was cold. She'd seen the fire in his eyes. She'd seen the desire, the longing on his face, along with something that came close to adoration. She'd felt his controlled tension and the throbbing of his pulse. And the sheen of perspiration glowing on his skin had betrayed his own fever.

Kyra bit back the sob of disappointment coming from deep inside her, but she couldn't stop the tears from flowing. She felt betrayed by Mac's departure. How could he have left her so raw with desire and not done anything about it?

She shivered despite the heat making her body sweat. The motion hurt, setting off a chain reaction of fatigue. Her whole body suddenly felt like a massive bruise. As she turned away from the noise of the bathroom, she blinked rapidly to clear the tears, and took her first glance at Mac's room.

The massive walnut dresser alongside the bed was topped by a huge mirror. Two matching night stands flanked the walnut-framed bed. The window held no drapes. It was covered simply with bare hunter green blinds that were open and let in the golden late afternoon light. The bookcase by the door was cluttered with a multitude of books and electronic gadgets. Piles of magazines littered the floor, and in one corner a laundry basket overflowed with clothes.

There were signs of life everywhere, but oddly enough no signs of belonging. There were no pictures on the walls, no photographs on the dresser. Even on vacation, she always carried a little three-sided frame that held a picture of her mother, one of her father, and one of Misty to place within view. Despite the clutter around the room, she would never have guessed Mac had lived here for two years. Had his training also taught him to call no place home?

Kyra's eyelids drooped and her limbs were heavy when she tried to move. She heard the spray of water stop, and then, a few minutes later, the door unlocking. As Mac opened the closet door, it squealed. She wanted to turn around and fill her gaze with the sight of his body, but she couldn't—her body was too stiff and her will too weak. If she saw him, she'd want him, and she didn't want to grovel in front of Mac. Definitely unladylike.

Mac came around the bed. As he crouched beside her, his knee cracked. Kyra forced her leaden eyes open. He was dressed in a red sweat suit.

"Do you have a whole closet full of those red sweat suits?" She tried to smile, but her skin felt as if it would crack.

He reached a finger to her cheek and wiped away a half-dried tear. The scent of his soap filled her nostrils.

"I never meant to hurt you," he said with a catch in his voice.

"You haven't." The tears had flowed in regret at what might have been, not pain.

"How are you feeling?"

He pushed away a strand of hair from her forehead, and the prickle of tears stung her eyes once more. "I'm a little tired."

"I'll let you rest in a minute. Let me take your temperature first." He unsheathed a thermometer from its casing. "Open wide."

Kyra did as she was told, and Mac placed the hard plastic under her tongue.

"Do you want a pillow?"

She nodded, and he placed one under her head. Wanting a connection, she tried to restrain his hand with hers, but he swiftly pulled it away, turning his gaze away from her. She swallowed her sob and ordered her tears not to fall. The thermometer beeped, and Mac smiled at the reading.

"Your temperature's back to normal. Why don't you try and sleep for a while?"

"Misty?" Kyra asked with a yawn.

"Don't worry. I'll call Debbie. She'll take good care of her."

Her energy suddenly vaporized. Her eyelids closed against her will and her brain fogged. "Stay with me."

Mac tucked the blankets around her, and she felt as if she were wrapped in a snug cocoon. "I've got to check on a few things. I'll be back later."

Her warm cocoon now took on a smoky layer of sadness, and she couldn't remember why, but she knew she shouldn't go to sleep—not without Mac by her side.

She felt the gentle warmth of his finger on her skin, and as the gray clouds of sleep enveloped her, she thought she heard him say, "I love you."

But it had to be wishful thinking because she was alone and cold, and the dark was trying to seep into her soul.

Chapter Sixteen

The shadow flowed out of the mountain and into the night, glittering silver under the filling moon. Like the shifting waters of a mirage, he glided over the snow. He hated to use the tortured soul haunting the shaft's entrance—his camp strategically placed for observation and quick action—but he had no choice. McKane's constant interference had lessened his own power. To make his plan work, he would need an ally.

This man had the black heart and the wretchedness of a man cheated of what was rightfully his, as he himself had been. The magic would work; it had worked twice already—after all, the man was spiritually damaged. But how much more rewarding it would be if this kindred spirit bore the torch willingly.

The shadow paused by the tent. The man inside thrashed about, victim of the demons of his soul. For a moment the shadow wondered whether this man might be too weak. He melted through the nylon sides of the tent, then probed a wraithlike finger into the man's mind. He found the fabric of his psyche filled with holes. The shadow retreated to a corner of the tent. Not good. This man was like a keg of gunpowder with a lit fuse attached to it. Loose gunpowder was so much harder to handle than contained dynamite.

But what choice did he have? Kyra's will was strong, and McKane kept a vigilant post at her side, making his victim accessible for only short spells. The incident at the pond had been unfortunate; a miscalculation on his part. He'd simply wanted to remind her that she could have no peace until she visited his home at the bottom of the mine. He hoped the icy bath hadn't damaged his prize. The kill must be his.

He had to wrest this last piece of vengeance before that interfering fool McKane sealed the mine. To exact his revenge, he needed Kyra in his grave. To get Kyra to the mine, he needed outside help. He had to strike now, while she was weak.

There was no time to waste.

The shadow fluttered angrily around the tent. Since he couldn't guide Kyra into the mountain himself, he'd have to use this man. There wasn't enough time to find anyone else.

With a little luck the man wouldn't explode until his job was done. But then, Lady Luck had never deigned to smile down on him. He couldn't take any chances.

The shadow hovered over the restless figure of the man, then melded with him. Using some of his precious energy, he knitted a few of the wider rents together; then he inscribed his wishes. With an unbinding of etheric threads, he disentangled himself from the man's human carcass and floated above him for a few minutes.

The man slept in peace. The repairs had worked.

As the dark silhouette of his essence moved once more across the snow, the shadow rejoiced. In exchange for peace the man had agreed to everything.

He had chosen well after all.

The shadow slipped back to the mountain. He would soon be free. Now he needed to renew his depleted energy. He wanted to be at his best to receive his guests.

The gray mist swirled, turning white as it rose. It looked like dry ice on a stage, Kyra thought abstractly. Then, just as surrealistically, a figure dressed in a long, flowing white nightgown materialized. She beckoned with a finger, and Kyra saw herself in a similar dress. As she neared the figure, Kyra recognized Hallie.

"Don't be afraid, child." Hallie pointed to a rock rising out of the steam. "Sit down. There are a few things you should know for your own good. Things that should have been told to you years ago."

Kyra sat down silently and looked at her surroundings. The mist smoked around and through them, but Kyra couldn't see anything past its thick bluish-white curls except Hallie's vaporous image.

Was she dead? Is that why Hallie had come to her? She'd read about things like this before. Kyra looked down at her body, touched her legs. They felt real enough. Surprisingly, the thought of death brought no sadness, only disappointment that she'd missed out on a life with Mac. She looked up at Hallie once more.

"Am I dead?" Kyra's voice echoed eerily in the damp haze.

Hallie chuckled. "No, dear. We must have a talk. There isn't much time if you are to have a future. You have felt Rolf Schreck?"

"The wolf-shadow?" Kyra nodded. "Yes, I've seen him."

Hallie sat on a rock facing Kyra and reached out for her hands. Kyra expected the ghostly hands to be cold, but she felt warmth from the pale skin, and something else—love.

"You must stay away from the mine." Hallie's face was filled with worry. "He wants to kill you, and no one can protect you there. It's the center of his power. No one is strong enough to break through it."

"But I have to go. I have to stop his curse." Kyra squeezed the hands holding hers, willing Hallie to understand.

Hallie shook her head. "Your intentions are honorable, but Schreck doesn't understand honor. I'm not going to whitewash the truth by letting you believe I was a saint. I wasn't. I made a lot of mistakes in my life. But Schreck . . . well, Schreck was just plain evil. His hatred followed him to his grave and beyond, and this hatred has caused him to kill off our entire family. You're the last. The curse is written on your shoulder."

Hallie reached to the small crescent-shaped mark at the juncture of Kyra's neck and shoulder. "All the children born after Schreck's curse have carried the mark." Hallie's hand moved to Kyra's cheek. Her fingers followed the double wavy line. "And this is his kiss of death."

Kyra looked up to Hallie and for the first time noticed that a matching freeze burn marked Hallie's cheek. "Oh!"

But instead of pacifying her into flight as she thought Hallie had hoped it would do, seeing the mark and understanding its meaning made Kyra even more determined to end its power.

Kyra grasped one of Hallie's withered hands. "Don't you see, that's why I have to go. Someone has to stop him."

Hallie shook her head. Her pale green eyes took on a sad, downward cast. "Don't you think I've tried? You cannot fight him."

"Why not? If something has a beginning, it must have an end."

Hallie stood up and turned away from Kyra. She cleared her throat. "His original claim has a basis in truth."

She whirled back to face Kyra. "But I swear I knew nothing of it when I appeared before the court."

"You mean the mine did belong to him?"

Hallie shrugged and lifted her hands in a helpless gesture. "Half of it. I found out much later. He was already dead, and I was packing the house to move to California. After Elizabeth died, I knew I had to move away and save Rebecca from Schreck's curse. I found Emory's original grubstake agreement hidden in a false-bottomed drawer that fell apart when I dropped it by accident. He never told me. His secret cost me so much."

Hallie's features drooped with a heavy sadness that seemed to permeate the mist surrounding them. In the cottony silence floating around them, Kyra felt regret mingle with love, disappointment mix with longing. She was loathe to break the quiet in which Hallie seemed lost, but the questions building inside her couldn't wait.

"If Rebecca lived in California, how did she end up in Park City?"

Hallie sat back on the rock and folded her hands into her lap. "Like you, the brave fool had the urge to put the past to rest. She wanted you to grow up safely." Hallie shook her head and shifted her gaze downward. "I tried to stop her, but I was too late. He got me first—strangled me while I slept in a hotel in Heber. I hadn't realized his power could take him that far." Her gaze returned to Kyra's face. "It grows with every kill, you know."

221

"What does this power give him?"

"He thinks it will bring him the life he lost."

"Will it?"

Hallie shrugged. "I don't know. But you must leave."

"I can't if I ever want to live in peace. You killed him in the mine. That's where he has to be stopped."

Hallie's hand reached for Kyra's cheek. "Brave, foolish child. How do you plan to do that?"

"With Mac's help I'll figure out a way."

Hallie's hand dropped back into her lap. "Why didn't you heed the message in the box?"

"What box?" Kyra asked, confusion floating through her mind.

"The one the moonstone key opens."

Kyra unconsciously fingered the filigreed silver key on the chain hanging around her neck. Her mother had given it to her when she graduated from college. Kyra had seen it as the key to open her future. "I didn't know it opened a box."

"That key opened a box I gave your mother. I gave it to Rebecca so she would understand the curse. Pity she didn't pass on the secrets along with the key."

Kyra left her seat on the rock and crouched at Hallie's feet. She placed her head on the older woman's lap and felt courage flow through her from her great-grandmother's caress.

"My mother," Kyra said. "My adoptive mother never dealt with the truth. She hid it from me all my life. Even when I was a child I could sense some unknown fear eating at her. She knew about the wolf-shadow, didn't she?"

"I'm afraid so."

Her mother's fear of this unseen shadow, Kyra realized, had fueled the few arguments she'd overheard between her parents. Her father had wanted to tell Kyra "the truth"—the word *adoption* was never mentioned—and her mother had remained adamant that she couldn't break her promise. Kyra hadn't understood what they had fought about until after her mother's death. This fear would also account for her mother's controlling behavior. Knowing her fear would have made her mother's behavior understandable, if not acceptable.

"Running away from Schreck didn't save you or Rebecca," Kyra said with resignation. "The only way to stop him is where he lives."

Hallie stopped stroking Kyra's hair and gave a heavy sigh. "Perhaps you're right. But even your courage might not be enough." She stood. "There is only one thing evil cannot destroy."

"What—"

"Kyra!"

The disembodied voice, wafting through layers of mist, sounded like Mac's. Kyra stood up abruptly and looked around for its source. It came from all around. She looked right, then left, behind and ahead. Still she couldn't find him.

"Mac?"

Hallie's face brightened at the sound of Mac's voice. "Go to him, Kyra."

Hallie's body grew thinner, more pale, until Kyra could barely see it against the mist.

"Hey, wait! You can't leave without telling me the answer. What can't evil destroy?"

"Look to your mother." Hallie's voice resonated through the thickening haze, and she vaporized.

"Which one?"

"Both."

Kyra ran to the last spot she'd seen Hallie. "Don't go. I don't understand."

"Look . . . inside." The voice rippled and floated away like dandelion seeds.

"Kyra!" Mac's voice called to her once more.

Whirling around, Kyra pinned down Mac's position and started toward it. "Mac! Wait for me!"

She ran blindly, hands before her to part the thick clouds. The mist turned black. In the pitch darkness she saw pictures swirling around her. Pictures of death. *Not again.*

Panic drove her forward. "Mac!"

John Barrett, Hallie's second husband, appeared out of the left. As his image passed over her head, Kyra saw him being killed by a runaway coal truck. When he disappeared to the right his image was immediately replaced by that of Matthew, Hallie's son, raping his half-sister, Sarah. An outraged Hallie disowned her son and sent him packing. A car struck him head-on before he reached the town limits, killing him instantly.

She ran faster, trying to dodge the images assaulting her.

As they got closer, the pictures were more garish and more real. Sarah gave birth to a daughter, then killed herself. Kyra gagged at the smell of ether emanating from the woman, dressed in black, lying on the bed with a bouquet of flowers clasped in one hand and a white towel draped over her face. An empty bottle of ether still rolled on the floor in the breeze from a half-opened window. A suicide note silently slipped from the dead woman's free hand, hanging over the edge of the bed.

The appearance of Otto Stern, Hallie's third husband, quickly followed Sarah's vignette. The man was sucked into a giant saw at his mill. Kyra veered away from the blood raining overhead like a sudden summer storm.

She gagged.

"Mac!" she cried desperately. Tears flowed freely down her cheeks, but they couldn't cloud the grisly pictures that drew closer and closer, trying to absorb her into their mad whirlpool.

Hallie, crying over Otto's grave, swore she would never marry again. Marrying for protection was an illusion; it only brought more deaths.

Sarah's daughter, Elizabeth, her husband, and two of their three children followed the sweep of blood. They were trapped in their car on a railroad crossing, with a train approaching at full speed, as if they were invisible.

Running as fast as she could away from the nightmare, Kyra clamped her hands over her ears and shut her eyes. But it wouldn't let her go. The sounds and the pictures penetrated her barriers and dogged her every move like hungry wolves on the heels of a kill.

Hallie desperately packing, hiding the sick child who'd stayed behind, not breathing a sigh of relief until the train reached California.

Hallie fighting off Schreck's attack was quickly followed by Rebecca's suffocating death.

Each of the dying bore the double wavy line on their cheek.

Each had agreed to be taken, believing others would live.

Each had found out too late that their sacrifice had been in vain.

They had died. They had all died.

Like Bluebeard's murdered wives, their spirits rattled in the dark closet of Schreck's cave. And she was next because she'd given in to the curiosity of the dreams. She'd seen the skeletons. He could not let her live knowing the truth. Because knowing the truth would give . . . what? She lost the rapid train of her thoughts. She stopped and looked back.

She had found the key, opened the forbidden door, and now she could never pretend she hadn't seen the ravages hidden in its dark recesses. She understood her past. But she'd missed something, brushed against it and recoiled from it before she could grasp it. Something important. Something she needed to know.

Kyra froze, panting, listening, trying to recapture the moment that had passed her by.

Nothing. There was nothing. Except a silence deeper than any she'd ever experienced. Even her labored breaths had no sound. When she tried to call Mac once more the scream shaking her body didn't make any noise.

When she looked down at the silver key hanging from the chain around her neck the notches were red and the steady drops dripping from the tip stained the front of her white dress.

While she swiped at the stains, a new darkness descended like a heavy theater curtain, surrounding her until she couldn't see the hand she waved before her eyes. She'd missed it, missed the clue pratically dropped into her lap. And now she was going to die because of her stupidity. Sheer panic swept through her.

Then she started falling.

Chapter Seventeen

Kyra fell dizzily, like a sky diver without a parachute, through the blacker-than-black sky. Moist, heavy air dampened her hair and whipped it painfully across her eyes and into her mouth. Her limbs flayed help-lessly, at the mercy of the wind and the occasional ineffectual command of her brain, which frantically tried to regain order over the chaos.

"Kyra, come back to me." The vaporous voice that sounded like Mac's, and yet didn't, penetrated the murky smog of her mind.

As she fell, the black lightened to gray, and gauzy, cloudlike hands caught her and held her close. Soft lips on hers reeled her back from the darkness into the light and breathed life into her battered body. As if she'd been on a long trek through the Mojave with-out water, she drank in the energy. Her hands, fin-gers splayed wide through the white fog, reached out and landed on something solid, then hung on for dear life; she didn't want to fall anymore.

When she looked at the solid wall, Mac's smiling face beamed at her.

"You're here," she whispered, finding it hard to catch her breath.

"Where else would I be?"

"I can see you. I can feel you." She clamped her hands on his shoulders while she looked around herself at the white fog still surrounding them. "You're in my dream with me."

He chuckled, holding her lightly in the circle of his arms. "Of course."

"Do you believe me now? Do you believe in the dreams?" She peered deep into his eyes and held her breath.

"I always did."

This had to be an illusion. Mac was agreeing with her about something as wispy and unbelievable as a dream? She pinched him to make sure he was real.

"Ouch!"

The sound jarred her eyes open wide. Her fingers gripped Mac's sweat suit–covered shoulder. Her breath rasped rapidly through burning lungs. The sound of her heartbeat ricocheted off her ribs and pounded loudly past her ears.

As she lifted her gaze to meet his, she noticed the blankets were pooled at her waist, stopped there only by Mac's weight on top of the bedcoverings. Her upper body was bared to the too warm air of the room, and the heat of Mac's hand seared the skin of her lower back.

They stared at each other silently. She watched the haze of confusion in his eyes lift. Shock and embarrassment replaced it. Then, slowly, the molten silver turned into bottomless black, reminding her fleetingly of the wingless flight of her nightmare.

She couldn't catch her breath, couldn't calm the wild hammering of her heart. Nor could she stop the sweeping need that had her blood on fire. But it wasn't terror she felt. She lowered her gaze and it fell on Mac's lips, still moist from their union with hers. A hunger, deeper than any she'd ever known, rocked her to the core.

She lifted her gaze to his eyes once more, noting the coiled tension stiffening the tendons around his temples into tight cords. The blinds, still open, showed off the pink and purple dawn painting the sky in soft watercolors and framing Mac's head.

"Don't push me away this time," she said, in what to her sounded like someone else's voice. "I have a clear mind. I know exactly what I'm doing." She lifted a tentative finger to Mac's lips and traced the moist trail shining there. "I want *you.*"

With the groan of a defeated warrior, he closed his eyes and possessed her mouth. His ardor swept away the cold, dark clouds of her nightmare and filled her with the flaming heat of desire.

He pulled away from her. She saw the storm of emotion pass through the bared soul in his eyes. "You don't know what you're doing," he said shakily.

"Yes, I do." She wanted to replace all the cold death she'd just witnessed with the warmth of love—however temporary it might prove to be.

He pushed away the remainder of the covers and leaned up on one elbow to give her the look he'd promised. And as he'd predicted, it had her blushing from head to toe.

"You're beautiful," he said with reverence, the admiration written all over his face lending credence to his words.

She'd never felt as beautiful as she did at that moment. She didn't feel too tall and awkward, as she often did, but feminine, sexy, and desirable. And those feelings fueled her hunger. She held her breath, afraid to move, afraid the moment would disappear, afraid Mac would leave.

Slowly she let out her breath as his hand reached

out and barely skimmed the skin of her arm, raising goose bumps and setting off a series of firecrackers along her limbs. He continued his delicious torture for a lifetime, the look of adoration never leaving his face. He teased her breasts until she thought her strained nipples would burst if he didn't touch them, and when he did she couldn't help the sigh of pure pleasure that had her closing her eyes and arching against him.

She reached for him, clumsily trying to remove the barrier of his sweatshirt. When she couldn't get rid of it she let out a frustrated growl. "Take it off!"

He stood up slowly and faced her as he took off his shirt, then his pants. Mac, naked in his full glory, and bathed in the pale morning light, had never looked more magnificent. She invited him back beside her with a glance.

He kissed her with a restraint she longed to see shattered. She kissed him back with an abandon that had the muscles of his stomach rippling, his hard heat pulsating a caress against her, the spicy scent of him driving her wild. She let her hand roam freely, exploring each taut muscle, discovering the ticklish spot where his hips cradled his flat belly.

She loved the feel of him, the hard softness of his body. She drank in the earthy musk of him. He tasted like wild honey and she savored him greedily. She feared she could never get enough of his natural sweetness. With seductive pleasure, she noted the frantic beating of his heart matched hers. His breath was as ragged as her own.

Never had she felt like this. Never had she allowed herself such vulnerability. Even as enchanted as she had been seven years ago she'd reserved a part of her from him. Had she known then he couldn't stay? She wondered, in the brief moment Mac chose to move away from her, if this wantonness had been brought about by the nearness of death. If she hadn't feared for her life, would she have been able to abandon her reservations about his departure so quickly?

She heard the scrape of a drawer and the rip of foil; then he returned to her. He tasted her and touched her with such thoroughness, she soon felt as if she was a fireworks shell confined to a tube. The powder of her resistance burned rapidly, making her temperature zoom. The pressure of the chemical reaction expanded to fill her until she thought she would burst.

"Mac," she whispered breathily into his ear. "Please."

He groaned as he rolled on top of her, but still he resisted her attempts to rush him. He positioned himself so that the tip of him rested against her moist invitation, teasing her until she thought she would die from the wondrous torture. She arched against him and tried to guide him into her. He answered by giving her a sample of what she wanted.

As he allowed the hard hot satin of him to glide inside her, her whole body throbbed with pleasure. She anticipated his full length filling all of her and curved to meet him. As he eased himself out again, a cry of frustrated surprise escaped her. She strained toward him, demanding he finish what he had started.

"What's your hurry?" he asked in a husky voice. The seductive smile gracing his lips told her he enjoyed her torture, but the sheen of perspiration on his brow belied his levity.

He grasped both her hands in his, holding them beside her head in such a way that she had no choice but to look deep into his eyes as he continued to tease her into a frenzy again and again.

And as he joined her once more with his full length, it happened.

Mac surrendered his control.

And she took flight.

The lifting charge propelled her like a fireworks shell into the sky. The bursting charge ignited her and scattered her into brightly colored sparks and stars. As a life of dancing light exploded around her, her soul caught on fire, burning her body until she thought only the spent shell of her would be left. She fell back to earth in time to receive the tremors of Mac's own explosion.

They lay there for a minute, each struggling to regain some of their shattered control. When he eased his weight off her, she made a sound of protest until he held her in his arms again. The possessiveness of his embrace choked her with emotion.

He was hers.

Whether they had a thousand tomorrows or only one there would never be anyone else for her. Mac had possessed a piece of her soul from the first moment they'd seen each other seven long years ago. She returned his embrace with a covetous hug of her own, twining her legs around his, snaking her arms across his chest, wanting to be a part of him once more.

"Without you, a part of me will always be missing," Kyra said in a voice filled with emotion.

As soon as she'd uttered the words, she knew she'd made a terrible mistake. He stiffened in her arms. Her words had cornered him. She quickly looked up and watched in horror the emotions playing in the bottomless depths of his eyes. Watched as shock replaced desire. Watched as the molten silver slowly hardened and shut her out. He was leaving even then.

"What's wrong?" she asked frantically, hoping against hope to keep him near.

He gently pushed her away from him and sat on the edge of the bed, his back to her.

"This was a mistake."

Mac's words cut straight to her heart.

"No, no! Something this good can never be a mistake." She placed a tentative hand on his shoulder, but he shrugged it off. "I feel better. I wanted you."

He turned to her, and for an instant she saw his eyes flicker with pain.

"Mac, please. Don't leave."

He didn't answer. He got up and with leaden movements took clothes out of his dresser. Kyra watched, frozen in place by disbelief. How could he possibly leave after what they'd shared?

As he shut the bedroom door behind him, she flopped back onto the bed. Her throat was constricted with pain and anger. Her heart ached with an anguish she knew would never be quelled.

She slammed both her fists beside her into the mattress. She'd be damned if she'd cry for him again. She'd asked for his love with open eyes; she'd known the risk before she started. Why was she surprised by the results? Mac didn't like to be cornered. He wasn't the staying kind. What had made her think time had changed him? Silly, frivolous, stupid, stupid hope.

The quiet, orderly life she'd created for herself had been shattered by Mac's return. Now she'd allowed the raw healing of her heart to be ripped open again.

With great effort she swallowed her emotions and locked them deep inside—so far into the corners of her soul, her heart wouldn't find them again.

There was one last thing she had to do before she left Park City. Then, with some semblance of balance restored to her life, she could return to her job, to try to expunge Mac from her heart.

This time forever.

Mac waited for the sound of water to stop before he gently knocked on the bathroom door. A tentative "Yes?" came from the other side.

"I . . . your clothes are in the dryer. You can use

the bathrobe on the back of the door until they're ready."

"You're leaving," Kyra said flatly.

"I'm going to go fix the generator." He laid a palm against the door and wished he had the courage to face her. He knew he'd hurt her. He also knew there was no way he could explain his behavior. How she'd scared him. How he'd scared himself. Not in a satisfying manner, anyway.

"You won't go down into the mine without me, will you?" she asked, and he could imagine her holding her breath for his answer.

He didn't know how to respond. He didn't want to lie to her, but right now he couldn't see any other way around it. He'd brave even her rejection to seal the shaft and the mountain's evil before she could get lost in its bowels and be snatched away from him forever. As long as she was alive he had a chance—they had a chance.

He heard Kyra fumble with the lock; then the door opened. She speared him with her glance, the green of her eyes almost colorless and completely devoid of life. He looked away, unable to bear the emptiness.

His lie was for her own good.

"Promise you'll come back for me," she said.

"I'll come back," he said.

"Promise!"

"I said I'd be back," Mac said gruffly, striding toward the bedroom door. He couldn't blame her for doubting him. After all, he wasn't planning on keeping his promise. But still, it hurt.

"Help yourself to whatever you want in the kitchen. I should be back sometime this afternoon." He had to get away from her, from the wildfire of emotion she'd ignited, from the unnatural fear her love had spawned deep in his soul.

Mac slammed the door behind him to relieve some

of the incongruous anger building up in him. He was mad at himself for caring, mad at Kyra for making him so vulnerable, mad at Alek for endangering them both.

He needed to get away from her. If he stayed, he feared he would let her talk him into going with him. Taking care of his mission would vent his pent-up angry energy and keep Kyra from sacrificing herself in the mine. He jerked on a pair of winter boots and snatched his coat off the floor. It was for her own good. He banged the front door shut, then jogged down to the resort chalet, where he'd left his truck.

After a quick conversation with Debbie, he found the package of parts he'd ordered and borrowed one of the plastic sleds they rented to parents to pull their young children along the ski trails.

A quick stop at Brad's house allowed him to retrieve his backpack; then he headed for the mountain. He set a grueling pace for himself, pulling the heavy sled behind him. If he concentrated on movement, he wouldn't be able to think, and right now the last thing he wanted to do was think; he knew he'd think of Kyra, and if he thought of her, he wouldn't get any work done. And the faster he took care of the mine, the faster he could get back to her and make up for the lie he'd been forced to tell her.

Kyra would be safe while he was gone. The painter would be by to finish the trim work in the living room. He'd arranged for Phyllis Vorel, Shana's medium, to spend the morning with Kyra. By the time they were done with their talk about Kyra's wolf-shadow his mission should be accomplished.

He hadn't seen any sign of Alek on his way up, but that didn't mean anything. The barricade he'd built over the shaft entrance seemed undisturbed; but then again, he and Alek had been trained by the same people. Once in the cave, Mac set up a powerful lantern and directed its beam on the generator. He hated to waste time fixing the damned thing, but a working elevator would make his task of sealing the mine safer.

Next he took off the oilcloth covering the machine and laid it on the ground beside it. He arranged his tools on the cloth and sat down to work.

As he started to clean the dirt and debris off the engine with a brush, his thoughts wandered back to Kyra.

"Go away!" he said out loud. But the harder he tried to keep her out of his thoughts, the stronger the images became. He saw her naked beside him, her soft, pliant body molding itself to his, and groaned in frustration.

"She's not perfect, you know," he told himself as he attacked the engine's dirt, trying to dissolve some of her grasp on his mind.

She'd blinded him. That was it. Just as she had seven years ago. And he'd let her—as he had that morning on the crater. So much hope lay in the spring green of her eyes that it infected him like a virus. She made him forget who he was, what he'd been trained to do. What he had to do still. *You arranged the meeting,* he reminded himself. *Yeah, and look where it got you. In a royal mess, that's where.*

"I didn't know." How could he have known the mountain would come between them?

But that was no excuse. He should have been prepared. He'd been trained to be prepared, to anticipate the unexpected, to shift his life around without a backward glance, at a moment's notice. Like a shadow, he thought, and sneered. Wouldn't Kyra get a good laugh at that notion!

She'd been more than a preoccupation for the past seven years, he realized with a reluctant sigh. An obsession he hadn't been able to drive out of his mind no matter how hard he'd tried. An obsession that had caused him to question everything in his life and caused his world to come crashing down around him. And his obsession had now put both their lives in jeopardy.

So how do you get rid of an irresistible fixation like Kyra?

"Why, you marry her, of course." His brother's smiling face entered his mind. "Then she either turns into your worst nightmare or she makes you wish eternal life existed on this earth, because you want to be with her forever."

Mac smiled at the memory. "I don't have to ask which Lynn is."

"Lynn is heaven," Brad had said.

To cover his own embarrassment, Mac remembered laughing at the besotted look on his brother's face. Now he knew exactly how Brad felt, and his soul cried because he'd found heaven and, to keep her safe, he'd had to push her away.

He'd had to make the same hard choice he'd made seven years ago. And this time he feared there would be no more second chances.

After this was all over he'd take a long vacation, he decided. Get her out of his system for good. He'd go to Hawaii—to that little house by the sea . . .

He shook his head. No, that wouldn't do. The house would remind him of happier days. The flowers would remind him of Kyra. And the sounds of the sea would forever remind him of making love with her.

What were the chances she'd let him crawl back into her bed and take up where they'd left off? What were the chances they could pretend they'd never heard of Alek or evil shadows on the mountain?

Slim to none.

Not after she found out he'd lied to her once again.

He doubted he could make her believe it was for her own good. Even a woman as generous as Kyra could take only so much betrayal before her trust was shattered irreparably.

Thinking of making love with Kyra had been a tactical error, he realized. His body responded strongly to the mere idea. As he remembered the feel of her skin on his, he cursed hotly. He could have sworn their bodies had actually melted one into the other. He could still smell her passion-flower fragrance and taste the warmth of her mouth.

He roughly tossed the brush aside and started to remove the old fuel filter. Making love with Kyra had been an experience he wouldn't soon forget. It was almost as if there were an added dimension this time that hadn't existed between them seven years ago, a binding of ties on a level beyond the physical one. He'd flown clear out of this universe and seen worlds he'd never dreamed existed. She'd left him feeling as if she'd read his soul. Such ungrounded notions had frightened him. They were so unlike him, so incomprehensible.

When she'd told him she'd never feel whole without him, it had reflected his thoughts so perfectly, his fear turned into panic. All the emotions coursing through him were unfamiliar, and knowing without a doubt that life without Kyra would be unbearable made him realize he'd have to save her from herself. He'd have to lie to her again—a breach of trust that might never be mended.

She'd given of herself so freely—then and now— he thought as he cleaned the cooling system. She'd brought out the human side of him all over again, the part the Institute had tried to train out of him. And that scared him more than his coming confrontation with Alek. Because, until he'd met Kyra, feelings had never come into play when he made a decision. Until Kyra, he'd forgotten the taste of failure. It weighed on him now like a cumbersome cross that seemed to span time itself.

The machine had a heart. A wound to the heart was always lethal, he knew from experience. And now was definitely not the time to develop soft spots. Alek would know, and Alek would go straight for it. A month ago Mac would have called them equally matched, but now . . . he knew Alek held the upper hand.

He swore.

That would leave them both losers. Even though he understood Alek's twisted sense of honor, he knew neither of them could accept anything less than their best effort. But with Kyra's safety on his mind, could he give anything more than a halfhearted attempt to deliver Alek from his ghosts? Yet anything but his best could see him dead.

Mac replaced the spark plugs, changed the spark arrester screen, and scraped the combustion deposits from the cylinder with a wire brush. Each scrape of the brush brought new images of Kyra—her smile, her eyes, her laughter. After a while he stopped fighting them. As he cleaned the oil pan, then refilled it with fresh oil, he relived each moment with her.

Remembering their lovemaking once again had his hands shaking as he tried to align the air cleaner. As he adjusted the carburetor, the memory of her long hair on his chest made him open the valve too far. He took a long, cleansing breath before he finished the fine-tuning and went on to the equipment controls. Even the gasoline fumes pouring from the can as he filled the engine's tank couldn't eclipse Kyra's scent from his mind.

You'd better shape up. Alek's not going to make any allowances for your love-blind mind. He rested the gas can on the sled. On the contrary, he thought, Alek would understand exactly how to use that weakness against him.

Mac stood back and looked at the generator. Now came the moment of truth. As he opened the fuel shut-off valve, moved the stop switch on and the choke lever to start, he sent a small prayer above. He pulled the starter and held his breath.

A dark cloud seemed to pass over him. He shivered involuntarily, breaking his concentration. The engine sputtered, coughed, and stopped. He swore, then bent down and made a few adjustments.

He brushed away an invisible bug and tried to start the engine once more. As the generator's tentative putt-putts were replaced by a full roar, he let out a whoop of triumph. With a few more tweaks here and there he soon had the engine purring.

After inspecting the cage and its related cables, he sent the elevator for a test run. It creaked and groaned but held firm. He brought the cage back up, then put his tools away.

Loading the tools on the sled, he wondered how long Alek would wait before springing on him. When they'd been partners he could have forecasted a blow-by-blow description of Alek's movements, but the years had made Alek unpredictable. How far had the workings of his mind degenerated over the past few years?

At least he'd made sure Kyra would be safe. She wouldn't be alone. The painter would be there. Phyllis, the medium, would be with her. And Debbie was just down the road. She'd promised to keep in touch with Kyra at regular intervals and to check on her at lunch.

Mac decided not to wait. He inspected and rebalanced the load in his backpack. Just as he was getting ready to climb into the elevator cage, he froze.

A thread of fear unraveled along his spine, bringing with it the unshakable feeling that a part of him was being ripped away. The pain in his head screamed for attention.

For an instant the past and present blurred. Another time on this mountain, another crushing blow.

"Use the key, Hallie. Give him what he wants. The papers. Use the key."

"You've got to lie still, Emory. The doctor's on his way."

Gentle fingers probed at the crushing wound pouring blood down his face. A voice reverberated through his mind. Hallie. What was she saying? He couldn't lie still. He had to make her understand. He had to keep her safe from his mad partner. Darkness swam into his head. "Use the key, Hallie." A painful gasp, not his own, yet he felt its echo through his body. "I've failed you, my darling. I've failed you."

Disoriented, Mac shook his head to dispel the incongruous thoughts piercing him like shrapnel. Sweat trickled down the side of his face. The powerful lantern's beam burned through him. Dread nauseated him. Distant failure paralyzed him.

"No!"

His pack fell unnoticed to the rocky floor. Then he knew. And fear as he had never before known propelled him forward, pumping a surge of adrenaline through him. Like a green recruit, he stumbled into the sunlight.

He couldn't fail her this time. This time? He cast the thought aside. No time for that. He had to get to her. He had to keep her safe. But as he raced down the mountain like an elk with a wolf shredding its flank with sharp fangs, he knew he was too late.

Alek had played his trump card.

"Kyra!"

Chapter Eighteen

The shadow hated daylight; it was so much harder to be inconspicuous. As he slunk up the shaft, he hoped his rest had been long enough. He didn't feel quite up to par yet, but the fool in the cave insisted on rushing things.

Didn't McKane realize waking up the dead was never a good idea? And trying to revive that rusty elevator, he was certainly making enough racket to stir the wretched souls lost in the cesspool at the bottom of the shaft. Didn't he realize sealing the mine would do him no good? It would only make things more complicated for everyone concerned—himself included.

No matter; the sunlight would soon fade, and the shadow knew his strength would be restored. He couldn't be stopped—not until his full vengeance had been exacted. Not until Kyra was his.

He filled the cave with his presence and saw McKane bent over the generator. As the engine sputtered tentatively, the shadow smiled and inserted a finger into the whirling parts. As the engine died, he roared with laughter.

The man didn't even notice his presence. What a pity! The shadow inserted a probing finger into the fabric of McKane's mind. McKane brushed the intrusion aside, but he was there long enough to find the reason for the distraction: Kyra. It was pathetic to see a man so besotted with a woman. A particular failing to which he'd never fallen prey.

A thought entered his mind. In this weakened state, perhaps McKane's mind could be tampered with. But no, the other was already engineered. Redrawing his plans would take too long and use too much of his precious energy.

Killing McKane, as pleasant as it would be, would also drain his stamina. He needed to conserve. He couldn't afford to squander even an ounce of vitality, not when he was so close to victory—no matter how sweet the kill.

What a shame! The potential was so much greater here, the opponent so much worthier in strength than any he'd encountered over the past eight decades. Fighting between equals brought a certain amount of respect—something he hadn't felt since his attempt to reclaim his due from Hallie. And she'd been a woman.

The shadow sighed. Better stick with the other. McKane wasn't the issue anyway. He would die before sunrise, one way or the other. And Kyra would come to him like a willing sacrifice—as they all had. She was a strong woman, but like Hallie, her weakness was her emotions. In the end she would want the blanketing oblivion he would offer her.

The shadow carefully set a path in the shelter of the trees and found the man on his belly, watching the cave entrance through a pair of binoculars. As a puffy cloud temporarily covered the sun, the shadow eased over his servant.

The time is now.

The man nodded and got up.

Red Granger will arrive at 9 to finish the trim in the living room. Mrs. Phyllis Vorel, the medium, will arrive at 9:30 to talk with you. Debbie will bring you some lunch. I'll be back as soon as possible. Mac.

Kyra was still staring at the terse note Mac had propped between the salt and pepper shakers on the table when the doorbell rang.

Debbie had already called twice to check up on her, once on the pretense of giving her a report on Misty and once to ask her if Mac had left her with enough food to make a decent lunch. The painter was already at work in the living room, so this latest intrusion must be Mac's medium. How kind of him to have arranged so many distractions for her, she thought bitterly as she strode toward the entry hall.

He didn't trust her anymore than she'd learned to trust him. What did that say about the chances of their relationship lasting longer than a holiday? They looked grimmer than the divorce statistics for the population in general.

She flung the door open with the intention of sending the medium tripping right back to her crystal ball. She had an open mind when it came to things that couldn't be explained or seen. She believed in ESP, ghosts, and angels, and she had a new appreciation for things unknown. What she didn't like was being manipulated like a child who was too stupid to take care of herself. If she heard the phrase "for your own good" once more in her lifetime, she would throw a tantrum even a two-year-old would envy.

The small, colorless woman standing before her

was the last thing Kyra expected to see. The cheerless effect of her faded brown felt hat, calf-length brown coat, and scuffed brown boots was lightened only by the drab beige scarf tied around her neck and the beige gloves on her hands. The only spots of color were the artificial rouge reddening her cheeks.

"Mrs. Vorel?"

The woman's smile was tentative at best, and Kyra wondered if she'd come on this visit of her own accord.

"You must be Kyra."

Kyra stepped aside and opened the door wider, inviting her visitor in. "Come on in. Can I get you a cup of coffee?"

Mrs. Vorel's eyes darted about before she entered the condo. "No. I can't stay long."

She wiped her boots on the mat but refused to take them off, or to let Kyra hang her coat in the closet. Reluctantly, she perched on one of the kitchen chairs.

"I don't know how much help I can be." Mrs. Vorel sat in perfect finishing school style, back straight, hands daintily laced in her lap, and ankles crossed.

Making an exception to her usual tea rule, Kyra poured herself a cup of coffee. She needed the caffeine jolt. "I'm not sure how these things work. Mac said you came highly recommended, and that you've had experience with redirecting spirits to their proper planes."

"I have." Mrs. Vorel concentrated her gaze on her twisting thumbs.

"But . . ." Kyra urged, sensing hesitation on the woman's part.

Suddenly the woman looked up, brushed one hand in the air in dismissal, and smiled. "I'm just being a silly old woman."

"If you have any reservations, I need to know."

245

Kyra took a sip from her mug and leaned her backside against the counter.

"What's happening here is wrong, terribly wrong."

"What do you mean?"

The woman's hands fluttered before her like startled birds. "Driving up the mountain to meet you, I sensed a strength to this spirit that frankly scares me." Her eyes widened. Her voice lowered. "It's suffocating."

Great: a medium who was afraid of ghosts. A lot of help she would be. "What can you tell me about him?"

Mrs. Vorel hesitated, opened her mouth, and closed it again. Hefting up her shoulders, she seemed to regroup. Her tawny eyes took on a brightness that did nothing to lessen the chill this odd woman's presence imparted.

"There are two strengths in this world," she said. "Darkness and light. One exists only if you believe in it. The other is salvation. But because darkness seems insipid it seeps into small gaps and spreads rapidly. Before you realize it's there, it blinds you. It breeds fear. And fear feeds on itself and grows. This spirit has accumulated enough darkness to swallow souls whole."

Mrs. Vorel's eyes implored understanding. Kyra couldn't quite follow the nonsense prattle.

"So how do I stop him?" Kyra asked, mug level with her lips, ready to take another sip.

Mrs. Vorel stood restlessly, poised as if for flight. "I don't know." She twisted her hands together as she spoke. "I sense you are the key."

The coffee's aroma mixed with the paint fumes, making her slightly nauseated. "The key to what?"

"To the end. To the beginning. The images I'm getting don't quite make sense."

Kyra set her mug solidly on the counter. "I don't understand."

"Unless you can ask the right question you must leave and never come back." Mrs. Vorel's voice was harsh, practically spitting out the words.

Kyra recoiled from the urgent plea in the woman's eyes, from the violence in her voice, from the chord of recognition they stirred inside her. "What question?"

"You alone know it."

"No, I don't. Help me."

"I'm afraid I can't." The slight shake of Mrs. Vorel's head and the deepening of her frown made her seem genuinely sorry for her impotence.

"I can't leave," Kyra said.

"If you leave, the spirit's strength will die."

Something was wrong. But what? "How can that be, when he's managed to live all this time? You're wrong; there's no point in leaving. As you said, without me there can be no end. I must stop it."

She felt the force of this inner knowledge punch her in the stomach. If she left, there would be no end—for her, for Mac and Alek, for the people living on the mountain. Yet a restlessness settled over her.

"Can't you see all this started with your arrival?" Mrs. Vorel inched toward Kyra one slow step at a time until the toes of her boots touched Kyra's stockinged feet. "You woke him, don't you see? And his waking has stirred more than you can comprehend."

She remembered Mac's explanation of the experiments in the mountain. Had her arrival in Utah over a month ago reawakened the shadow, causing the Pandora protons' mutation? Hadn't Mac said the trouble with the equipment had started then? Could it be possible that the shadow and the Pandora effect were the same? She shuddered at the thought. No, of course not.

"Like what? What can't I understand?" Frustration coursed along the tensed muscles of her body.

The tawny eyes narrowed to slits. "Your husband

is right to worry about you. Many lives hang in the balance, including his."

"My husband? Who, Mac?" She shook her head in short, rapid strokes. "Mrs. Vorel—"

"I cannot say which way it will go. The spirit has a strong will, and what he plans for you is beyond imagination. It is pure evil. Do you understand?"

Mrs. Vorel was too close. The woman's intrusion into her personal space had her throat tightening and her nerves jangling. She escaped with a sideways turn, grabbing her mug as she went. Twisting the sink's faucet to wash the cup, she tried to make sense of the words. There was none. She was letting herself get caught up in dramatics. *Get back to basics.*

"What can I do to help him find peace?" Kyra placed the mug on the drain board on the counter.

"I cannot sense anything, only evil."

She whirled around, crossing her arms beneath her chest. "Would it help if you got closer to him?"

Mrs. Vorel became agitated. Her eyes widened. Her hands fluttered. She cleared her throat. "I cannot in all good conscience get any closer to his source. I have a family of my own, you understand. My daughter is about to make me a grandmother for the first time. I only agreed to the consultation because of your husband's insistence, and because I owed Shana a favor. . . ."

"I understand."

"I must leave now. I sense the cresting of a wave. There is much danger here. I would advise you to leave, too."

The woman skittered to the front door. Grabbing the knob, she turned back to Kyra. "You have reached a crossroad, and only you can choose the path. You must find the key."

Kyra's mind wanted to scream in rebellion. She was tired of hearing about this damned key everyone wanted her to find. "What key? Where do I find it?"

"I sense a great capacity in you to transcend. If you insist on facing this wretched soul, perhaps . . ." She shook her head, pursing her lips.

"Perhaps what?"

The woman sighed heavily, reached for Kyra's hands, and squeezed them. "Your heart will be your guide. Listen. You must listen."

Exhausted, baffled, and more than a little irritated, Kyra let out a frustrated sigh. She ripped her hands from the woman's strangling hold. Her temples pounded and a dizziness, whirling the world around like a spinning top, made her believe this discussion would drive her into pure madness. She wanted nothing more than to turn back, to shut the door on this horrible daytime nightmare getting more complicated by the minute and run, to pretend none of this had happened at all.

But it was too late for that. She had no choice but to go and confront her deepest fears, confront the shadow on his own ground.

Mrs. Vorel crossed the threshold into the sunlight and kept walking down the short path to the road. "You must ask yourself one question, dear."

"What?" Kyra held on to the door, seeking support.

Mrs. Vorel threw open her battered Volvo's door and paused, looking at Kyra over the car's roof. "Can you risk the life of the man you love?"

"What do you mean?"

As if being ingested, Mrs. Vorel slipped into the car. "I see the shadow of death black all around him."

Kyra wandered restlessly around the kitchen, wiping already clean counters, sweeping an already crumbless floor, straightening an already neat pile of newspapers in its green recycling bin. Could Mrs. Vorel be right? Was she putting Mac's life at risk by staying? Could she save him as easily as walking away from this mountain and staying away forever?

Then why did it feel wrong? Why did her instincts insist she had to go to the mountain, to face the shadow, to save Mac?

Placing the dried mug into the cupboard, she knew she couldn't stay here. She either had to leave and keep going, or she had to swallow her fears and face the mountain.

If only the medium hadn't added the cost of Mac's life to the balance, making her feel that whichever road she chose would be the wrong one.

Remembering her vow of decisiveness, she headed for the laundry room and retrieved her outdoor clothes. In the end she had no choice at all. The destructive energy had to be dismantled. Being its target, she was the only one who could do it. If she left Mac alone to deal with it, the shadow would suffocate him. If she went, she could divert the shadow's attention to herself, and save Mac.

This silver shadow had stolen everything from her—her family, her heritage, her inheritance. She'd be damned if she let him steal anything more. If Mac was ripped from her life once more, it wouldn't be because of an angry man who'd died decades ago. Maybe they could never sort out the differences between them, but at least Mac wouldn't die another of the shadow's victims.

Rounding her shoulders against the wind, she headed down the narrow, winding road leading to the chalet.

She couldn't help smiling when she walked into the Mountain Swift resort and spotted Misty half-buried in a box beside a toddler. Misty's bottom wagged her pleasure, and the little boy giggled as he tried to catch the dog's nonexistent tail. The sight lightened her gloomy mood.

"No! My ball, Mifty. Mine!" the little boy exclaimed as Misty emerged from the box with a bright blue ball.

"Hi!"

Kyra turned at the sound of Debbie's voice.

"Looks like they're having fun." Kyra smiled and returned her attention to the boy and the dog.

Debbie, elbows on the counter, leaned her chin into her hands. "They are. Misty's a great baby-sitter. Her energy level and her curiosity match Cameron's perfectly. Yet somehow she manages to keep him out of trouble. I don't suppose you'd consider selling her?"

"I've kind of grown used to having her around. I'd miss her."

"Well, it was worth a try. Mom usually takes care of Cameron, but she had an appointment in Salt Lake this morning. Mike—that's my husband—will come by after lunch to take him home. It's a good thing we're not too busy this morning." Debbie paused for a minute. "How are you feeling?"

"I'm fine." Physically, anyway. Mentally, she was a mass of contradictory voices. She wasn't sure she'd made the right decision. If she gave them half a chance, the what-if scenarios would drive her crazy before the shadow could kill her. "I'm still a little tired, but I guess that's to be expected."

"You should be in bed resting," Debbie said in a motherly tone. "Mac said he expected you to take it easy today."

"I'm fine, really." Kyra watched as Misty and Cameron fought over the slobbered-on ball, wishing she could share in their unadulterated pleasure. "Mac's been making too many decisions for me lately."

"Really?" Curiosity danced in Debbie's brown eyes.

"I've discovered he's not very good at keeping promises." Kyra leaned her weight against the counter on one elbow, watching the show the boy and the dog unintentionally put on for her.

"That doesn't sound like the Mac I know." Debbie fiddled with an already neat display of sunglasses, then rearranged the bright red Christmas bow on top. "You're good for him, you know."

Kyra turned to look directly at Debbie. She wasn't sure how to comment. She knew Mac cared for her in his own way. He couldn't have loved her so tenderly this morning if he didn't. And she loved him. But love didn't seem to be enough, and it didn't necessarily mean there was a future for them.

Debbie pushed the plate of Christmas cookies toward Kyra. She took one for herself and split it in half. "He's not an easy person to get to know," she ventured after swallowing a bite of the shortbread star.

"No. He certainly isn't." *Romancing a stone would be easier.*

"I've never seen him worry about anyone the way he worried about you last night. That's saying a lot about Mac. He's not very good with people."

"No kidding."

Debbie crumbled off another bite of cookie. "Just because he can't tell you how he feels doesn't mean he's not feeling."

"Umph." Kyra turned away and looked out the wide windows toward Eaton Peak. Another time, another place, their love would have had a chance to bloom. But with so much mistrust between them it had withered before it had a chance to flower. Now she had to make the most important decision she'd ever made—a decision where life and death literally hung in the balance. "It's just not that simple."

"What do you mean? If you love him and he loves you, what's the problem?"

"What do you know about Mac's life before he opened Mountain Swift?" Kyra turned back to the counter and absently took one of the cookies from the plate.

Debbie shrugged. "Not much. Like I said, he's not an easy person to get to know. I do know that you're bringing out his softer side. When he phoned last night, we had the longest conversation we've ever had, and if he's shutting you out, it's because there's a good reason."

The cookie stopped halfway to her mouth, her appetite for it gone. "You're married. Do you trust your husband?"

Debbie nodded emphatically. "With my life."

"Does he trust you?"

Debbie didn't hesitate. "Of course."

"If you didn't trust each other, do you think your marriage would last?"

"Probably not."

Kyra absently rubbed the green sugar from the tree-shaped cookie. "There you have it. Mac doesn't trust me. And I'm not sure I can trust his promises any longer. He lied to me once. I have a feeling he's lying to me again."

Debbie reached for Kyra's hand, stilling its nervous action. "Don't give up on him. He loves you."

"But is love enough?" Kyra looked into Debbie's brown eyes, half hoping she'd find reassurance in their liquid warmth.

"There's something else, isn't there?"

She looked at the boy and the dog playing so well together. She wanted that scene unfolding in her own home—a baby of her own, a devoted husband like Debbie's, ready to take over its care when needed, the roots both would give her. The longing almost tore her heart from her chest.

She wanted this with Mac for however long he would stay—a year, a decade, a lifetime.

Kyra searched her pockets for her gloves. "Would you mind if I left Misty here for a little while longer?"

Debbie smiled brightly. "You'd be doing me a favor."

"Thanks."

When Debbie found out Kyra was planning to

walk to Brad and Lynn's home, she insisted that Kyra eat some lunch first, then got one of the resort workers to give her a ride up the mountain in his truck.

As Kyra waved John, the trail groomer, good-bye, the skin along her spine prickled. She fished her key out of her pocket and shook the feeling away, putting it down as a reaction to being outside after her ordeal yesterday. She'd change, putting on lots of warm layers. Then she'd feel better. She'd go find Mac. Lies or no, he needed her, and to end the shadow's reign of terror she needed him. She might not trust him with her heart, might not be able to trust him to stay, but she did trust his strange code of honor, and therefore trusted him with her life.

She closed the door behind her. The air in the house seemed foreign, thick. She stomped her snowy boots on the small rug before removing them. The house seemed oddly dark for all the sunshine outside the drapeless windows. She shrugged out of her coat and hung it on a peg. She shivered. Mac must have turned down the heat. A deep sense of inevitability burned in the pit of her stomach and radiated out.

So it had started.

Someone was here. She wasn't ready. How far had Mac gotten on his repairs? Where was the key? What was the key? Her mind whirled. Her body shook. She wanted to flee, fast and furiously. She wasn't strong. Never had been. She never made a fuss. She didn't confront.

Swallowing thickly, she stepped into the hallway. Mac could die, and it would be her fault. She should have left when he'd asked her. Then none of this would have had to happen.

Hearing breathing ahead, she stopped. The shadow was here. Could she find the right question? Could she find the key? Could she end the curse here?

Anticipation of a resolution drove her forward into the hall. A cold, unexpected voice jelled the blood in her veins.

"There you are. I've been waiting for you."

Chapter Nineteen

Kyra froze at the sound of the cold voice, which seemed to come out of nowhere. Not the shadow. It took her a second to place the voice.

Then she shuddered.

As Alek rose from the recliner, she heard the almost silent sigh of fabric against fabric. He appeared as a dark silhouette against the backdrop of an ice-blue sky.

In her thoughtless rush to reach Mac, she'd forgotten all about Alek. Where had this act-first-think-later attitude of Mac's gotten her except in deeper trouble? What now? *Buy yourself time to think.*

"Now look what I've done," Alek said in mock remorse. "I've frightened the little rabbit." He approached her, his footsteps as quiet as Mac's on the maple wood floor. "Don't be scared, Kyra. I won't hurt you."

Those words brought back a flood of warnings. *He won't hesitate to use you against me. He cracked. He has no conscience anymore.* She moved reflexively, matching Alek's forward movement with a step back.

"You can't leave, darling. I need you."

A mantle of black ice settled over her shoulders, making her shiver as violently as she had last night. Something about Alek felt ominous. He exuded a cloying darkness that seemed to suck the heat from the air. Whatever game he had in mind could only be dangerous. Abandoning her plan to stall for time, she whipped around and raced for the door.

"Now, sweetheart, don't make me hurt you."

Strong arms wrapped themselves around her torso, wrenching her away from the door. As her fingers slipped from the knob, Kyra gave a cry of protest and found herself pinned against a rock-hard chest.

She tried to push herself away from him but couldn't. Darkness and despair flowed into her like a murky river. She was drawn into the swift current, pulled by an undertow. What was happening? Why was she feeling this way? Sadness engulfed her, threatening to drown her. Never had she felt such dire bleakness. With horror, she realized that the more she fought this suffocating darkness, the more she was drawn into it. She stopped struggling.

"That's better," Alek said. As he moved her limp body to the living room, the overpowering feelings receded.

She sat docilely on the sofa where he had placed her, waiting for her heart and her breath to return to normal, waiting for her jangled thoughts to slow. *What is happening? Why?* The rhythmic motion of her hands on her thighs stroking away the dark emotions helped calm her.

Kyra looked up at Alek, who sat on the coffee table watching her. His dull blue Siameselike eyes appeared as dead as a corpse's. The sweep of black feelings had shown her Alek's soul, and she hadn't liked what she'd glimpsed. The man's heart had been eaten away by melancholy. Misery had spread like a disease, leaving only the shell of a man who played cruel games.

Ordinarily, she would've felt sorry for Alek, but she'd felt the shadow seep into him, she'd felt the evil intent, and she knew that if she were to survive, she'd have to tread carefully. Alek wasn't totally himself. He wasn't merely a complication. He was part of the shadow's plan, for her and for Mac.

What had caused this new sensitivity, she couldn't have said, but it frightened her and gave her hope all at once.

Kyra swallowed hard. She needed time to think. Making quick decisions and acting on them had never been her strong suit. But mulling over the situation in this instance was out of the question. Her future was in her hands, and the rest of her life depended on quick and accurate action.

Overwhelmed by the dark remnants of emotions still shredding the atmosphere, she closed her eyes and rocked back and forth, rubbing her thighs with the palms of her hands. The fingers of feelings eased their grip on her. Alek said he wouldn't hurt her, but the man had no heart, no conscience. She had to assume he was lying. What she had to do was buy herself time.

She stopped rocking, stopped rubbing, and opened her eyes. No matter what she did, someone would die. It might as well be someone who wanted to. Understanding cleared away the doubts from her mind. She realized Mac had wanted to keep her away from the mine so she wouldn't be caught in the middle of his struggle with Alek. A struggle in which Mac hoped to give his friend the peace he'd sought since his wife's murder. A struggle to the death.

"I'm glad you've decided to cooperate," Alek said. He glanced down at his watch. "The time isn't right, but we've gotta move. Your lover might come back, and that wouldn't work at all. Come on."

Alek rose and gently pulled on her elbow to help her up.

"I'm cold," Kyra ventured, trying to buy time. "I need to change."

Alek considered her request for a moment. As if deciding he needed her warm and alive, he nodded. "All right, but leave the door open so I can see you at all times. Don't try anything stupid. I'm not a patient man."

She walked to her room slowly to give herself a chance to work out a plan. With a leisure she didn't feel, she opened a drawer and selected several layers of clothes. Alek watched her every move. She knew he'd pounce on her without a moment's hesitation.

She shut the drawer with an angry slam. She had to act fast; act on her strengths. Obviously, she wouldn't be able to overpower Alek. He was much stronger, and she had a feeling his mental instability added to his physical strength. Her ability to build things wouldn't do her much good. But, she thought with a slow smile, I am good at one-on-one relationships with clients. She often heard the meaning behind the words uttered, and she could keep someone talking until she was sure she understood what he wanted.

Kyra pulled off the sweater she wore and added several layers before she replaced it. If she could keep Alek talking long enough, she might be able to delay his plans for Mac, and if she was very good, she might even be able to make him change them. Standing before the mirror, she distracted Alek's attention to her face with one hand running a brush through her hair. All the while her other hand furtively reached for the decorative obsidian cutting tool on the dresser. It was part of Lynn's collection of pottery and primitive tools, spread over nearly every piece of furniture in the house.

She looked straight at Alek in the mirror. "You and Mac were good friends, weren't you?" She infused her voice with as much warmth as she could muster. The hand clutching the adze carefully placed the cold object in the waistband of her pants.

"The best." Alek leaned against the doorframe and watched the movement of Kyra's brush in her hair.

"What can you tell me about him?" She kept each stroke slow and seductive, letting the gold in her hair catch the afternoon light shining through the window.

Alek smiled, bringing a faint glimmer of warmth to his cold eyes. "I see the Ram hasn't changed. He never was one to talk much, but he never missed a beat. Always the action man. What's he told you?"

"Not much," she said, forcing a sigh of regret. Hopefully, Alek wasn't as schooled as Mac was in the subtle art of deciphering the nuances of body language and would react as she planned.

"He's never cared for anyone before you."

Their eyes met and held in the mirror. Perhaps Alek saw too much; she couldn't afford to have him see through her plan. She smiled warmly. "He said you were very observant."

"We know each other too well." He shifted his weight and crossed his arms over his chest.

"He called you 'brother.'" She held her breath, hoping she'd taken the right tack.

"I was." He broke the eye contact and looked down at his well-worn boots. She let her breath out slowly, gaining confidence with her small success.

"I've never had any family," Alek continued. "I grew up in the foster home system. But I was a handful; I never stayed in one place long. Mac had alienated himself from his family with all the trouble he got himself into." Alek glanced up again and smiled. "So you see, we were two of a kind. Before the Institute got him, he was a real rebel without a cause.

After . . . well, he had a cause, all right, and that made him very dangerous. They funneled his idealism—our idealism—until we were blind."

"What did they do that was so bad?" She placed the brush on the dresser but didn't let go of it.

"They used us." Alek sneered. "Like robots. And we were just as expendable. One dies, grab another one off the assembly line. What does that say about our society? There are so many lost souls out there, trying to find a way to make their mark on the world, all ready to be snatched up by empty promises."

"I don't understand." God, she seemed to spend her life saying that lately.

As he approached her, Alek's gaze never left hers in the mirror. "I can see how you wouldn't. You're full of ideals, too."

When Alek reached for her hair she forced herself not to shrink from his touch.

"It's beautiful," he said. His eyes glazed with a faraway look. "Anna had long hair, too. And soft, just like yours. But hers was midnight black."

Kyra turned around and faced him, leaving the brush on the dresser. "How did the Institute kill your idealism?"

As he moved a step back, faint regret registered on his face. The hard edge framing his mouth returned. She'd made a tactical error.

"They had us believing we were helping people and the environment. And don't get me wrong, sometimes we were. But their methods often put the very people we were helping in danger. They never warned anyone of the risks."

He gave her a crooked smile that held no cheer. "Let me tell you about your lover, darling. Let me tell you how we tried to save the world and failed. Like the time we were sent to rescue a small town in Colorado. It was wiped out by mercury poisoning from a runoff we thought we'd taken care of. Bet you never heard of it. Things like that never make the news. You know why? Of course not. Things like that never make the news because we also make sure nobody knows about them. Not even the people dying because of us."

His eye contact deepened, his chin thrust out, his arms folded across his chest, giving him a defensive look. "Then there's the town in Idaho that was never told they were exposed to high levels of radiation from some illegal testing. We stopped it, but for those people we were too late. Most of them have cancer now, and they'll never be told the real reason why."

"What about all the good you did do?" Kyra held on to the edge of the dresser for courage.

Alek whipped his hand through his greasy blond hair, turning away from her, then spinning back to face her. He caged her against the dresser by leaning his weight on the hands he'd placed on either side of her. "The last year I was there, we handled two hundred and sixteen special projects. *Two hundred and sixteen.* What does that tell you?"

She tried not to flinch at the sour breath fanning her face. "That you helped a lot of people."

"No!"

Alek pushed himself away and paced an agitated, tight half circle around her, allowing her no escape.

"It tells you there are more people out there interested in making a buck now than there are trying to preserve what we've got so our families can enjoy it later. For generations and generations. It tells you that a few have power, and the rest of us are at their mercy."

"You're wrong." She played with the hem of her sweater, wondering if she should try to use the adze now, or if she should keep trying to distract him.

Stopping his pacing, Alek looked at her with disbelief. Then he tipped his head back and laughed.

"You haven't been hurt enough to understand the truth."

Not hurt enough? She supposed against his losses the betrayals she'd suffered would pale. But yes, she'd been hurt enough to understand more than he thought.

He reached for a strand of her hair again and let if flow through his fingers before letting it fall back into place. His eyes took on a blank look. "Life is so precious, but our failures snuffed it out as if it had no worth."

She picked up the brush and tried to wipe away the dead feel of Alek's touch with the rough bristles. "So why do you keep doing it?"

He blinked as if he hadn't understood her question. "Because I must. If the balance isn't evened out, there will always be this skewed power. I can't stop. Not until there are no more secrets. Until everybody is equal. Then . . . then there'll be peace."

Kyra grew uncomfortable at the feverish blush coloring his face and the nervous excitement making his cheek twitch. His eyes opened wide, allowing the white, visible all around the bright blue pupils, to give him a fanatical look.

"That's what I want, too," she said calmly, while desperately hoping Alek wouldn't choose this moment to become completely unglued.

Once more, Alek looked at her without recognition, blinking as if he was trying to focus on something he wasn't sure was there.

"Killing won't bring you peace," she continued, edging her hand toward the adze pinching her waist. Just in case; she'd be ready.

"Peace . . ."

As Alek's eyes became wilder and more unfocused, her breath quickened.

"I can help you," she said in a soothing tone.

"No one can."

Oh God! Now I've done it. I've sent him over the edge. Fear rippled through her like a rock disturbing the surface of a pond.

His eyes darkened until none of the dull blue showed. They were a marked contrast to the prominent yellowed whites. His skin looked deathly pale against the black of his jacket and pants. He reminded her of one of those living-dead characters in a horror movie she'd once tried to sit through with a friend. She'd been able to leave the theater then. Today there was no escape.

The brush she held fell to the floor with a sharp thump. The noise distracted Alek and brought back some of his reason.

"Tell me about Anna," Kyra said before she had a chance to think through the wisdom of her decision.

"Anna," Alek whispered. His eyes softened. His hand reached for her hair and she held her breath. "Beautiful."

Suddenly he clasped her against his chest, squeezing the breath out of her with his ardor. "Anna, I'll be with you soon."

As Alek's eyes took on a pained, haunted look, she held herself still. He stroked her hair, and the unfocused pupils seemed to go back in time.

"Anna," he whispered, and smiled lovingly.

"Alek." He seemed to think she was Anna, and Kyra seized on his confusion to try to rectify the situation. "I want you to stay. I want you to stop killing."

Alek pushed her at arm's length. He brushed the side of her face with a cold hand. His head cocked to one side, his brows raised with resignation. "I have to fight for you. I have to make sure no more innocents die."

Kyra forced herself to hold him in a comforting way. "There are other ways, Alek."

"Not with these people." He shook his head sadly.

"Life means nothing to them. Killing them is the only way to stop them."

"But you can't kill Mac; he's your best friend."

"He was." Alek nodded woodenly, then squeezed her into another hug. "I'm so tired, Anna. I want to be with you. Mac will see to my honor."

"Mac won't kill a friend," she said softly, pushing away the knowledge that Mac had promised to honor his friend's wish.

"He will."

"Set Kyra fr—"

"I won't hurt her. I promise, Anna. I need her. When Mac's given a choice he'll make the right one. I wasn't given that chance with you." Alek kissed her then. Revulsion built in her stomach. "Wait for me, Anna. I won't be long."

"Alek . . ."

He placed a trembling finger on her lips. "Shh, my love. Soon."

Alek's hands slipped to her wrists and held them in a painful grip. A heavy silence reigned for several minutes. The faraway look disappeared. When he finally spoke his voice startled her.

"It's time to go," he said flatly. He dropped one of her wrists and pulled her along by the other.

He herded her into the small hall like a well-trained sheep dog. He helped her with her coat and boots, then prodded her along to the kitchen door. Before he opened the door he slipped a pair of handcuffs from his coat pocket and clipped one side of the loop to one of her wrists, the other around one of his.

"For your safety, you understand," he said.

She didn't understand, but didn't know how to get herself out of this situation. Praying desperately for inspiration, she hoped against hope that Mac had somehow managed to fix the generator and had already sealed the mine.

She'd forgive him for having lied to her. She'd be forever grateful. She'd made a mistake thinking she could handle the shadow and its evil. A terrible mistake. As Mrs. Vorel had predicted, she'd put Mac's life in danger.

Alek turned toward the living room and tossed something that landed on the wooden floor with a dull clang. He opened the door and jerked her wrist. "Let's go."

"Where are we going?" Kyra asked as Alek dragged her down the snowy deck stairs.

"Why, darling, I'm taking you to your lover. You should be thanking me."

His wide smile sent dread careening down to her knees, making them shake slightly. She swallowed hard. Alek turned back from her, pulling her along with him. They headed out into the snow at the back of the house. He barely left a track, while she sank to her knees with every step.

"How do you do that?" she asked, puffing as Alek waited impatiently for her to extricate herself from the snow.

"It's a matter of weight distribution. Think light and spread your weight over your whole foot, not just your heel or your toe."

She tried to follow his instructions without much success. She sensed his growing impatience but couldn't do anything to lessen her awkwardness. With each step she willed Mac to leave the mine, willed him to leave the area, all the while knowing her wishes would be futile because if he did make it back safely, he would find her gone. With Alek's calling card on the living-room floor, he would know what had happened. She had no doubt he would come for her—and walk right into Alek's trap.

The frigid metal slapping her wrist with each movement had her whole arm throbbing with pain. Alek took a different route to the mine than Mac had taken. It wound furtively around the dark shadows of the trees, making her jump involuntarily each time one moved in her peripheral vision. She tried to engage him in conversation several times, only to be told in terse clips to keep silent.

Despite the layers of clothes she'd put on and the fast pace Alek set, she felt as if ice water covered her body. She turned to look back and saw the wolf-shadow carefully tracking their progress from behind the rows of dark pines.

"Come on!" Alek jerked her cuffed wrist forward, making her stumble forward in the snow.

"I'm trying my best." She scrambled to her feet and defiantly took the time to brush the snow from her pants with her free hand.

Alek lashed his free arm out like a bullwhip and caught her chin painfully in his hand. "And I'm trying very hard not to lose my patience with you. I've got an appointment to keep and I don't want to be late."

"If you're in such a hurry, then go without me."

The wind blew a lock of greasy blond hair into his face. That, added to the crazed look in his eyes, made her immediately regret her impulsive words.

"Unfortunately, sweetheart, you're the door prize. I need you. Let's go."

He yanked her forward again, but this time she caught her balance on his sleeve and managed to keep up with him.

As they neared the entrance, he slowed. He placed her before him and pressed down heavily on her shoulders to make her crouch. Then he covered her mouth with his gloved hand. She tried to move away from the dirty taste of the leather, but he only tightened his grip, making the icy handcuff chain dig painfully into the side of her neck.

Still as one of the towering pines surrounding them, he watched the entrance.

She closed her eyes and concentrated her energy into a single thought. *Mac, watch out!* She willed him to hear her. She willed him to take heed. Tears of frustration prickled her eyes. Why had she been so stubborn? Why had she been so stupid? Why had she been so selfish? She'd placed all of them into an impossible situation. And all she would have had to do to avoid this was to turn her back on it and walk away, never to return.

So simple, so easy.

Knowing Mac was alive and safe, she would have learned to live with the ghosts left behind.

She would do anything to turn back time and reverse her decisions.

But she couldn't. And if she couldn't, she'd have to find a way to get out of this mess. Mac shouldn't have to die because of her mistake.

When she opened her eyes, it wasn't the mine entrance that drew her attention; it was the silver threads shining brightly on the dark wolf-shaped shadow only a few feet away from them. He shimmered away, leaving her feeling as if she'd seen a hallucination. The heavy knot in the pit of her stomach denied her thought. She'd seen him again. And he was waiting for her.

Alek nodded and tugged her to a standing position. "It's safe."

They stood inside the entrance, waiting for their eyes to adjust to the darkness. Kyra took in the blue plastic sled with the dirty engine parts and the tools, the abandoned backpack still heavy with its load, and the gleaming machinery by the elevator cage. The smell of gasoline and grease mixed with the dank, dusty air of the cave. The shaft wasn't sealed. Acid swirled up from her stomach. But Mac had left. Relief washed over her, tamping down the nausea. For now, Mac was safe.

"What now?" Kyra asked.

Alek smiled malevolently down at her, his crazed blue eyes black once more. "Now we wait."

"What makes you think Mac'll come back?"

Pushing her onto the elevator platform, Alek laughed wholeheartedly. He unlocked his half of the handcuff. She tried to jerk the metal cuff away from his hold, but he was too quick. Before she had time to realize what had happened, he slammed her against a rusted post on the cage. Metal clanged against metal and chained her wrist to a ring on the post. Her struggles were met with iron resistance.

"There's no use fighting, sweetheart."

Alek dangled the small key he'd used to free himself in front of her face. He moved to the edge of the platform. With great ceremony he held the key over the black abyss of the shaft.

"No!" Kyra stretched toward the key, fighting wildly against the impossible strength of tempered steel secured on iron, cutting her wrist in the process.

"Bye-bye." He laughed as he dropped the key. It disappeared with a series of pings decreasing in pitch. Then the sound died, and all she could hear was Alek's demented laughter.

Chapter Twenty

Mac rushed down the mountain at reckless speed, cursing himself with every step. How could he have assumed that Kyra would be safe in his home? He should have known Alek would have looked for her and found her if he thought her unguarded.

Well, it was all her fault, he tried to rationalize. All he'd thought about this morning was getting away from her, putting space between them so he could sort through all the powerful, unfamiliar emotions she'd managed to uncover, and sealing the mine so they could put this behind them and start exploring the future. If she hadn't muddled his mind so much, he'd have been able to think clearly. That wasn't fair to Kyra, of course, he immediately realized, but what if he lost her? He couldn't stand the thought and dismissed it firmly.

He couldn't lose her. Not this time.

His mind whirled like a top. She was still weak from yesterday's ordeal, and he knew his abrupt departure without explanation had hurt her. Even though he'd warned her about Alek, chances were she wouldn't be on the lookout for him. And, unlike himself, she hadn't received Alek's training—she wouldn't stand a chance against him. As he sped down the hill, a sinking feeling made his feet feel like lead blocks. Kyra was in terrible danger.

His truck waited at the bottom of the path he'd made to the mine shaft. He jumped into it and gunned the engine to life. He raced down the road, nearly plowing over two cars in his haste. The last stopped, brakes shrieking, its driver shaking an angry fist at him. But he didn't care. He had to find Kyra. He had to keep her safe.

He left the engine running and the truck door open and sprinted to the front door of his condo. He knew before he entered that Kyra wasn't there. No lights were on. No warmth blasted him. He searched with guarded expediency for clues to Alek's presence but there were none. Alek hadn't been here.

The tousled bed brought back images of the love they'd shared. His chest tightened. Panic edged into his bloodstream. He loved her. He couldn't bear to lose her. He tightened his fists by his sides and forced himself to breathe deeply. To help her, he had to stay grounded. He had to outsmart Alek.

Maybe Alek didn't have her. Maybe she'd gone looking for Misty and, knowing how worried he was about Kyra, Debbie had invited her to her home. Renewed hope had him bounding down the stairs two by two. He grabbed his cell phone and headed for his truck.

When Debbie answered her phone Mac launched into his interrogation without preliminaries. "Is Kyra there?"

"No, she's at your brother's. What's wrong?"

He should have explained. He should have warned Debbie not to let Kyra leave. But no, all he'd done was give sparse orders. He couldn't blame Debbie; the fault was all his. "When did she leave?"

"About an hour ago. Mac, what's wrong?"

Mac punched the off button without answering her question. He slammed the truck onto the mountain road, heading up toward Brad's house. For the first time, he noticed the late hour. Where had the time gone? Repairing the engine had gone smoothly, but he'd taken much longer to do the job than he'd thought.

The house sat unnaturally quiet in the dark of the long afternoon shadows. He parked his truck next door and walked cautiously around the house. He eased himself silently through the garage, and once his eyes had adjusted to the darkness, he slipped without a sound into the deathly silence of the house.

The housekeeper had been here. The scent of lemon furniture polish hung in the air. The breakfast mess he and Kyra had made yesterday morning was cleaned up.

He strained to hear, listening pointedly for breaths and heartbeats. He heard none. The sunflower clock on the wall seemed to beat in time to his nervous pulse. The refrigerator cycled on, puffing a wheezy hum. If Kyra had been here, she was gone now.

Or worse, Alek had beaten him to her.

In Kyra's room he saw her brush on the floor. The top drawer of her dresser was slightly ajar. Kyra had been here after the housekeeper had left. She'd gone in a hurry.

He was too late.

Controlling his rage, he sprang into action, letting his trained eye follow Kyra's trail. A shiny object, gleaming in the dying day's light, caught his attention. He crouched and reached for the small metallic piece. His fingers closed around the raised *V* on one side and the blind Lady Liberty on the other.

Alek had Kyra.

Mac's fist turned white around the coin. "If you hurt her, I'll make sure you suffer."

His gaze lifted to the picture window. A dagger of red pierced the horizon. In a few minutes the world would plunge into darkness. Even the rising full moon, half hidden in black clouds, wouldn't light his way to Kyra. He knew without a doubt that Alek had taken her to the one place on earth she shouldn't be—the mine.

And Alek would dangle her as bait.

If he wasn't careful, Mac knew he could easily fall for the trap.

Everything was going according to plan, the shadow thought as he hung in the dark pines near the cave entrance. At this very moment the final player trudged his way through the snow.

Even the wind had unwittingly helped by blowing away the cloud over the full moon to illuminate the last pawn's path. Did this mere mortal really think he could stop a need for vengeance as deep as his?

Will you walk into my parlor? said the spider to the fly. 'Tis the prettiest little parlor that ever you did spy. The shadow laughed heartily. *Yes, dear guests, welcome to my parlor. Feed me my last meal and set me free.*

My vengeance will be done.

He glanced at the patch of shimmery light by the cave entrance where Mac had just disappeared. The scent of lavender water filled the night air. Hallie, the poor fool, fluttered there. What did she hope to accomplish? If she couldn't reach Kyra away from his center of power, how did she expect to protect her while she was in his home?

As he approached her, he burst out laughing once more. *Even your love for your great-granddaughter won't be able to spare her her fate.*

Don't underestimate the power of love, Rolf.

What good is it doing you? My shield is too strong for you. You can't penetrate my home.

If ghosts could shiver, Hallie was shivering, her fear plainly etched in the vaporous planes of her face. Her anguish dissipated her power, rendering her to nothing more than an ephemeral white film against the snow.

Watch me, Hallie! Watch me as I kill the last part of you. Watch me buy you your place in hell!

Defeat weighed heavy on Kyra's shoulders. She leaned against the rusted post holding her prisoner, seeking reassurance from its strength, searching out its weaknesses. She closed her eyes and felt the quiet desperation of thousands of men eking out a living in the bowels of the mine. These ghosts couldn't help her. She'd have to come up with her own answers before time ran out.

For now there was nothing to do but watch the setting sun bleed red shadows onto the mountain's white snow and listen to the eerie whistling of the wind whipping through the cave opening.

And wait.

And hope Mac wouldn't come searching for her.

The shadows lengthened and clouds played peek-aboo with the moon, alternating her view from pitch darkness to a picturesque winter night's scene, then back again.

She felt Mac before she heard him. She started to yell out a warning when Alek's rancid glove clamped over her mouth.

"Now, now, darling," he whispered into her ear. "We can't have a party without the guest of honor."

Kyra aimed the heel of her boot at Alek's shin, but he neatly avoided her kick. He chuckled softly and tightened his grip around her, making it impossible for her to move.

Mac! Go! Please, Mac, go! She put all her energy

into the mental plea, then whimpered with disappointment against her leather gag when Mac stepped into the cave.

At that moment, Alek flipped the switch to the halogen lantern he'd hung beside him, bathing the cave in bright light and giving everything around it sharp, ghastly shadows.

"Glad you could join us, old friend," Alek said.

Mac blinked once against the unexpected bright light, then stood immobile by the cave entrance. Not an emotion, not a thought played on his well-guarded face.

When she realized how little she knew about the man she loved, her heart did a quick flip. When he was with her, his closed appearance was imposing enough, but here as he faced his friend—his enemy—his body had taken on a whole new stance. One that sent cold ripples fluttering through her body.

"See what I have for you?" Alek continued when Mac didn't answer his taunt.

"Let her go." Mac's voice was cold, impassive. She shivered.

"Now, you know I can't do that. Without her here, how else would I convince you to take a little ride with me?"

"You have my word of honor."

Alek shook his head. "I can't trust anybody's word. Not even yours. Not where she's concerned."

"If she gets hurt, I promise I'll prolong your hell."

"If you cooperate, she won't get hurt."

Alek's hand left Kyra's mouth. She heard the quiet slip of metal against leather. She wasn't surprised to find the cold point of a knife against her throat a moment later. She swallowed hard.

"Go, Mac," she ventured. "He won't hurt me if you're not here."

Alek chuckled. "Now you know that's not true, don't you, buddy?"

Mac's gaze never left Alek's face. He didn't say a word, but she sensed that the computer of his brain was going through computations of odds.

"Go," she pleaded.

"Why don't you slide that gun of yours over. Nice and easy now. Remember, I've got a very sharp knife right along your lady's carotid artery. So no tricks, no acts of bravery, no sudden movements."

To make his point, Alek pressed the knife's tip where Kyra's ear met her jaw until the skin broke. She heard a drop of blood splatter on the front of her light green jacket. Remembering Mac telling her that Alek had found his wife with her throat slit from ear to ear, she understood his unvoiced threat.

Please, Mac, don't buy into his intimidation.

When she saw Mac ease the gun from his waistband and hold it by the muzzle with two fingers, she felt her heart drop.

"Nice and easy now, slide it on over."

"He's not going to hurt me," Kyra said with a firmness that belied the jelly weakening her knees.

Alek swiftly moved the knife to the other side of her face and left a matching cut. Mac slid the gun toward Alek. Alek kicked the weapon into the shaft. It hit the side of the shaft, then broke uselessly apart as it fell.

"Why don't you start that engine for us and join us for a ride?"

When Mac didn't move Alek slid the knife to the center of Kyra's throat. "Five, four, three . . ."

Mac moved with controlled caution toward the generator.

"No, Mac, don't," she pleaded.

He ignored her. Within a minute the whole cave vibrated from the whir of the engine.

"Join us, won't you," Alek shouted to Mac above the din.

Mac stepped onto the elevator cage. Alek, using

Kyra as a shield, gestured toward the control lever that would set the contraption into motion.

"Take us to Pandora," Alek ordered.

Mac glanced at his backpack, askew on the cave floor.

"What's in there?" Alek asked.

"The Institute's seal."

Alek stood silent for a minute, then nodded. "Take it. However this ends, the job will be done."

Mac carefully set the pack on the elevator floor, then took his position at the controls.

The cables and wires, unused to activity, stirred to life. The elevator groaned and creaked. Kyra wondered absently whether the ancient cables were strong enough to hold their combined weights. Would the lines break at any moment and plunge them to their deaths? Fear numbed her. Her helplessness to do anything to save Mac, to save herself, sent her morale plummeting.

Someone's bound to make a mistake, she thought, fighting her discouragement. The knife's sharp blade against her neck was a vivid reminder that a mistake on Mac's part might cost her her life.

The elevator crept slowly down the shaft. The lantern illuminated the black walls, glistening with water. As the noise of the generator faded, the dripping water became more audible. The dizzy pings of the drops, falling but never ending, did nothing to calm Kyra's raw nerves.

The black walls soon gave way to green patches of fungus, glowing under the cold glare of the light. Dark shadows gyrated a pagan ritual on the moving walls, inviting the occupants to join the dance with their primitive movements. Fear, cold and raw, writhed along her spine and lodged in a solid lump at her throat.

With each passing level the timbers shoring up the walls grew damper. She'd expected to feel colder as the elevator went deeper into the mountain; instead she found herself growing warmer with each level they passed. Soon the elevator disturbed great curtains of wet slime, hanging like squirming serpents. The snakes threw their sludgy fangs at them. They whipped their oozy tails in anger at the provocation the elevator's passage made.

Closing her eyes against the gory spectacle, Kyra swallowed her revulsion. Echoes of the past reverberated through her brain in a schizophrenic whirlwind. Misery, so much misery. It clung to her like an octopus's tentacles, reaching for her heart, searching for her soul.

"Stop!" Kyra raised her free hand to one ear to block out the noise. As she doubled over reflexively, the knife dug into her throat and left its mark.

"Kyra?" Mac's voice, filled with worry, brought her back from the despair of ghosts past. She opened her eyes and saw him lunging toward her.

"Ah-ah-ah!" Alek warned, lifting Kyra up and repositioning the knife at her jugular. "Get back to your position, old man. The time for chivalry hasn't come yet."

Alek turned his sour breath closer to her face. "And you—try that again and you'll bleed to death. Tell her, Mac; tell her how long it takes someone to die with a severed carotid artery."

The squeaks of the elevator cables took on gargantuan proportions in the silence that followed.

"Do as he says, Kyra," Mac finally answered, his voice flat and even.

As they descended deeper into the squalid bowels of the mine, the temperature increased. By the time Mac slowed the elevator to a halt the shaft felt like a sauna. The manacle at her wrist now burned as if it had been heated by a flame. The musty air, unbearable as it was, would have been welcome compared to the rank smell of Alek's sour sweat, which gagged her as it fell in a steady stream into her hair.

As Mac eased the brake on, the elevator clattered a final grunt. Kyra lost her balance on the slippery surface and pitched against Alek, who held her firm.

"That's right, darling," Alek chuckled into her ear. "Lean on me. I've got the power. Your lover always had too much heart to be the best."

Alek angled Kyra slightly, clearing a path to the black tunnel carved into the rock. "Why don't you be a good boy and go get me Pandora's brain."

"That's not what you really want," Mac said calmly.

"Just in case." She felt Alek's smile against her cheek. "You were always second best."

In the interminable pause that followed, she thought her heart would beat right out of her chest.

"I'll need the lantern," Mac said coldly.

"Be my guest. Just remember, my knife is very sharp, and it's resting on her jugular. And it's a long way down into the sump." Alek chuckled. "Did you know that when someone fell in the olden days, even if they reeled them out right away, they died? Their flesh boiled away from their skeleton that fast. It would be a shame for such a pretty girl as your lady to meet such a grim end."

Kyra shivered involuntarily as the clear picture of grappling hooks, kept on the very ring from which she hung, came into her mind. She saw them being used to fish for the mangled remnants of fallen men. The pieces of body were rolled into sheets of canvas and placed in candle boxes to be taken back above. Nausea churned her stomach; acrid bile burned the back of her throat.

Mac unhooked the lantern. As he walked by, she could read nothing in his cold demeanor.

Eight beady red eyes stared back at her from the depthless black into which Mac headed. They shrieked and scampered away from the approaching light. As the light faded, and a heavy darkness settled around her and her captor, Alek started to whistle tunelessly.

She closed her eyes against the blackness and tried to block out Alek's discordant din. *Think, Kyra. There's got to be something you can do.* The germ of an idea took root.

"Alek?" Kyra made her voice as melodious and as calm as she could, acting on her idea before she had time to think it through.

"Um?"

"Tell me about Anna?"

Alek reached for a strand of her hair and fingered it. "Not now."

His voice caught. On and on he stroked. Kyra waited, as still as she could make herself, until a pitiful sound escaped him and she knew his thoughts had shifted. She said his name softly over and over again, hypnotizing him. He relaxed against her, and she sensed he thought he held Anna once more.

"It's time to go home now." She rubbed her head softly against Alek's cheek, thankful the darkness hid her distaste at the gesture.

He stroked her hair for what seemed an eternity. "Anna, what are you doing here?" His voice had taken on the faraway quality she recognized from her last encounter with it. He moved away suddenly. "You're all wet. You'll get sick."

"I-I don't feel so good." She added a few moans for effect. She had to play this role to the hilt. Mac's life might depend on it. "My stomach is cramping. I think it's the baby."

"No! It's much too early." Both of Alek's hands reached for her arms nervously.

"I need to go home and rest." Kyra sniffled.

"Yes, of course. Why is it so dark?"

Confusion laced Alek's voice. She knew she had to be convincing. "The power must be out. My hand is stuck. Can you do anything about it?"

She felt him reach for her manacled wrist. "How did this happen?" he asked.

"I don't know." She kept her words shaky and leaned on him. "I was asleep; then the next thing I knew I was shackled, and then you came in. I'm so grateful you found me in time. Help me, Alek. I'm so scared." She added a few sobs and hoped she wasn't overdoing it.

Alek held her tenderly and rocked her reassuringly for a few minutes. "It's all right. I'll get you out of here."

He sheathed his knife, then picked at the lock with something she couldn't see. To her horror, she saw the returning light. *No, Mac! Go back! Give me a few more minutes!*

Her mind worked frantically, trying to think of a way to warn Mac. If she could get Alek to call her Anna, maybe Mac would understand what she was trying to do and hang back until she was free.

She whimpered, doubling over as if protecting her stomach. "It hurts, Alek."

Her sobs were heartfelt when Alek whispered his concern tenderly in her ear. Mac was too far away to have heard. She had to try again before it was too late.

"Alek . . ."

"Shh, Anna, shh."

She felt Alek stiffen as Mac's light suddenly reached them. Despite the insufferable heat of the shaft, a cold wind blew and settled over Alek. The faraway look disappeared. All the tenderness and concern left his face. The shadow's influence had returned.

He whirled around, unsheathing his knife as he moved. He reached for her, grabbed her arms, and readied himself to pull her into position as his shield.

"No, Alek." Mac dropped the briefcase-sized box

he carried and placed the lantern on the ground beside it. "This is between you and me. How can I help you if you won't face me?"

Kyra could see the confusion on Alek's face. Then the dark shadow floating over them melded into Alek's body.

"He's not himself!" Kyra tried to warn Mac, but Alek's rancid glove silenced her.

"Remember Anna," Mac said, his eyes never leaving Alek's face. "Remember how you felt when they used her against you. Remember how you wanted to die."

Mac approached slowly. "Let me help you, Alek."

With a savage push that knocked her off her feet and left her hanging by her arm, Alek jumped off the elevator cage onto the tunnel floor.

As she tried to regain her footing, Kyra slid on the slimy surface of the cage bottom. Her arm felt as if it was ripping out of her body. Her wrist throbbed with pain. After several attempts, she managed to hang on.

Mac and Alek circled each other warily. Kyra saw that Alek, armed with his knife, held a distinct advantage. Then she remembered the adze at her waist. It wasn't much, but it was better than nothing.

"Mac, catch!" Kyra threw the adze in his direction.

He caught it deftly, but Alek chose that moment of distraction to charge. She gasped when she heard the rip of fabric, but Mac didn't seem hurt as he swiftly moved away.

As Mac and Alek parried and thrust, she spied the straightened paper clip Alek had used to pick at the lock. She strained to reach it, but even as she willed her sore shoulders to stretch and her fingers to extend farther, she knew her freedom lay just out of reach.

She changed position and tried to reach the makeshift key with her foot, to no avail.

As if it were a piece of clay, she worked feverishly at her hand, molding it and reshaping it to try to free it from the handcuff holding her prisoner.

Hearing a knife skitter on the hard ground, she stopped abruptly and whipped around to see who had lost the advantage. Disappointment flowed through her as she saw Mac on his knees, holding his right arm with his left hand.

Alek closed in for the kill. Mac rolled out of his way. By the time Alek recovered from his miss, Mac flowed to his feet and stood ready for the next attack.

Mac's well-aimed kick sent Alek's knife flying in Kyra's direction. It clattered on the metal platform and bounced against the iron column before coming to rest in the opposite corner from where she stood. A weighty silence filled the air as all three pairs of eyes followed the knife's travel.

A moment later, Alek knocked Mac to the ground with a ramming blow to the head. Mac groaned in pain. Alek launched himself at the knife.

"Mac!" Kyra called.

He tried to rise but fell back to the ground with a moan.

She strained her tether to kick the knife over the edge. She slid. Her arm jerked painfully against the handcuff. She scrambled up again.

"Mac!"

Alek recovered the knife from the far end of the platform. His gaze glued on Mac, he advanced maliciously toward the prone figure.

She cowered against the iron beam.

He's forgotten about me, she realized, controlling her urge to call to Mac once more. *Now's my chance.*

As Alek crossed her path, she jumped up. With all her might, she aimed both her feet at Alek's legs. As she fell, her arm jerked once more in its socket. The skin on her wrist tore. She skittered to regain her footing.

The slimy sweat on the metal, the slickness of his clothes, and the force of her blow propelled Alek toward the abyss of the shaft.

In a last desperate attempt to save himself, Alek reached up and caught the base of the iron beam. He hoisted himself back on the platform. Carefully avoiding the feet kicking at him, he raised himself up.

"Stand up," Alek said, panting. He waved his knife ominously in her direction.

Kyra tucked her feet beneath her to obey. When she wasn't fast enough Alek reached down and yanked her up like a rag doll. Her feet tried to find purchase on the slippery surface, but the rubber of one sole skidded from beneath her. It caught the side of Alek's boot.

He lost his balance.

Kyra, down on her knees, watched as surprise registered on Alek's face.

The knife dropped from his hand. It disappeared in the dark pit beneath the elevator cage. It fell, and fell, and fell. Then it hissed as it finally plunged into the hot water with a resounding splash.

Alek hung on to the edge of the elevator platform for an instant longer.

As she watched, he fell away in slow motion.

His eyes grew round with the inevitability of his situation. He understood his fate. He understood the pain waiting for him. And he didn't want it.

In a last frantic attempt to cheat the end, he reached up. He caught her free wrist with his left hand. And pulled her down with him.

Chapter Twenty-one

Kyra desperately tried to keep her footing on the slippery surface of the elevator floor while Alek's struggling weight pulled at her. The pain in her shoulder was almost unbearable.

If she did nothing, her arm would surely sever from her body and she would follow Alek into the boiling pit below. If she helped him, they would both live—until he got his footing. Then he would more than likely finish the job he'd started.

She wasn't ready to die.

But she had no choice.

Letting go of a living being simply wasn't an option, especially when he was acting under the influence of an evil shadow.

She strained the fingers of her cuffed hand until they curled around the chain between the manacles. The fingers of her other hand wrapped around Alek's wrist.

Ignoring the pain in her arm, she pulled with all

her might until she could push her body on the iron beam to which she was shackled and use it for more leverage.

Alek's body inched up until his other hand caught the edge of the elevator bottom. He tried to kick his leg up to climb back to safety. Kyra heard his frustrated groans. As she eased her grip on Alek's wrist, she noticed the silver shadow separating from Alek's body.

Alek sprang up.

His forehead creased.

His jaw squared.

His gaze bored through her with murderous intent. Both hands splayed wide before him, he lunged at her throat.

An angry *"No!"* exploded in her mind. Her head whipped around to find the shadow morphing into its wolf shape, baring its spirit fangs at Alek. A low rumble started deep in the mine and simmered threateningly.

She's mine. The savage voice seemed to come from the dark shadow and projected straight into her brain.

In the next instant the wolf-shadow launched itself at Alek's neck. Through its murky shape, she saw it rip Alek's carotid artery open. Blood sprayed in every direction. Bright red drops splattered like rain all over her light green coat. She thought she'd faint.

Alek's body slid from the platform. His mouth gaped open in surprise. When he realized his fate was inevitable his face transformed into calm acceptance. "I'm coming, Anna," he said simply as he plummeted into the blackness below.

Kyra closed her eyes and screamed to drown out the dull thumps of Alek's body hitting the shaft walls, the rip of fabric, the breaking of bones.

"Anna!" Alek's final piercing yell drilled through her own cries. As the greedy sump devoured him alive, she wept uncontrollably.

Deathly silence followed. Even the constant drips of water ceased for a moment, as if in awe of the pit they fed.

She slumped against the iron beam. When she wrapped her free arm around herself, she realized that her hand still held Alek's watch.

Fetid breath fanned her face.

Kyra opened her eyes.

The shadowy beast stood before her, Alek's blood staining its muzzle and chest. Its silvery color glowed, taking on an eerie quality.

He sat down, curling his bushy tail around his paws. *The time has come,* liebliche *Kyra. You will expunge your great-grandmother's sins.*

His mouth didn't move, but his voice bounced macabrely off the stone walls of the tunnel.

Fear as she had never known trampled through her, making her cower against the metal beam.

"Mac!" Shivers of dread racked spasmodically through her limbs.

The shadow cocked his head sideways and grinned. *He cannot save you. With my help, your lover has been knocked unconscious. When he is found it will be too late for all of you.*

She jangled her imprisoned wrist, trying against reason to free herself. It couldn't be too late. She refused to believe it was too late.

Really, you must calm yourself, the shadow said.

She knew killing meant nothing to the shadow. If Mac stood in his way, he would think nothing of snuffing out Mac's life to reach her.

Mrs. Vorel's warning flashed into her mind. *Can you risk the life of the man you love?*

Her heart grew leaden. A deep, dense darkness filled her, making her shudder.

No, she couldn't. She would do anything to save Mac's life.

287

Come to me. The shadow's voice cajoled her like an enraptured lover.

She stood on the edge of the chasm that was the shaft. There was nowhere for her to go. This would be the end. With the shadow sated, there would be no more death. The mountain would be safe. Brad and Lynn would be safe.

Mac would be safe.

With her gone, there would be no one else. The shadow of evil would disappear.

But she hesitated. Was her death the key?

No! a soft voice feathered in her mind. Hallie? *Listen!*

The shadow slithered up her body. *Come to me.*

Something was wrong. But what?

"No!" she screamed, backing away from the edge. With a jolt, she knew she couldn't surrender.

Roaring with anger, the shadow seized her.

Icy pain numbed her body; fear tumbled freely into her heart, pounding a zigzagged drumbeat into her veins. A band tightened around her chest. She couldn't breathe.

Anger seeped through the fear. It roiled in her chest. She gathered its power and pushed on the shadow with all her strength. Her action caught him by surprise; he fell back. He was still for a moment, then advanced toward her once more.

Come to me.

"Why?" Her fingers curled around the iron beam. "To make the job of killing me easier for you? Well, I have news for you. I'll fight you every inch of the way."

The shadow cocked his head. *You remind me so much of Hallie. She had fire in her veins. Just like you.*

He was right, she decided. She burned with the raging fire of anger. And the more she burned, the more the shadow's silvery edge seemed to glow. "Was the mine really worth killing all those people?"

He eyed her confidently. *The mine, no. My life, yes.*

"But you cursed Hallie before you died."

It was the curse of a man. It held no power.

"Then—"

In the mine, as Hallie killed me, I made a bargain. Your family's souls for mine.

"What will killing me get you?"

You are the last, liebliche. *With your death comes another chance at life for me.*

She heard a faint moan coming from Mac's direction. She knew she had to buy him time. "What happens if you let me live?"

Then I suffer in this hell forever.

"But you're alive now. I can see you."

The wolf-shadow paced the small rectangle of the elevator floor, his gaze never straying from hers. *Is this life? I think not. I want to be a man again.* He stopped before Kyra. *I want what I missed.*

"The world's changed a lot since the last time you were alive. The silver mine doesn't produce anymore."

For a clever man there is always a way to earn his fortune.

"The ways of the Old West aren't looked upon favorably these days." She knew she was repeating herself, but she had to give Mac a chance. Out of the corner of her eyes, she saw him roll over and rub his temples.

The wolf-shadow stopped his pacing and faced her. *You have much to learn,* liebliche. *The ways of men never change. Since the beginning of time the strong have survived. Whether by knife, by gun, or by wit; the strong always survive. And I am strong.*

Despite the humidity in the tunnel, her throat felt dry and tight. Out of the corner of her eye she caught Mac's struggle to stand. She jiggled her shackle loudly to cover the noise.

You must stop that nonsense, the shadow said. He

sat once more. *Contrary to what you think, I do not enjoy killing.*

"You could've fooled me."

It is my duty.

"No, you only think it's your duty. What has killing gotten you so far?" Noting Mac's drunklike stagger, she rattled her cuff once more.

I have earned privileges.

"Like what? I didn't know ghosts had privileges." She raised her voice louder than necessary.

I am not a ghost! he said.

Anger built in the cruel, straw-colored eyes. She cowered as far as she could from the shadowy gaping mouth advancing toward her.

I am caught in limbo, he said between snarls. *My freedom can only come with your death. It is my contract. It is my duty.*

"Kyra, are you all right?" Mac's strangled voice startled both Kyra and the shadow. "Who are you talking to?"

You! The shadow's feral growl echoed in the hollow tunnel. He crouched low on his back legs. *You have interfered for the last time!*

"Mac, watch out!" Kyra warned. She jangled her bracelet madly.

As the shadowy beast pounced, her shriek of terror reverberated against the shaft walls.

He knocked Mac to the ground.

Mac rolled away and scrambled up, looking around for his attacker. His gaze darted in a wide arc around him.

He can't see the shadow, she realized with horror.

"To your left," she said. Her hands curled into tight fists.

Mac swiveled to his left into a defensive pose. "Where?"

She had to help him see the shadow.

Shimmery images hovered on the edge of her

mind. The rumble of the mountain deepened. Kyra saw that the shadow, not Pandora, had caused the surge on the Institute's instruments.

You have the key, Kyra. Use it. A weak voice, like the tendrils of a breeze, brushed into her mind.

"Hallie?"

Listen. Listen to your heart. The voice faded and drifted away.

"What key? Listen to what? Hallie, help me."

She thought she heard something else but couldn't decipher the words. Tears streamed down her face. What key did her heart hold? How could she help Mac see the shadow?

"He's circling you to the left," she called to Mac.

Mac followed her direction, but Kyra could tell he still didn't see his attacker. Her mind ran quickly through all the dreams she'd had since her arrival in Utah. She closed her eyes. Images passed in misty vignettes. She dismissed them until she caught the one she'd been looking for. The one with Hallie. *What is not as it appears?* Her mind instantly focused on one picture.

Then she knew.

She licked her lips and opened her eyes. Would Mac suspend his disbelief to survive, or would he stick stubbornly to his set ways?

Mac's head pounded from Alek's blow. His chest ached from the latest attack. But for some reason his fuzzy mind refused to focus on his foe. Kyra called out directions, but he still couldn't locate Alek.

Had the blow to his head blinded him? No, he could see Kyra in the elevator, could see the walls of this damned tunnel. Where was Alek?

Mac whirled around to face his unseen opponent. Something came at him. He twisted out of the way. "Alek?"

"No, Mac," Kyra said. "Not Alek. The shadow."

"Shadow?" Mac shot Kyra a doubtful look.

"The wolf-shadow. Watch out! Behind you."

The warning came too late. Mac felt the definite imprint of paws connecting with the middle of his back. The power of the blow sent him flying forward.

He twisted around in midflight, fell on his side, and dissipated the impact by rolling. He sprang up.

"Where?" he asked.

"In front of you," Kyra said. "Mac, listen to me. You've got to close your eyes."

"Are you crazy?" How could he possibly see anything with his eyes closed?

"No, listen. It's the only way. Close your eyes. Hear the sounds that make no noise. Feel him. Trust me, Mac."

The *whoosh* of a paw scratched his face. Mac reached up to his stinging cheek. He stared in disbelief at his reddened hand.

"He's what's causing the mountain to shake, not the Pandora project," Kyra said. "His energy is making the scientists' instruments go crazy. If we defeat him, the mountain will be safe again. You've got to listen to me, Mac. Close your eyes. Feel him. *Please.*"

He caught the desperation in Kyra's voice, the mad jangling of her handcuff against the iron bar holding her prisoner. What did he have to lose? He couldn't see whatever was attacking him now. And yet closing his eyes to face his enemy went against all of his carefully trained instincts.

"Trust me, Mac."

What did he have to lose? His enemy appeared to be invisible. Mac closed his eyes.

He forced his mind to clear, his breaths to calm. Instantly, he sensed a shadowy presence hovering in front of him. An opponent he could see. How could that be? He snapped his eyes open to find himself staring at a black wall.

Impossible!

"To the right!" Kyra yelled.

Mac wasn't quick enough. His thick jacket caught the brunt of sharp claws and ripped to shreds. He moved aside to regroup.

"Close your eyes!" Kyra entreated him.

Mac closed his eyes. He found his center. As the swish of a tail brushed his hand, the smell of wet fur filled his nostril. The low, rumbling growl grew and set the mountain trembling deep in its core. Hot, gamy breath pulsated in noisy spurts near him.

The shadowy presence of the wolf materialized against the black screen of his lids. He fought the impulse to open his eyes and focused on the immaterial sounds of the beast's footfalls.

This couldn't be happening. This wasn't real. How could he feel and hear something that wasn't there with his eyes open? It made no sense. But there it was. A wolf.

He stopped fighting the impossible and concentrated on his opponent; that was something he could deal with.

The animal's menacing snarl guided him. He followed the wolf's sideway motion, poising himself defensively.

The wolf retreated to the other side of the tunnel. Mac followed the path of its heavy presence.

"He knows you can feel him now," Kyra said softly, as if she was attuned to his thoughts as well as the wolf's. "Careful. Concentrate. Think of love."

What was she talking about?

He had no time to ponder. He heard the wolf crouch and launch himself in his direction. Deftly, he sidestepped him. When the wolf threw himself in his direction once more, he was prepared. This time he connected both his elbows to the wolf's flying form with a loud thud.

The lunging wolf yelped and fell in a crumbling mass to the tunnel floor. Then he scurried back up, snarling, menacing. He circled Mac once more. Gathering speed in the narrow corridor, the wolf hurled his weight at Mac.

Jaws clamped around the arm Mac raised protectively before his throat.

The blow's impact brought them both to the ground. Mac swallowed his cry of pain and clamped his eyes shut tight, afraid to lose his edge by opening them.

"No, Mac! He's feeding on your fear." Kyra's frantic cry echoed all around him.

As he struggled with his concentration and the phantom wolf in his arms, his foot banged against the adze. If he reached for it, he'd lose his advantage.

He grabbed an ear and twisted it.

A leathery piece of skin broke off, but the wolf didn't loosen his hold.

Mac couldn't let this beast win. He couldn't leave Kyra at his mercy. He loved her.

With a roar of power, he brought his balled fist down repeatedly in the direction of the wolf's tender nose.

The wolf yipped and released his deathly grip long enough for Mac to push him away. Moving swiftly, he straddled the squirming beast.

With one rapid movement, Mac captured the wolf's lower jaw with one hand. By feel, he placed his other on the side of the neck, kneeling into the beast for leverage.

As he snapped the spine, a loud crack reverberated in the hollow chamber.

The wolf lay still, his head limp in Mac's hands.

Mac slowly opened his eyes and found the beast was real.

From his matted gray fur to his vacant yellow eyes to his lolling tongue, the wolf was as real now as he'd been a shadow with his eyes closed.

He scrambled away from the dead body, panting

as he caught his breath. How could this be? It didn't make any sense.

"Mac?"

Kyra's voice brought him out of his thoughts. It was then that he noticed that the rumbling had stopped; the pinging of water drops had once more become predominant.

"Are you all right?" Kyra asked.

Tears streamed down her face, diluting the blood splatters, replacing them with streaks. Her eyes were filled with concern, and he felt a wave of relief pound through him.

Kyra was safe.

"I'm fine," Mac said, ignoring the throbbing pain of his right forearm. He made his way to Kyra and held her for a long moment.

"He's gone," he said. "It's over."

She shook her head against his chest. "No. He's still here."

Chapter Twenty-two

Dragging itself from the floor, the shadowy form re-shaped. The material wolf dissipated like a magician's illusion. The indistinct form glowed dully, flickering brighter and brighter with each passing moment. A low rumble shook the floor.

You are mine! The voice boomed like dynamite.

Pieces of rock broke free from the tunnel's ceiling. The walls started crumbling. Dust like blue-black rain trickled around them.

Come to me!

Mac stepped forward to protect Kyra.

"No, Mac. Turn toward me. You can't fight him with your fists. He can't die that way."

"Then how?" He gripped the sleeves of her coat, placing her firmly behind him.

The shadowy form advanced toward them.

"Think of love," she said, so calmly it stirred something deep in him. "The only thing that can destroy evil is love."

The form encircled him, tightened around his neck, crushing the breath from him.

"Mac, no! Don't think of him!"

Pain pulsated through him like an electric current, growing stronger and stronger with each squeeze.

"You are not real," Mac croaked.

The jaw at his neck grew more powerful, gaining strength as Mac lost his own. He struggled against death, fought against surrender.

"He's feeding off your fear," Kyra said. "Please, Mac."

He twisted his body and looked at his beloved. *I love you!*

He thought it with all his mind, with all his heart. *I love you!*

The grip on his neck loosened. Something clicked inside him. Think of love.

He understood.

He surrendered.

"Not this time," a voice not quite his own said.

He concentrated his thoughts on his love for Kyra. A bond stronger than any man-made material connected them. In the spring green of her eyes, he'd felt life. In her arms, he'd discovered he could feel. With her love, he'd dared to hope for a future.

The grip fell away. An anguished cry tore from the shadow. Gasping for breath, Mac kept his thoughts focused on his feelings for Kyra. The shadow lurched back.

Then Mac saw him launch himself at Kyra.

She gulped, faltering back. The shadow crept over her.

"No!" Mac moved to protect her.

Understanding the shadow's ploy, he surrendered once more, stopping in his tracks.

"I love you, Kyra. Do you love me?"

She nodded. The shadow shrouded her. Pain wavered across her face. A gasp escaped her.

"Look at me!" he ordered. "He can't hurt you."

Her gaze locked with his. "I know." The fear washed from her eyes. A heavenly smile curled her lips.

He kept his own gaze firmly fixed on the love shinning in her eyes. Love for him. Waves of warmth flowed through him, enfolding his heart. The world seemed suspended in time, suspended in their love.

The shadow thinned. The veil of evil slipped away.

No! Anger mushroomed from the shadow like a nuclear bomb. The edges folded and refolded, collapsing within themselves. He fought against imminent destruction. After all this time, he couldn't lose. Not when he was so close to victory.

He gathered his strength, struggled to hang on to his essence, shredding before him.

"Not this time."

The shadow heard the out-of-time-voice ping against him. He whirled to face it. For the brief flash of a moment Emory Eaton's ghost superimposed itself on McKane's body. Emory smiled, saluted, and vaporized, leaving the shadow staring at McKane and Kyra.

Conserving his remaining energy, he launched himself at the couple. He clashed against them as if they were covered with armor. Repelled, he floated above the silvery-white form etched into the rocky floor. His fading strength folded inward.

Wrapped in the protection of their love, he couldn't harm them. His power spent, he couldn't pierce their shield.

Kyra was out of his reach. He couldn't kill her. He couldn't harvest her energy and regain his stolen life.

He had lost.

He would spend eternity in hell.

His fast dissipating life force folded in one last time, and the shadow gave a final cry of outrage.

*   *   *

A rip tore the air. The fine blue-black dust sifting from the ceiling turned into a shower of pebble-sized rocks.

From her vantage point Kyra saw the silvery-white form of a man lift from the rocky ground. The silver man-shadow mixed with the darker floating one, each consuming the other with its own anger until there was nothing left except shining silver pieces. They fell like rain down the shaft to rejoin the bones of Rolf Schreck's body.

"He's gone." She sighed deeply. "Can you feel that?"

"Yes . . . I can."

"Spirit and shadow got separated when Schreck died in the mine all those years ago. They're reunited now."

They'd done it. They'd broken the curse. With Schreck returned to his rightful place, there would be no more nightmares. Tears of relief burned her eyes. Her muscles started to shake and weariness crept over every inch of her body. It was over. It was really over.

Falling rocks peppered them. She followed Mac's gaze to the timbers shoring up the walls and saw them starting to buckle. The tunnel wouldn't hold for much longer.

"We've got to get you out of here," Mac said.

His face took on the same blank expression it had when he'd walked into the cave and seen Alek holding her prisoner. He looked like a warrior, making her realize that the war wouldn't be over until they were safely out of the mine.

He reached for his backpack, rummaged inside, and came out with a camp knife.

Using the saw blade, he worked on the chain linking her to the iron beam. After an eternity her arm fell loose. He rubbed the bruised flesh of her wrist, avoiding the crusted cuts on both sides.

"Lovely bracelet," Mac said. He smiled and played with the chain's broken link tenderly with one finger.

"It's not my style," she said lightly, shaking the chrome-plated steel cuff. "I prefer gold."

Her smile hid her pain, but the look in his eyes told her he knew how much the levity was costing her. He wrapped her in his arms. She collapsed into the comfort he offered. Soon they would be out of here. Soon they could talk. Soon they could think of the future and what it might hold for them.

"Let's get out of here," he said.

"Good idea."

Mac felt humbled by Kyra's strength shining through her fears. While his strength had been drilled into him, hers came from deep down. That was true courage. If he hadn't loved her so much already, he'd have fallen for her at that moment.

"I love Christmas, don't you?" he said as he walked across the elevator platform.

"I prefer Easter myself. All that chocolate." Kyra slid down the iron beam and sat watching his movements.

"Well, I've got a special present for the Eaton mine." Mac gave Kyra his best smile. "I'm going to make sure the people living here have hundreds of Christmases together."

He reached for his pack. He hadn't lifted it more than a few inches off the platform when he dropped it. The weight was too much for his injured arm. He fell to his knees, cradling his pain.

Kyra was by his side in a flash. "You're hurt. Why didn't you tell me you were hurt?"

She peeled away the shredded mess of his coat sleeve to uncover the bloody, mangled flesh the wolf-shadow's powerful jaws had created. She gasped. "We've got to get you to a doctor."

"Not before the mine is sealed."

"Why? The shadow caused the mountain tremors. He caused the equipment's surge."

"Because the mine is about to collapse, and if we don't seal it, innocent people will die."

He pointed to the wood braces cracking under their load.

She turned resolutely away from the menace. "Tell me what to do."

"It's dangerous," he said, knowing the task would be hard enough for him to accomplish.

"You don't have too many options right now."

"No, I don't."

The sense of powerlessness that fact created was unfamiliar and downright unpleasant. Mac McKane was always in control. Or at least he had been until he'd met Kyra.

He smiled. Losing control with her had been wonderful. He trusted her, and with his help she could set the boxes as well as he could—especially in his condition.

She was his partner. He liked the warmth the thought and the feeling brought.

"Right," he said. "Get the backpack to the middle of the elevator. Then unpack all the red boxes."

She lifted the pack. When it reached waist-level her left shoulder dipped down, turning her heat-reddened complexion ash-white.

He sprang up to help her. "What's wrong?"

"I'm fine. The shoulder muscle's a little sore, that's all." She smiled. "Looks like we'll have to work together to get this mission of yours accomplished."

His heart swelled with pride. "Have I told you how much I love you lately?"

"No. As a matter of fact, I do believe it's been at least ten minutes since you've mentioned it. But you can keep saying it over and over, and I won't ever get sick of hearing it."

"I love you," he said, and kissed her. "Let's get this show on the road."

"There's just one more thing I'd like to do."

"What?"

She reached into the neck of her coat, yanked on the moonstone trapped in the filigreed head of a key, breaking the silver chain's clasp, and dropped the piece of jewelry into the shaft.

Mac squeezed her to him. She rested her head on his shoulder for a moment. "Let's go."

They retrieved the Institute's recorder and the lantern from the tunnel. Then, working in perfect unison, they unloaded the boxes. Mac could run faster, but with his swollen arm he wouldn't be able to set the boxes. He showed Kyra how to deploy the boxes' mechanism, and told her where to place it.

"Once the pin is pulled, you've got one minute to get back to the elevator. Then we've got one minute to get to the next level and do it all over again. Got it?"

"Got it."

With his heart pounding heavily in his chest, he took his position by the elevator control, then sent Kyra on her way with the first box.

The *pssh* sound, like shaving cream coming out of an aerosol can, told him the first box had been set. Kyra's hurried footsteps told him that she was on her way. He held his breath until she jumped onto the elevator, then shoved the lever up. The elevator cables complained. Agonizingly slow, they crept into action.

As they left the two-thousand-foot level, the mountain started to rumble again. He smiled. The boxes were working. This rumble wasn't ominous; it was a rumble of satisfaction as each tunnel filled and became part of the mountain once more. When he slowed the elevator at the next level, a feeling of rightness settled over him. Everything would be all right.

"Now," he said. Kyra promptly jumped off to set the next box.

They repeated the procedure thirteen more times. Only five more to go.

"You're doing great," he said as he set the elevator in motion once more.

But his words were an empty gesture. Her pallor worried him. Each outing seemed to drain her already weakened body.

At the five-hundred-foot level, Kyra slipped on her return run. White foam billowed all around her. If it hardened around her, he knew she would die.

He jumped out and grabbed her by the waist with his good arm just as the foam reached her, dragging her back to the elevator.

"My turn to set the boxes." He jerked the elevator into action.

"No, I'm fine. You can't take the pin out with your arm."

"And you're getting too tired."

"There are only a few more left."

He grabbed Kyra's good arm and dragged her to his corner. "When this knob shows you you're fifty feet from where you want to stop you slowly start bringing the lever back to this position here."

"No. I'm fine. I'll do the boxes."

"Kyra—"

"We don't have time to argue. Go on, slow the elevator."

The platform hadn't stopped before she rushed out with another red box. He swore and kicked at the rusted iron beams. He'd never seen anybody so stubborn in his life.

"Go!" Kyra yelled as she jumped back onto the elevator.

As they made their way up the shaft, the comforting purr of the generator increased and the temperature decreased. As Kyra placed the second to last box in the level below the mine entrance, Mac sighed his relief. One more to go and they would be free.

Fifty feet from the top, he began to lower the lever to slow the elevator down. When the generator's purr turned into a sputter his heart jumped to his throat. The cables groaned and creaked. He mumbled encouragement as he coaxed more mileage out of the dying engine.

"Come on," he said, grinding his teeth.

Ten feet from their destination, the sputtering generator stopped. The elevator ground to a halt.

Chapter Twenty-three

With the hum of the generator gone, the hissing of the white foam, gaining ground below them, took on a new urgency.

Mac fished a leather glove from his pocket. With the help of his teeth, he yanked it over his good hand. He jumped up, caught the top bar of the elevator cage with his good arm, and pulled himself up.

"I'll be right back," he called down to Kyra. He hated leaving her down there, but he had no choice.

He hiked himself up the greasy cable, using his good arm on the twisted steel and bracing his legs against the shaft wall to hold his upward progress. When he reached the top, his muscles cried their protest, but he ignored them.

The foam was gaining on Kyra. He had to hurry.

Mac sped to the blue sled. He jerked off the rope he'd used to hold his gear in place. With a knot tied on the bottom half, he threw it down to Kyra.

"Twist the rope into a figure eight. Slip an arm into

each loop so that where the rope crosses rests between your shoulders. That's it. I'll pull you up. Don't forget to grab the last box."

"What about the briefcase?"

"Leave it."

If Schreck had caused the equipment surge, then the data inside the black box wouldn't do the Institute any good. They weren't likely to believe in ghosts any more than he had.

While he waited, Mac wrapped his end of the rope around the base of the generator for leverage.

"Ready," she yelled from below.

He strained his weight against his makeshift pulley and pulled the rope with all his strength. The sweat he'd acquired deep in the mine froze in the cave's cold air, numbing his fingers and his toes. He couldn't tell how much pressure he exerted on either his feet or his hands. He didn't care. As long as Kyra was safe.

When her head finally popped past the shaft entrance, he fought his urge to let go of the rope and run to her. He waited patiently for her to gain sure footing. With a sick lurch in his stomach, he noted that her boots and calves were covered with a white crust from the foam.

He'd come too close to losing her all over again.

After deploying the last box in the middle of the cave, they spilled out the side of the mountain into the blessed light of the full moon.

He grabbed her hand and urged her forward. "Keep running."

They ran until Kyra tripped and fell. As he helped her up, he noticed the echo of the rumbling foam was waning. He looked up at the white mound sealing the mine forever. Already the cold air around it had hardened the foam into rock.

"It's over." He clasped her close to him. "Come on; let's go home."

"Home," Kyra whispered wistfully into his shoulder. "I've been confused about where that was since I found out I'd been adopted." Her gaze moved to his. "I know now that home is wherever you're loved." She laughed. "I may sound like a greeting card, but my heart belongs to you, Mac. It always has. It always will. And my home is wherever you are. I love you, Mac."

"I love you, too."

A swelling ache filled his heart at her words. She looked awful with her sweat-matted hair and blood-splattered jacket, but to him she'd never looked more beautiful. The light and the love in her eyes was more brilliant than any sun, and it was all for him.

He turned away from the sealed mine, and for the first time since he'd left Kyra seven years ago he found peace. The past was no longer a shadow to be feared, but a conscious picture in a photo album where the pages could be turned at will. He turned the page forward.

Somewhere in those tunnels, he'd put his days as the Institute's machine behind. Now he could concentrate on his future—on all those feelings Kyra had woken from their long slumber.

He had his freedom. He had Kyra's love. What else could he possibly ask for?

"With all my heart, Kyra. I love you." Emotions choked his voice as he turned back to gaze into Kyra's green eyes, so filled with the promise of life.

Kyra's grip on his shoulder tightened. "I have to go back to Florida . . . to say good-bye to Mom. To tell her I understand."

He nodded slowly. With the sealing of the mine he'd buried his last ghost. She wanted closure; he couldn't begrudge her that. "Do you want me to come with you?"

"No. This is something I have to do by myself."

He raised the collar of her jacket against the bitter

wind howling through the pines. "I'll be waiting for you. You know that, don't you?"

"Yes." Her smile said more than any words could have. "Let's go home."

"Yeah, let's."

As they walked slowly down the mountain's side, no shadows followed them.

Epilogue

Inside her room in the hospital's maternity ward, Kyra held the tiny bundle containing her infant daughter in her arms and smiled. When the baby fidgeted, rooting hungrily for a nipple, Kyra offered her her breast. The little girl sucked greedily.

The late December sun shone through the opened curtains, cheering the room's plain decor.

Mac, grinning like a fool, sat on the edge of her bed, one arm cautiously wrapped around her shoulders. Ever since he'd found out she was pregnant he'd been treating her like cut glass. No amount of telling him she wouldn't break had been able to convince him not to fuss over her. Now he treated his daughter with the same reverence. With an index finger, he gently stroked his baby's miniature pink hand, resting on Kyra's breast.

"She's so small," he said, fascination with the child

he'd helped create evident in his voice and in the glowing silver of his eyes. "So perfect. Ten toes. Ten fingers. Everything where it ought to be."

The tiny infant was a miracle Kyra couldn't help but be in awe of. But even more than what the baby had, Kyra was thankful for what she lacked. As if to make sure she hadn't been mistaken, for the hundredth time since her daughter had been born, Kyra pushed aside the green and yellow receiving blanket and examined the baby's rosy skin.

No crescent-shaped birthmark marred her skin.

And for the hundredth time, tears of joy slipped from her eyes.

The nightmare that had followed her family for over eight decades was finally over.

"Hey, are you okay?" Mac asked, concern filling his voice as he tenderly wiped the moisture from her cheek.

She smiled. "Everything's just perfect."

The curse was gone. Her daughter would continue Hallie's line without having to fear for her life. She would be free to go where she wanted, when she wanted. She would never have to fear silver shadows.

The circle was truly closed. In a dusty corner of her mother's attic in Florida, in a strong box, she'd found Hallie's letter to Rebecca. She'd understood her mothers' fears. They had both loved her. They had both wanted what was best for her. They had both tried to shelter her from pain.

A child could ask for no more.

She'd had a long talk with George. He'd listened to her impossible story, and when she'd tendered her resignation he'd countered by handing her a bright red and white box tied with a green ribbon. Inside, she'd found partnership papers. For the last year she'd been in charge of the west-coast operations, while George had run the projects on the east coast of Hadley and Kirtland Restoration Services.

And, as promised, when she'd flown back to Utah Mac had been waiting for her. Every time she'd had to be away for a project, when she returned she'd found him waiting for her. Her eyes were moist with tears, but she held them back. He was here to stay. Her heart was so full of love, she thought it would burst. There were no more shadows of the past between them.

Kyra tipped up her face, asking for a kiss. Mac obliged.

"Get me my clothes," she said, rewrapping the blanket around the child sleeping contentedly in her arms. "I want Joy to spend her first Christmas at home."

"Don't you want to rest? It's going to get pretty hectic in a few days. Mom and Dad are coming up. So are George and Janice. Add Brad and Lynn to the mix, not to mention Debbie and her family. And I think we may have to deal with a bit of jealousy on Misty's part. According to Debbie, she's been pouting since we left for the hospital. We'll have a regular zoo on our hands."

Family—all of them. They were her dream-come-true. "I know. Isn't it wonderful?"

A slow smile spread over Mac's face, dazzling her as it always did. "You're right. Let's go home."

Their own home had been built at the base of a quiet Eaton Peak—designed by Kyra, constructed by Mac, and filled with their love.

You can write to the author at the following
address:

Sylvie Kurtz
P.O. Box 702
Milford, NH 03055-0702

Shadows on a Sunset Sea

Sabine Kells

**A Haunting Love Story
By The Bestselling Author Of *A Deeper Hunger***

"A major new voice in the supernatural/fantasy romance subgenre has arrived!"
—*Romantic Times*

*A shadow in the dark, a whisper in the night, a man reaching out to her....*Surely, Carolyn is dreaming. The ghostly legends of Thornwick Castle can't be true. Tiernan O'Rourke lived nearly three hundred years earlier; he can't still walk the great halls, waiting for the return of the woman he lost. Carolyn wants to deny the irresistible spirit that calls to her from a wondrous realm of rapturous passion and unknown peril. But in the fading echoes of her ancestral Irish home, secrets of the past sweep Carolyn to a time she's never known—and into the arms of the lover who is her destiny.

_51984-4 $4.99 US/$5.99 CAN

BESTSELLING AUTHOR OF
THE PANTHER AND THE PEARL

He rides from out of the Turkish wilderness atop a magnificent charger. Dark and mysterious, Malik Bey sweeps Boston-bred Amelia Ryder into an exotic world of sultans and revolutionaries, magnificent palaces and desert camps. Amy wants to hate her virile abductor, to escape his heated glances forever. But with his suave manners and seductive charm, the hard-bodied rebel is no mere thief out to steal the proper young beauty's virtue. And as hot days melt into sultry nights, Amy grows ever closer to surrendering to unending bliss in Malik's fiery embrace.

__4015-8 $5.99 US/$6.99 CAN

MADELINE BAKER

Beneath A Midnight Moon

**Winner Of The *Romantic Times*
Reviewers Choice Award!**

He comes to her in visions—the hard-muscled stranger who promises to save her from certain death. She never dares hope that her fantasy love will hold her in his arms until the virile and magnificent dream appears in the flesh.

A warrior valiant and true, he can overcome any obstacle, yet his yearning for the virginal beauty he's rescued overwhelms him. But no matter how his fevered body aches for her, he is betrothed to another.

Bound together by destiny, yet kept apart by circumstances, they brave untold perils and ruthless enemies—and find a passion that can never be rent asunder.

_3649-5 $4.99 US/$5.99 CAN